Ola Farmer's Road

Isaiyan Morrison

Books by Isaiyan Morrison

Deamhan Chronicles
Deamhan. Deamhan Chronicles #1
Kei. Family Matters. Deamhan Chronicles #1.5
Dark Curse. Deamhan Chronicles #2
Maris. The Brotherhood Files
Ayden. Deamhan Minion. Deamhan Chronicles #2.5
Deception. Deamhan Chronicles #3
Hallie. A Tit For A Tat. Deamhan Chronicles #3.5
Divination. Deamhan Chronicles #4
Remy. The Brotherhood Files
Veronica. Deamhan Chronicles #4.5

BEHESIANS
Behesians. Book One

THE DEAD SERIES
The Not-So Dead
The So-So Dead

You can also visit her: https://www.isaiyanmorrison.com/
https://www.deamhan.com/
https://www.bookbub.com/profile/isaiyan-morrison

Maybe that's what life is... a wink of the eye and winking stars.
-JACK KEROUAC

Contents

CHAPTER ONE
Just One More

"Here we are."

Robert Ellsy turned off his car, removed the keys, and placed them in his breast pocket. He gazed into Allison's settled eyes and immediately turned away, careful to hide the concern that had lingered inside him for days. He lied to her, just like before. It'd become second nature. He knew she couldn't come with him because she wasn't leaving Old Farmer's Road alive.

Fog, thick and dense, blanketed the sky and billowed across the ground, blocking the view of the Mississippi River. The city of Minneapolis stood in the distance, casting an amber shadow over the lazy clouds. The air carried the cold breeze from the river's bank and it glazed across Allison's skin, making the tiny hairs on her forearm stand erect. She shivered and Robert assumed that she was starting to regret wearing her thin baby tee instead of her Green Day T-shirt with the long sleeves. Warm breezes accompanied Minnesota summers along with humidity and mosquitoes but not at Old Farmer's Road. On the entire drive she questioned why he wanted to bring her to a remote swamp on his last day in the city instead of taking her to the movies.

Allison rolled up the passenger side window and folded her arms over her chest. She turned her head left to face him and her

1

thick auburn curls bounced from behind her shoulder. "This has to be one of the most ridiculous places you've ever taken me. I still don't know why I decided to come here with you."

"Because you love me." Robert coolly nestled his body closer to her but she moved away. "Aw, c'mon Allison. Don't be that way." He grabbed her wrist and she immediately pulled out of his grip.

"I don't like it here Robert. Take me home." Allison eyed the hazy environment around them.

He wiped away the condensation covering the car windows in a slick white residue, revealing lighting bugs in the distance, beyond what looked like an impenetrable line of tall pine trees. The sound of a cop siren in the distance broke through the uncomfortable silence that filled the air around them.

"Scared?" Robert's comment sounded more like a tease to Allison.

She rolled her eyes and turned away from him. "I'm not scared. Just irritated."

"Why?" He asked with a hint of hostility in his voice.

"It's your last day in Minneapolis before you leave for New York." She puffed out her lower lip.

"It's only temporary. I told you, once I graduate you can move out there and live with me."

"How do I know you won't dump me for some other chick?"

"I won't babe. Promise."

While he thought about his devilish plan, a familiar voice jabbed into his brain like the sting of needles, making his stomach cramp. The coarse voice spoke, telling him to do terrible things to Allison; things beyond his imagination.

The past few weeks had been exceptionally hard. The moment he found out that he was accepted to college, the voice became constant and forceful. He tried ignoring it along with the cramps, but it only made things worse with each passing day. The voice always drew him back to the silent trees and the algae filled swamps of Old Farmer's Road.

"I love you Allison. I always will."

Allison turned back to him and glared into his brown eyes. She placed her palm against his cheek. "I love you too." She moved in and kissed him gently.

Still entangled in their embrace, Robert closed his eyes. He wholeheartedly wished things could be that simple. He wished that he had never agreed to come to the area in the first place.

He pulled back. "I can't."

"What are you talking about?" She dropped her hand and returned to her irritated behavior.

"Nothing. I think I just need some fresh air."

"Fresh air?" She pouted. "Out there?" Her eyes skimmed the scenery.

Robert exhaled but before he could speak Allison spoke up again. "I still don't understand what you and your friends see in this place."

"I don't think you'd like to know." He hands gripped the steering wheel as if he prepared to drive off. He had parked facing the old rickety bridge that ran across the river to the other side of the swamp. This way he had a full-length view of what was ahead of them.

"What do you mean?" Allison asked.

"Nothing."

"What's going on Robert?" She leaned against the car door, giving him her full and undivided attention. "Every time I ask a question or mention this place you always say 'It's nothing'?"

"I just think there's really nothing to tell you."

"Really?" Allison tilted her head to the side in defiance. "Nothing to tell me? Your girlfriend?!"

Robert stepped out of the car and closed the door behind him. He stretched his arms overhead and closed his eyes, listening to the wind flap against the leaves of the trees nearby. Allison had a right to know what had happened, but by telling her, he would place her at risk. He didn't want her to know anything: the monstrous voice that plagued his thoughts, what he and his friends did across the bridge, the hunger, and most importantly, the murders. He already mentioned these things to his older brother, Derek, and Derek didn't believe him.

Allison knocked on the windshield and he turned back. She spoke loud enough for Robert to hear her muted voice telling him to get back into the car, but he motioned for her to come out and join him instead.

She rolled down the window and leaned her head out. "Robert, please come back inside."

He ignored her. "Allison, get out here."

She shook her head, defiant.

"There's a breeze coming off the swamp."

"I don't want to smell swamp water. I want to go home."

"Fine, but just, come out here with me first." He crawled onto the hood of his car, startling her. Feeling the adrenaline pumping through his body, he closed his eyes and heard the voice whispering in his thoughts. He felt it pushing with such magnitude that he covered his face and immediately slid off the roof of his car.

Just one more.

One more.

He turned back to the bridge, noticing a ball of light circling through the trees ahead.

"Robert, what's gotten into you?" Allison called out.

He turned back to face her. "I want to show you something." He playfully waved.

She sighed again. "But it smells like old dirty water out there."

Robert sniffed the air and shrugged, unable to locate any odor. "No it doesn't." He approached the passenger side of the car. "You've always asked what my friends and I do down here." He opened her door and extended his hand to her. "Let me show you."

Allison released a low audible breath, took his hand, and left the car.

"I swear you better not scare me." She eyed the area. "If you do, I'll never forgive you."

Robert placed his hands on her hips and pulled her in closer. "I swear I'm not going to scare you."

She smiled. "You better not." She snuggled in tighter and whispered. "I don't understand why you would come out here anyway."

"You're scared of the Old Farmer, aren't you?"

"I don't believe in urban legends."

"I don't either." He pointed to the old withered bridge ahead. "Let's cross it."

They heard a loud howl in the distance and Allison immediately gripped him tightly around the waist. "What was that?"

Robert chuckled. "It's just a dog."

"That was not a dog." Allison cringed.

"Maybe a coyote."

"This close to the city?"

"I've seen deer in downtown Minneapolis," he said. "It's not abnormal."

She placed her head against his ribs and they remained silent. He heard her breathing increase and when she put her arm around him, she squeezed, pulling him in close. He kept his ears opened, waiting for another howl.

"Robert, what's that?" She pointed into the darkness.

He watched a flickering white light deep within the trees, just pass the old bridge, moving slowly from right to left. "That's just a lightning bug."

"Someone's down there watching us." She elbowed him in the ribs.

"Stop being so scared." He walked forward and felt her hesitate. "Allison, I swear. It's just a lightning bug. I see them all the time down here."

Allison picked up her feet and soon they walked to the edge of the bridge. The mysterious blinking light didn't increase or decrease in size. Instead its rhythmic pulsating pattern began to confuse Robert as well. While the light's appearance didn't startle him, its long exposure to him did.

The wood, warped and twisted from years of exposure, with old iron beams rusted brown from the elements, gave the bridge a ghastly look. Allison placed one foot on the bridge, testing her weight on the board. It creaked slightly and she hesitated before placing her other foot down.

"It doesn't look safe to cross," she said to him.

He ignored her statement and stepped forward. "It's safe." He held out his hand to her and together they trudged over the bridge. As they reached the end, the light suddenly disappeared into the darkness. Crickets in the bushes near them chirped endlessly and the rapping noise of dragonflies traveled through the air.

This is it, Robert thought to himself. They had crossed over into the unsafe zone.

He took off his jacket and held it in his hands. He glared into the darkness, to where the pulsating light used to be, and he moved forward following the path ahead, that looked as if it'd been paved the night before.

"Okay, it was a lighting bug. I believe you." Allison tugged at his arm. "Now can we go please?"

"This isn't right." Panic began to fill his voice. "This path is different."

"How?"

"Nothing changes around here Allison without their doing." He stepped forward and he felt her pulling on his belt.

"Whose doing?"

He pried her hand from his belt and watched as two red dots appeared in the darkness followed by a low, ferocious growl. His eyes focused and he could barely make out the outline of a German Sheppard with its ears at full alert. The bushes rustled and the dog stepped forward, revealing itself to him. He then heard the voice inside his head and it broke through his concentration.

Just one more.

One more.

The dog remained still. Foam collected around its mouth and its upper lip quivered. They heard the low rumble of aggression as the animal crept toward them, revealing white rib bones covered with tinny maggots and stringy flesh.

Allison screamed but Robert didn't panic. It was the sign he'd been waiting for. "I've brought you what you've asked for," he spoke to the dog. "She's the last one. After this I'm out. I'm done."

Allison jumped back. "Robert, what's going on?"

Suddenly the voice spoke but this time its voice didn't generate in Robert's head. It came from the darkness just beyond where the dog stood.

Just two more.

Two more.

"Two more?" Robert repeated, confused.

The dog hoofed its legs forward and Allison turned to run. All of this happened so quickly that he couldn't react as the dog sped past him and chased after Allison.

"No! I thought we were going to share her!" He spun around watching her run back over the bridge and toward the car with the dog close on her tail. She tripped over an upturned wooden beam and fell. The dog jumped on top of her and she let out a high-pitched scream that echoed through the air.

Robert stood still but he couldn't watch. He covered his face, hearing Allison's muted screams as the dog began to rip into her flesh. He felt his body shake uncontrollably.

Just two more.

Two more.

The dog turned to face Robert and its hideous eyes locked onto him.

He lowered his hands from his face. "I did what you asked. You have to let me go."

The dog lumbered a low growl.

"I'm done!" He screamed at the dog. "No more!"

With its head low, the dog ran toward him. Robert quickly moved back but he found himself tripping over his own feet. He fell onto his back and now the dog stood a few feet away from him with its lips pulled back and Allison's blood dripping from its pointed fangs.

"You can't kill me." He attempted to stand back on his feet but the dog's growl made him freeze. It continued to pace toward him.

Robert closed his eyes, feeling the dog's roasting breath on his right cheek. The dog's sharp claws dug into his stomach and he felt searing pain throughout his body. He tried to fight back to protect what the dog wanted; the three stones that gave him life and that made him what he was. The voice inside his head spoke for the final time.

Just one more.

One more.

CHAPTER TWO
The Boy Next Door

Cecilia Richardson awoke to the constant pounding on her bedroom door. It increased in its intensity as she slid from her bed. From the other side she heard her mother's annoying voice.

"Cecilia, get up. You're father's leaving for work in a couple of minutes."

She didn't understand why her mother wanted her to see her father off. She opened the door and shot her mother an evil yet tired stare.

"I made breakfast." Her mother stood in the doorway, wearing an apron that looked straight out of a Betty Crocker manual. Her hair was pulled back in a ponytail and a streak of flour ran across her right cheek. "How many pancakes do you want?"

"Seriously?" Cecilia rubbed her eye. "Mom, you look ridiculous in that outfit." She expected her mother to turn irate. Instead the smile didn't waver from her face.

"It's too early to start this. Now get up. You're not going to sleep until noon." She turned and walked back to the kitchen.

Cecilia peaked out from her bedroom and watched her father, dressed in a business suit with a black and white checkered tie, sitting at the kitchen table. He sipped quietly from his coffee mug while skimming through his cell phone. She took zombie like footsteps into the living room and watched as mother frantically moved back and forth from the kitchen to her father.

"You're going to brush your teeth first before you eat, right?" her mother asked.

"No mom. I thought I'd do something different today," Cecilia replied sarcastically.

"Don't start that tone with me. I don't need any of your lip."

Since moving to Minneapolis, her mother had attempted to distance themselves from the environment they left behind in San Diego. She dealt with settling into their new quiet suburban neighborhood by spending his hard earned money. Yesterday she bought expensive black and white furniture and matching black and white photographs. Last week she purchased brand new placemats for their black polished dining room table. Her father never said a word about her ridiculous shopping sprees and her attempt to get rid of anything that gave off a "bad vibe."

Yet neither of them asked how she felt about the move.

They didn't allow her to have her say. They gave her a week to say goodbye to her friends and her boyfriend, Glenn who she missed terribly. Now that he wasn't around, she had no one else to vent her frustrations to.

Mr. Richardson gulped the last drops of his coffee. "I have to go." He grabbed his suitcase and headed to the front door.

"What time will you be home?" Mrs. Richardson dried her hands on a soaked dishtowel.

"Around six." He kissed her on the cheek and rushed out the door.

Cecilia dragged her feet along the carpet and over to the dining room. "So you woke me up just to watch him eat?" She stared at the half eaten eggs and pieces of bacon left on her father's plate.

"Today is your father's first day at work." Her mother wiped down the kitchen counter. "Plus I thought we could have some quality time together, just you and me." She placed the dirty dishes in the dishwasher and when finished, she draped her apron over the handle on the stove.

"I'll pass if you don't mind." Cecilia turned around and headed back to her bedroom. In her closet she grabbed a pack of cigarettes tucked behind a stack of board games on the top shelf. Afterwards, she headed out through the front door.

It took some time for her eyes to adjust to the sun's glare. She sat on the concrete footsteps and examined her new neighborhood. All the houses looked the same to her with their white and tan façades, mowed front yards, and neatly trimmed green grass. Every house had flower pots placed on their front steps. Any screen door not properly secured swung back and forth in the slight wind. She also didn't see any cars parked along the streets. She heard kids yelling and playing down the street.

When the coast was clear she lit her cigarette and inhaled. Her attention was diverted by a metallic sound coming from the house next door. The front screen opened. A scraggly clothed boy emerged dressed in a dingy shirt and frayed jeans. The screen door slammed shut behind him. He swiped back his brown hair and plopped down on the concrete stairs before lighting his own cigarette. She watched as he inhaled with his head titled back, peering at the clear blue sky. He mumbled incoherently to himself.

Since moving into her new house, she'd never seen anyone enter or leave from the house next door. Also, he was the first attractive boy she'd seen since moving to Minneapolis, nowhere near Glenn's rugged good looks, but dateable. He intrigued her.

He pivoted to his left side and away from her. Healed cuts covered his left forearm from his elbow down to his wrist. She squinted to get a better look just as their eyes met.

Immediately she turned her attention forward but still watched him from her peripheral.

He placed his cigarette up to his lips. "Hey."

She slowly turned her head in his direction. "Hi."

He inhaled. "You just moved here, didn't you?"

"Yeah, a few weeks ago."

"I haven't seen you around," the boy replied. "My name is Isaac."

Isaac. Cecilia repeated his name in her head a few more times before replying. "I'm Cecilia."

He flicked the ashes from his cigarette. "Nice to meet you."

"Likewise." She tucked a stray lock of hair behind her right ear.

"Do you go out Cecilia?" Isaac asked.

"Go out?"

"Yeah, like with friends."

"I don't have any friends here."

"We could hang sometime if you want."

Cecilia heard the front door of his house open. A girl with curly brown hair and immense hazel eyes appeared and she sat next to Isaac. When she placed her hand on his back, his demeanor changed and she scooted away from him.

"Stop acting like a prima donna." Again, she placed her hand on his back but this time she playfully pushed him forward.

"Why is this funny to you?"

"You're doing it again." She yanked the cigarette from his fingers.

"Elsie, not now." He reached to take back his cigarette from her but she moved her hand.

"Nope. Not until you promise to behave."

"You're making me angry." He reached for it again, this time taking it. "And I'm not in the mood." With his head he nodded in Cecilia's direction. "This is Cecilia."

Elsie leaned forward, gazing at her. "We have a next door neighbor? Since when?"

"She just moved here," he replied. "Elsie, this is Cecilia. Cecilia, this is my older sister, Elsie."

Cecilia waved but Elsie rudely didn't return the gesture. Instead she returned back to her brother. "See what I mean? You're doing exactly what father said you'd do."

"I don't care. I'm tired of his rules."

"Isaac, let's talk inside." She placed her arm around his shoulders and he rejected her advance.

"Where are you from?" He turned his attention back to Cecilia.

"California."

"I've always wanted to go there. Where exactly in California?"

"Los Angeles."

His eyes lit up and he looked at Elsie. "We should go someday."

"That place is overrated." The expression on Elsie's face changed. "Too many people."

"So what. It'd be perfect for us," Isaac said.

Suddenly Elsie stood to her feet. "Go inside."

Isaac stood up slowly and she pushed him toward the door.

The conversation took a downward turn and surprised, Cecilia remained where she sat and watched as Isaac gave his sister the evil eye. Their behavior toward one another stunned her, but she thought that it was simply sibling behavior; something she didn't understand since she was an only child.

Isaac flicked his half smoked cigarette and he walked back into his house, leaving Elsie behind.

"It was nice meeting both of you," Cecilia said.

Elsie's eyes narrowed. "Stay away from my brother." She opened the screen door. "I'm not going to tell you again." She entered her home and slammed the door shut behind her.

CHAPTER THREE

Out there, everything thrives

Her high pitched giggling echoed through the wall.

The morning sunlight slithered beneath his yellow stained curtains and onto his floor, slightly touching the small pile of newspapers near the bathroom door.

Derek Ellsy yawned, taking in the smell of mold and bile that polluted the air. She's at it again. He thought in a hazy daze. At seven in the morning she's at it.

He wiped the sleep from his eyes and looked to the discoloration on the ceiling of his apartment. He shivered as a cold breeze tickled its way up his back to the tips of his fingers, an annoying side effect that he had grown used to. He contracted his right fist to match the rhythm of her giggles, hoping it would steer his mind away from his aches and from his desire to start hitting the bottle. He thought about his younger brother Robert and immediately his mind snapped to his list of things he had to do today.

The sun's rays filled the room with warmth and light swam past the pile of Robert's clothing. It shined over a brown withered box full of Robert's high school football trophies. It invaded the bathroom and glistened off the grime on the tiles. It also illuminated an empty whiskey bottle near a picture of his ex-fiancé, Jan.

Derek squinted at the water stains on the ceiling and rubbed the prickly hairs on his chin. Every day it was like this, trying to muster up energy to get out of bed and start the day. He had to check in with Jan and see if she had any new information regarding his younger brother's disappearance.

I need a drink.

He sifted through crumpled papers, empty beer bottles, and a circular ashtray filled with used cigarette butts on the night stand. Behind the debris, in a solid oak frame, was a picture of him and Jan taken during the winter at a cabin in northern Minnesota. Her hair blew to the right, forever frozen in the cold arctic wind. He remembered that day clearly. On that day he asked her to marry him and she said yes.

However, the image also reminded him of how things had gone sour since that moment. Jan found out that he'd cheated on her with Rosie, his next door neighbor, and that very same night, she walked out on him and their relationship. Since then he buried his sorrow and guilt in bottles of whiskey and any other type of alcohol he could afford. It was the only way to numb the pain and his feeling of loneliness.

Before his infidelity he consider himself to be a good man. Yet all that changed when Robert disappeared. He blamed his depression and his severe bouts of loneliness for taking up Rosie's offer. Now he considered himself lucky that Jan, who worked for a private detection agency, agreed to look into his brother's case. After all, her sister, Allison, went missing along with him.

Derek carefully swept the crumbled papers to the floor, leaving the picture in place. The wetness dripped from his index and middle fingers as he found a half empty beer can. He drank and its warm, flat contents traveled down to his stomach, snapping his mind back to reality.

His bed creaked from underneath his covers but he confused the noise with the giggling he heard next door. With his back against the wall, he leaned over to reach for his cell phone on the counter while the bed covers pulled themselves back to reveal a mess of tangled brown hair grouped together in a black hair band. A woman looked up at him with her eyes glazed over from sleep.

She stretched out her tiny arms, pricked with small black holes, a jigsaw pattern of blues and blacks underneath her pasty and milky skin. Her skeletal figure lengthened while she stretched. She glanced at him before slapping her hands on his chest.

"Whatcha doin?" she asked.

"Nothin," he replied. "Who're you?"

She giggled. "You're funny." She lay her head on his stomach.

"No, really—who are you?"

Her lips, stained with dried mauve mocha lipstick, left a small faded streak on his chest. "It's me," she said. "Remember?"

He took a closer look. *Who is she?* Suddenly he remembered. He'd gone out last night to a bar in downtown Minneapolis. He must have met her there.

"You need to leave."

She giggled again. The sound of screeching tires from outside his apartment window drowned out the noise coming from the apartment next door. He briefly turned his attention to the world outside and became lost and forgotten in his own hell. Out there everything thrived.

The woman placed her head on his chest but he pushed her away. He examined his own body, his small but noticeable beer belly, his chest littered with small black hairs. He had let himself go since high school. "You really need to go. I'm expecting company."

"In this dump?" She looked around and giggled again.

He pushed her off the bed and stood up. "Don't forget your clothes." He pointed to a pile near his closet. She stomped over to them and began to get dressed, all the while cursing at him underneath her breath.

After she was done she opened the front door.

"I'm sorry but it was a mistake for you to come here," Derek said.

"Yeah. Whatever." She slammed the door behind her.

He sat on the edge of the bed. His stomach gurgled from the warm beer and he tossed the can across the room. He glanced around his apartment. Dirt covered everything around him. His mind fluttered and again he remembered his goals for the day. He couldn't waste any time.

He saw the late edition of the Sunday newspaper on the floor. Last night, during his drunken stupor, he circled the headline in red ink. Another teen went missing at Old Farmer's Road.

Something about that place irked him to no end. When Robert started visiting the place, Derek noticed a change in his behavior. He and his new friends spent a lot of time in the swampy area which angered him—and Allison. Shortly before he vanished, he told Derek that the disappearances weren't coincidences and the police were dealing with something they could never understand.

Derek grabbed his cell phone and looked up Jan's number. He stared at it, debating whether or not to call even though he didn't have any time to lose.

CHAPTER FOUR
Welcome to the Neighborhood

There were a few things Cecilia loathed doing in the world: homework, chores, and wasting an entire day with her mother.

First, she loathed how her mother drove. She allowed other drivers to cut her off, she refused to go over the speed limit, and she never removed her hands from the ten o'clock and two o'clock position on the steering wheel.

Mrs. Richardson pulled into the parking lot, turned off the car, and searched her purse for her shopping list. "Sweetie, you need anything besides shaving cream?"

Cecilia stared out the window at the tall buildings which towered above them. Her mother chose a superstore, Simpleton's, located in a large tan colored building right next to another small convenience store called Towley's.

"Did you hear me?" Her mother's voice broke through her thoughts.

"Just shaving cream." Cecilia exited the car. She waited for her mother, who still fumbled with her purse. Eventually Mrs. Richardson found her wallet and left the car.

Cecilia had never seen so many trees in one city. To pass the time, she started to count each one she saw. She also spotted small ponds, especially near the minor highways and exit ramps.

Minneapolis had so much space and the air didn't burn her lungs while she breathed, like in L.A. That was always a plus.

"Don't forget. We need eggs." Her mother pulled out a small piece of paper and began to read off her shopping list. "And butter. Your father likes butter on his pancakes. Oh and I was thinking about making an apple pie tonight."

"Mom. I don't care." Cecilia felt her phone vibrate in her pocket and yanked it out. A ring tone exploded in the air and she saw her boyfriend's name, Glenn, flash across its small screen. Careful to hide it from her mother's prying eyes, she spoke. "I'll meet you inside."

Her mother paused. "Who's calling you?"

She ignored the question and placed the phone up to her ear.

"Is it Glenn? It better not be Glenn."

Cecilia waved her away and walked to the far end of the building. She cleared her throat before she spoke. "Hey, babe."

"Hey." His warm voice tickled her ear and she leaned against the store's brick wall, giggling childishly. Just hearing his voice made her miss Los Angeles.

"How's Minnesota?" he asked.

She sighed. "There're a lot of trees around here."

"I bet. How you doin'?"

"I could be better," she replied. "I miss you so much."

"I miss you too."

She sighed in exuberance. His voice was so soft, like cotton candy.

"How's the weather?" he asked. "I heard it gets cold there."

"I think that's late in the year," she replied. "Right now it's extremely hot."

"Hot, like, L.A. hot?"

"More humid than anything."

"Well, I just called to see how you're doing," he spoke. "I wasn't sure if your mother confiscated your phone."

"She hasn't, yet." Cecilia giggled.

"Well, I have to get back. I'm cramming three classes in my summer schedule. School's been pure hell."

"Okay. Be safe."

"I will. Love you."

"Love you too." She hung up the phone and placed it in her pocket. Her eyes turned to Towley's.

To her surprise she saw Isaac leaving the convenience store with his sister Elsie following him close behind. Cecilia sulked back further, hoping to avoid their gaze.

Elsie lit a cigarette, inhaled, and lifted her head to the sky. "You can't be serious. You don't even know her."

"I want to get to know her," he replied. "Aren't you curious?"

"You say that to everyone you meet for the first time." Elsie jabbed her thumb in the direction of the convenience store. "You said that about Roger, remember?"

"He was a mistake," Isaac replied. "I'll admit that, but I don't think she is."

While they continued to walk, Cecilia sulked even further back. Her foot collided with a small bag of trash and the noise caught Isaac's attention.

"Hey." He stopped and pointed at her. "It's Cecilia, right?"

She lowered her head, hoping that he wouldn't recognize her but it was already too late.

"What are you doing here?" His eyes widened into a surprised stare.

She looked up and her eyes met his. "I'm waiting for my mom. She's in the store."

Elsie placed her hands on her hips. "Why are you waiting back there?"

She thought for a moment before coming up with a lie. "Smoking."

Elsie chuckled. "Well, smoke your lungs out." She grabbed onto Isaac's arm but he pulled away.

"Stop being rude." He elbowed her.

"Stop being so emotionally attached to people you don't know and I'll stop being rude." She argued back. "Now let's go. We need to decide what to eat tonight."

Emotionally attached? Cecilia stared at Isaac and he quickly looked away. Feeling obligated to speak on his behalf, she stepped out from her corner. "Maybe you should stop being so controlling?"

Elsie grimaced and stepped forward. "What did you just say?"

Cecilia swallowed hard. "Maybe you should stop being so controlling?"

"You don't know anything about us." Now standing face to face with her, Elsie lowered her voice. "You don't know me, little girl."

Isaac yanked on his sister's arm. "I'm sure she didn't mean anything by it."

"No, I don't know you and maybe that's the problem," Cecilia rattled her reply. "You're walking around like you have a chip on your shoulder. Maybe you should tone down that bad ass attitude you have." She watched as Elsie's lips pulled back into a devious smile.

"Let's go." Isaac pulled his sister back.

"No, if she wants to play this game, we can play." Elsie inhaled her cigarette.

"I'm not playing a game. I just think that you're a control freak." Believing that she'd attack her, Cecilia prepared herself. She'd seen this type of behavior before, back in high school in L.A. Girls who used intimidation to get what they want or to prove their superiority over someone else wasn't new to her. However, something didn't feel right about Elsie and Isaac, but she couldn't put her finger on it.

"You really don't want to test me," Elsie said.

Isaac positioned himself between them.

"I'm not scared of you," Cecilia replied.

Elsie flicked her cigarette. "You will be." She stepped back and suddenly laughed. "I like her. She has spunk." She playfully slapped her brother on the shoulder. "Isaac, she's not a perfect fit."

Perfect fit? Cecilia grew uncomfortable and started to think that maybe they were part of some neighborhood gang. Her first impression of Elsie just didn't feel right, but neither did her first impression of Isaac. However his cute looks made up for that.

"Usually all the other girls Isaac talks about are scared of me," Elsie said. "But not you Cecilia. You don't back down, even when you should."

"So I'm right," Isaac said with excitement in his voice. "I told you."

"I'm not going as far as to say that." Elsie sniggered. "I said I like her. Doesn't mean that I want to hang out with her."

"I'm not saying that I want you to." His eyes moved back and forth from his sister to Cecilia.

"You don't know anything about her. Maybe Miss Bernadette has already gotten to her."

"Who's Miss Bernadette?" Cecilia asked.

Isaac scrunched his lips and hesitated to reply. "She's an old woman who lives in that white house with the wooden fence just down the street from us. Have you seen her?"

Cecilia shook her head.

"When you do, walk the other way."

Cecilia folded her arms. "Thanks for the warning."

"Hey, wait up!" Someone called from behind them.

Cecilia looked toward the direction of the voice while Isaac and Elsie didn't flinch. A fat, pudgy teen wearing a red and white striped shirt which looked too tight for his body, jogged hastily toward them. He stopped just short of them and placed his hands on his knees to catch his breath.

"What do you want Roger?" Annoyed, Elsie rolled her eyes.

Cecilia watched Roger struggle to catch his breath as Isaac whispered in her ear. "Roger works at Towley's."

Still winded, Roger smiled and waved at her. "Hey, I'm Roger"

She held out her hand. "Cecilia."

He shook it. "You going to the party tonight?"

"Party?"

"An invite only party." Isaac finally turned around to face Roger. "We were going to tell her." His voice carried a snobbish tone. "Did I ever tell you that you have a big mouth?"

Roger scratched the back of his head and his smile withered from his face. "Sorry, I didn't know."

"Thanks for ruining our surprise." Isaac placed his arm around Cecilia's shoulders. "Wanna go?"

Roger looked dumbfounded. "I thought you were going to invite me?"

"Sorry Roger. Change of plans."

Feeling sorry for him, Cecilia spoke. "I don't know if I can go anyway. My mom is a little overprotective. You should take Roger."

"Roger can find his own way."

Cecilia's eyes widened and before she could retort, Roger spoke.

"It's cool." He forced a smile on his defeated face and his bloated cheeks lifted, temporarily shrinking the size of his eyes. "Maybe next time." He turned and walked back to the store.

As soon as he was out of range, Isaac spoke up again. "You can't be nice to everyone nowadays, especially people like him. Do something nice once, they think you're best friends with them or something."

"Don't you think you were a little mean to him?" Cecilia asked.

"He'll get over it. Plus, he'll show up to the party anyway." He changed the subject. "So we'll pick you up about ten or so?"

Cecilia looked at Elsie, noticing her hardened stare. "I'm not sure I can go."

"It'll be quick." He dropped his arm from Cecilia's shoulders. "See you then." He turned to walk away with Elsie following close behind.

After they disappeared around the block Cassidy immediately remembered that her mother was waiting for her inside the store. She hurriedly walked to the entrance just in time to see her pushing a cart filled with brown bags.

"Where were you?" her mother complained.

"Sorry, I was talking to Isaac and Elsie." Cecilia followed her mother back to their car.

"Who?" Her mother opened the trunk and she began to place the bags in the car.

"They live next door." Cecilia grabbed a bag from her mother's hands. "I'll put them in. Go and start the car."

Mrs. Richardson walked around the car and unlocked the driver's side door. After Cecilia finished, she jumped into the passenger seat, and they drove out of the parking lot.

Her mother readjusted her rear view mirror. "So, these kids live next door? What did they want?"

"They invited me to a party tonight."

Her mother's hands fidgeted on the steering wheel. "A party?" She stared straight ahead.

Cecilia knew exactly what her mother thought. By allowing her to go to this party, she feared that she'd fall back into the same type of crowd back in L.A. Glenn used to invite her all the time to frat parties on campus and sometimes she skipped school to be with him. But this wasn't Glenn and this wasn't L.A.

"I'll be back by midnight."

"You've broken your curfew several times," her mother repeated in a tired chuckle.

"That was in L.A."

"Cecilia, I want a fresh start here. I don't want anything ruining that."

She shot her mother a confused look. "Ruin what?"

"What we have here." Mrs. Richardson kept her eyes on the road. "I don't want you running with the wrong crowd. This is our chance at a new beginning."

"Dad forced us into this new beginning or did you forget?"

"You can continue to blame your father or you can start taking responsibility for your actions."

"Of course I blame him. He was the one who cheated on you," Cecilia argued back.

"We're done talking about this." Mrs. Richardson turned the corner sharply and the car shifted to the side, rocking around the groceries in the trunk.

"You're overreacting like always."

"How else should I act when I can't trust my own daughter?"

"I'm seventeen mom, not twelve."

Mrs. Richardson turned the car's wheel sharp to the left and the car swerved again. "You're not going to this party."

Cecilia scoffed and opened her mouth to reply, but her mother immediately cut her off. "End of discussion."

She felt her mouth drop and her voice silenced. Once again, her mother did a good job ruining her social life.

When they reached their house, they noticed a medium height, thin looking woman standing on the front steps. Bright blue eye shadow and rose red lipstick contrasted with her mocha colored skin. She wore a long brown dress with a black belt resting on her protruding bony hips. She held what looked like a cake covered in a red plastic container.

"I wonder who that is." Mrs. Richardson pulled the car into the driveway.

Cecilia knew exactly who, thanks to Elsie and Isaac. The woman, who had to be Miss Bernadette, wore a noticeable small silver pendant around her neck.

"Hi there." Mrs. Richardson stepped out of the car and made her way to the back.

"Good morning, neighbor," the woman replied in a coarse voice. "I'd like to be the first to welcome you to the neighborhood. I made this delicious lemon pound cake for you and your family."

Cecilia found it odd that after a few weeks that suddenly today, Miss Bernadette decided to welcome them to the neighborhood. She watched closely as Miss Bernadette handed the cake to her mother.

"Why thank you."

"Don't mention it. I'm Bernadette Peters." The woman introduced herself. "People around here call me Miss Bernadette." She held out her wrinkly hand.

"I'm Whitney Richardson and this is my daughter Cecilia."

"Nice to meet you."

Carrying two bags of groceries, Cecilia walked around Miss Bernadette and to the front door. Seconds later she overheard her mother excusing her rude behavior.

"Oh no worries. Moving is always harder on the children than the parents," Miss Bernadette said. "It's just you two?"

"Oh no. My husband's at work."

Cecilia snapped her head around and eyed the woman.

"Well, make sure he gets a piece," Miss Bernadette replied. "All of you. I'm the reigning baking champion at the Minnesota State Fair."

"Really?" Intrigued, Mrs. Richardson smiled. "How is the Fair? We were thinking about going in the fall."

"It's phenomenal. I suggest that you do."

Mrs. Richardson nodded. "Thank you again."

"Really, it's not a problem." Miss Bernadette clutched at her necklace and the silver stone pulsed in her hand. "Just my way of saying welcome to the neighborhood." Her smile slowly dissolved into a leer. "The people here and quite lovely and full of surprises."

CHAPTER FIVE
A Sucker for Pretty Faces

Cecilia stood in front of her full-length mirror, admiring the clothes she had picked out for the party. She turned to the side and sucked in her stomach, dropping a few pounds from her waist. Like most teenage girls, she found flaws in her body. In her mind her breasts sagged slightly which could only be solved by tightening her bra straps. She pulled back her hair and within seconds, she changed her mind and decided to let her curls rest freely on her shoulders. Throughout her attempts, nothing satisfied her.

She sighed and tossed her red shirt, still clinched on the hanger, onto the bed. She reached back into the closet, pulling out her favorite black shirt with a low V-neck. She convinced herself that her first impression didn't matter, but she knew that wasn't the case. Glenn loved her regardless of what she wanted to wear. Besides, she wasn't going to the party for any other reason than to have a good time and to get away from her nagging mother.

She put on the shirt and returned to the mirror. She smoothed down the strands of her brown hair sticking straight up on the top of her head and wiped her face.

The noise of pots clinging in the kitchen brought her briefly back to reality. Her mother cooked dinner but her father, who called to tell her that he was running late, ruined her idea of a sit down family dinner. Her mother blindly believed him, but for Cecilia, his past actions didn't make any of his excuses reliable. Running late meant only one thing. He ran with that excuse constantly, just like when they lived in Los Angeles.

She straightened her shirt and puckered her lips when she heard her mother's roaring voice from the kitchen. "Cecilia. Are you going to eat?"

"What?" Cecilia headed out of her room.

Her mother stood in the kitchen, wiping her forehead as if she'd just finished a long work day. "Are you going somewhere?" She eyed Cecilia from head to toe.

"I told you, Isaac and Elsie invited me to a party tonight."

"I thought I made it clear. You're not going." She grabbed a knife from the kitchen drawer and stared at the lemon pound cake resting on the counter, dissecting it with her mind before she began to cut. "Go back in your room and change."

The front door opened and Cecilia heard her father's distinctive voice. He dropped his suitcase on the floor and closed the door behind him. He loosened his checkered tie and he approached his wife. "Sorry I'm late. They had a huge meeting at the end of the day." He kissed her on the cheek.

"How was your first day?" She kissed him back.

Mr. Richardson shrugged slightly. "Great. A few employees had issues dealing with the new software the company bought last week."

"Dinner's on the stove. I made spaghetti."

He rubbed his hands together, slipped off his shoes, and placed his keys on the kitchen counter. After licking his lips, he turned to Cecilia. "Hey kiddo."

Cecilia waved lazily.

"What? You too busy to say hi to you father?"

"She's upset," Mrs. Richardson spoke.

"About what?"

"She was invited to a party tonight. I told her she couldn't go."

Cecilia shrugged, indifferent to her mother's explanation. She had made up her mind. She was going as soon as Isaac arrived.

"Why can't she go?" Mr. Richardson scanned his daughter admiring her wardrobe. "Is she grounded?"

"John, she doesn't know the kids who invited her."

"They live next door." Cecilia looked toward the window. *Isaac, where are you?* She hoped he'd appear before her mother continued riding her high horse.

"How can she get to know them if you won't let her leave the house?" Mr. Richardson pointed to the pound cake on the counter. "You made this?"

"A lady from the neighborhood brought it over as a welcoming gift."

He grabbed a plate from the cabinet. "She's a teenager, Whitney. It's a new city. Let her branch out a little." He piled the spaghetti on his plate then covered his mountain of food with garlic seasoning.

The sound of a car's horn interrupted their conversation. Cecilia stood up and looked out the window to see Isaac sitting in a dark four-door sedan with tinted windows parked right in front of her house. She thanked him under her breath for his superb timing.

She grabbed her purse and headed for the front door when her mother called out to her. Defiant, Cecilia ignored her and opened the front door.

"Whitney, let her have some fun." Mr. Richardson filled his mouth with a fork full of spaghetti. Sauce collected on his lips and he licked them before slurping a noodle string. "Be back before one, honey."

Mrs. Richardson sighed. "For once I would like you to agree with me John."

Cecilia didn't let their mild argument stop her in her stride. While they continued to talk, she closed the door and walked hastily to Isaac's car.

The warm summer breeze slapped against her cheeks and her hair blew along with it. She tucked the wild strands behind her right ear and approached the car. Isaac waved at Cecilia to get in. "Hurry up. We're going to be late."

"Yeah, hurry up, C." Elsie, who sat in the front seat, also spoke. "I don't want to be late for you."

C? Cecilia couldn't think of any other nickname that got under her skin. She climbed into the car and Isaac sped off before she closed the door.

Classic rock thumped from the car's speakers. Elsie inhaled from her cigarette and looked back at Cecilia. "Nice shirt."

Her compliment took Cecilia by surprise. "Thanks," she replied. "And oh, thanks for inviting me."

"Thank Isaac," Elsie said. "I didn't want you to come."

"Elsie, you said you'd be nice to her," Isaac spoke.

"This is me being nice."

From the rear view mirror, Isaac looked at Cecilia. "It's going to be a fun night. I think you'll enjoy it. You might even like the other place I want to take you."

"What other place?" Cecilia reached into her pocket, pulling out her pack of cigarettes.

Elsie laughed and elbowed Isaac in his side. "I doubt that."

Besides her rude behavior, Cecilia also noticed how different Elsie looked. Her hair was pulled up in a tight ponytail that bounced gently on her shoulders with each bump the car drove over. Dark eye shadow covered her eyelids and glittery dark purple lipstick covered her lips.

Cecilia lit her cigarette. "So that woman you told me about, Miss Bernadette. She was standing on my door step when I got back from the store."

"What did she want?" Isaac asked.

Suddenly, Elsie also became interested. "Did she say anything to you?"

"You think Cecilia would be in the car if she did?" Isaac continued to drive.

"No. She just welcomed my family to the neighborhood and gave us a pound cake," Cecilia replied.

"Good," Elsie said as she laughed. "She tells the new people in the neighborhood to avoid us because we don't put up with her shit. Supposedly, we're the bad kids your parents warned you about."

Isaac pressed on the brake with his foot, slowing down at an intersection. "Don't worry about her. She's just nosey."

Elsie jokingly smacked the back of Isaac's head. "You would say something as stupid as that."

Isaac rubbed the back of his head. "You worry too much about that woman, Elsie." He turned up the radio. A song by Jefferson Airplane blasted from the car's speakers and Isaac began to sing along to Grace Slick's howling voice.

Elsie exhaled and cigarette smoke curled inside the car. She turned back to look at Cecilia. "You know, I think we got off on the wrong foot."

"It's cool." Cecilia glanced out the window.

"No, it's not. I can be a bitch sometimes. It's just my nature," Elsie replied. "I'm very protective of my baby brother."

"Yeah, I can see that."

"So if he's interested in someone, I'm there to make sure he doesn't fall off track."

Her explanation sounded too broad for Cecilia and she peddled her fingertips together. "I guess I can understand where you're coming from."

"No. You really can't." Elsie scanned Cecilia's clothing. She then tapped Isaac on the shoulder. "I think my brother likes you."

Cecilia watched as Isaac turned around, nodded nervously, and turned back to the road.

"He's shy." Elsie whispered to Cecilia.

"I'm not shy," Isaac replied back.

"He thinks you're different, in a good way." Elsie lowered her voice to a whisper. "But you'll never be good enough for him."

The night air carried the smell of oncoming rain. As the car sped down the slick, wet roads, Cecilia realized that Minnesota weather wasn't all that bad, especially at night. She had heard about the severe thunderstorms and the story of a tornado landing near downtown Minneapolis, swirling through neighborhoods on the north side of the city.

Isaac drove madly, swerving in and out of traffic at 80 miles per hour. Eventually Elsie stopped with her weird questions and statements, which made Cecilia feel uncomfortable, and they remained quiet for the remaining part of the ride, listening to the Jefferson Airplane song, "Greasy Heart," before Isaac switched the CD, replacing it with The Doors. Jim Morrison's sensual voice poured out of the car and the song, "The End" was barely over when they pulled up in front of a white two-story house with a brown porch.

A long driveway lead up to an attached garage on the side of the house. The opened window blinds revealed a house packed with party goers. A group of teenagers walked up to the house. They opened the door and music from inside blasted out into the air.

"This is the place." Isaac turned off his car.

Cecilia stepped out of the car, seeing that Elsie and Isaac had already exited and began walking up the driveway. She looked over the house once more.

Elsie looked back at her. "What are you waiting for C?"

Hot stuffy air filled with the smell of cigarette smoke infiltrated Cecilia's nostrils as she entered. Three teenagers, who looked no older than her, stood in the foyer laughing at each other while sipping alcohol from their red plastic cups. Rap music blared in the background mixed in with the alcoholic chants of another group in the living room egging on a male , downing a bottle of Scotch.

Cecilia followed Elsie and they walked through another crowd before changing direction and heading toward the living room. Elsie walked by a couple sitting on a couch near the back window. She eyed them as they kissed, their arms rubbing all over one another. She crossed her arms in front of her chest and grinned in amusement. The boy slowly slid his hand up the girl's thigh and under her short, white skirt.

"I hate public displays of affection." Elsie whispered to Cecilia who stood closely behind her. "They can do this behind closed doors. It's stupid."

"Maybe they're just in love?" Cecilia replied.

"Bullshit, they aren't in love." Elsie continued. "That's lust." She continued to walk. A boy ran past them, screaming at the top of his lungs, tripping over his feet before catching himself. Near the opposite end of the room a group stood around a keg seated on top of a table. Elsie pointed and a wide grin appeared on her face.

"Wanna drink?"

Cecilia nodded. She wasn't a fan of beer but any available alcohol, especially free alcohol, she couldn't pass up.

They walked over to the keg, grabbing the attention of kids huddled around it. One female, wearing nothing but a pink bikini top and a short silver skirt flipped back her curly brown hair. "Hey." She pointed at Elsie. "I know you."

"Not likely." Elsie grabbed a plastic cup.

"No, I think I do." The girl giggled.

Elsie ignored the girl and she handed Cecilia the plastic cup.

"Oh I know." The girl smiled joyfully. "You were at Douglas' party last week!"

Elsie took a second look at the girl. "I don't think so."

"I think I saw you there. You were with that boy...what's his name again?" She paused. "Damn, I don't remember his name."

"Nope. You have the wrong person."

"Elsie!" The girl continued to point at her. "Yeah, you have a brother, right?" She held out her hand. "I'm Julie."

Elsie filled her cup with beer and she took a gulp. She then grabbed Cecilia's cup and filled it with beer. "You have me confused with someone else." She handed the filled cup back to Cecilia.

"Thanks." Cecilia had no intention of drinking at that moment. She looked around the room, wondering where Isaac had disappeared to. She felt more comfortable in his presence than Elsie's. Her eyes glanced over a large bookcase next to a flat screen television covered by a white bed sheet.

Cecilia followed Elsie away from the keg and they stood near the entrance of the room. Music thumped from a stereo system across the hall in the living room where a dancing crowd had gathered. Elsie remained quiet, eying the dancing crowd that moved in a synchronized rhythm. Cecilia also watched but she felt as if someone stared at them from behind. She looked over her shoulder, her eyes meeting Julie's.

"You sure you don't know her?" Cecilia gulped her beer, feeling it slide down her throat. "She knows you."

"Yeah, I know her." Elsie finally admitted. "I just don't like her."

"You don't like anyone, do you?" Cecilia asked.

"No, not really," she replied. "I especially hate attention whores and that's what she is."

"Lighten up a little." Cecilia felt the beer she had just devoured rush from her stomach and to her nose.

"She was all over my brother at that party," Elsie added. "Speaking of Isaac, where is he?"

Cecilia gazed around the room until she saw him standing in the corner. "He's over there."

Elsie followed Cecilia's gaze. "He's patrolling again."

"Patrolling?" Cecilia asked as she watched Isaac eying the crowd.

Elsie ignored Cecilia's question. "We're not staying long. Make sure you finish your beer."

"But we just got here."

"You can stay if you want." Elsie took a swig of her beer. "Actually, I'd prefer if you stayed."

Isaac walked through the dancing crowd and toward them. His eyes shifted passed them to Julie. "Did you see Julie?" Isaac looked at Elsie.

"Unfortunately," Elsie replied.

"I want to take her with us."

Elsie slapped Isaac on the shoulder. "You're kidding, right?"

"Stop hitting me." He rubbed the inflamed area.

"Isaac, think about it for a moment. She isn't your type."

"She is my type for tonight," he replied back.

"What are you guys talking about?" Cecilia asked them.

"It's always what you want Isaac." Elsie's rolled her eyes. "You just can't be happy with what you have."

Cecilia cocked her head. Before arriving at the party Elsie told her that Isaac liked her and now he wanted Julie. It didn't make sense and she brushed it off. She wasn't interested in him like that anyway.

"I thought you don't like the annoying types." Elsie briefly looked back at Julie.

"Then who else do you think I should choose?"

"Someone who isn't annoying and who is your type." Elsie shrugged and sipped her beer. "Isaac you've made some pretty crazy choices in the past. This is the worst one yet."

"To you, I'll never make the right choice."

They turned back. The group that stood around the keg had dispersed, leaving Julie who now walked toward them.

Elsie sighed and rolled her eyes. "Here we go." She gulped the remaining alcohol and tossed the empty cup over her shoulder.

"Isaac!" Julie wrapped her arms around Isaac's waist. "How have you been?"

Isaac stared back at her. "Hey Julie."

"Last time I saw you was at Douglas' party."

"Yeah, yeah." Isaac nervously scratched the back of his head. "Good times."

Julie looked at Elsie. "I don't think Elsie remembers me though."

"Oh I remember. I just don't care."

Julie paused. "What's your problem?"

Elsie leaned back and crossed her arms.

Julie then extended her hand to Cecilia. "Hi, I'm Julie."

"Cecilia." Cecilia introduced herself but she found her introduction lost as Julie began to rub her hand on Isaac's chest. Isaac whispered in her ear and Julie giggled slightly.

"I'll be right back." Julie waved the red plastic cup and smiled at Isaac before she walked away. "Gotta refill."

Isaac waited until Julie left the room before he spoke again. "Yep, she's my choice for tonight." He nodded as if he satisfied his own doubt. "You have to accept that Elsie."

Elsie walked off, leaving Cecilia with him. She remained reticent, unsure of what to do or say. Their behavior mystified her and their communication toward one another didn't resemble a loving sister and brother relationship. Cecilia blamed it on Elsie's lack of etiquette.

When she confronted Isaac, he shrugged. "She's just looking out for me."

"She's rude and obnoxious," Cecilia replied.

"She has to be." Isaac turned to her. "She's just making sure that I'm making the right decisions. She was right when she said that I've made some bad ones."

Soon Julie returned, holding two plastic cups full of alcohol in her hands. Isaac wrapped his arm around her shoulders and they walked away, leaving her alone.

Cecilia walked down the hallway to the kitchen. She peered into the doorway before walking in. Pieces of cheese, crackers, and meat were scattered across the kitchen counter. She saw a small pool of dried soda in the middle of the floor and six kegs stacked up against the wall.

"Hey."

She heard a familiar voice around her and she turned. She saw Roger standing in the doorway wearing a brown cardigan sweater, a white shirt, and black pants. His stomach slightly protruded over the waist of his pants and struck out slightly from underneath his shirt.

"Roger right?"

"Yeah, it's Roger."

"I guess you came after all."

"Yeah, why wouldn't I?" Roger tilted his head slightly, cocking his eyebrow. "I know popular people too."

Cecilia shook her head, clueless on how to reply.

"Elsie and Isaac aren't the only people who know people." He walked over to the fridge and he opened the door.

"Sorry. I didn't mean it that way."

He began to scan the fridge for food, pulling out a can of whip cream. He closed the door and began to shake the can. "I know just as many people as they do." A load of thick, swirly whip cream blasted from the can and into his mouth. Cecilia cringed as Roger began to chew.

"They're taking you to Old Farmer's Road, aren't they?" He licked his lips free of the billowy cream. When it came to Roger she now understood Elsie's reason for not wanting to be around him. He was an eyesore to watch.

"What's Old Farmer's Road?" Cecilia watched his highly unattractive mannerisms.

"It's a creepy place, but kind of cool at the same time, you know?" He squirted more cream into his mouth. "Some people call it the devil's playground because there've been a lot of murders and deaths down there." His cheeks were puffed and filled with the cream. "You want some?" He offered the can to Cecilia.

"Oh, no thanks." Cecilia edged her way to the kitchen entrance. She walked down the hall, excusing herself through a male group. Two boys ran by her to the kitchen, screaming at the top of their lungs with their arms raised in the air.

"Oh, you're still here?"

Cecilia heard Elsie who stood behind her.

"Why wouldn't I be?" Cecilia quickly turned around.

"I thought that maybe I'd scared you off."

"I don't scare easily."

"Yeah, that's what they all say." Elsie changed the subject of the conversation. "So, what were you and my brother talking about earlier?" Her eyes turned to Isaac standing across the room near the front door talking with Julie.

"You," Cecilia replied in a snarky tone.

"Oh, I'm flattered."

Cecilia gave Elsie an awkward glance. "Why are you so mean to everyone?"

"Because my brother is a sucker for pretty faces." Her eyes moved across the crowd until she found Isaac sitting on a couch in the far corner. With a quick nod, he stood up and approached them.

"I'm hungry," Elsie said. "Let's go."

Isaac nodded. "We're sharing tonight, right?"

Elsie looked at Julie again and she squinted. "Are you sure about her?"

Isaac turned back to Julie and with Elsie they continued their strange stare. Finally, Isaac nodded. "Oh I'm sure." He then walked back over to Julie.

Elsie looked to Cecilia. "Ready C?"

"Where are we going?"

"Old Farmer's Road," she replied as she elbowed Cecilia in her side. "You said you don't scare easy, right? Well, I'm dying to test that theory."

CHAPTER SIX

Old Farmer's Road

Old Farmer's Road was a misconception. To Cecilia, the road didn't look old at all, but she couldn't say the same for the area. They drove past a small local park next to a vast swamp. Old street lamps lined the dark street along with rotten wooden signs directing visitors to the location. The car's headlights briefly exposed a large metal sign connected to a metal chain blocking the entrance to the bridge that read "No Trespassing."

"This is it." Isaac parked the car, switched off the ignition, and looked back at Elsie and Cecilia in the backseat.

"Finally." Elsie opened the door. "I don't think I could've taken much more of Julie's giggling." She got out of the car and slammed the door shut behind her.

For the first time, Cecilia couldn't agree more. During the entire ride Julie sat in the front seat, giggling and sweet talking Isaac with her hand firmly placed on his leg. At one point she sucked on his earlobe and periodically stared back at Cecilia with a smirk to claim that he belonged to her. But when she rubbed her hand up his forearm, discovering his scars, she began to hesitate, so Isaac quickly changed the subject. The more Julie pried, the more annoyed Elsie became.

Cecilia left the vehicle followed by Isaac and Julie. The sky began to clear with only a few remnants of rain clouds partially blocking the moonlight. Cecilia blinked, letting her vision adapt to the darkness. Just beyond the "No Trespassing" sign she gazed at the old wooden bridge with rusted beams. The smell of river water overcame the smell of the asphalt. The wind picked up speed and the tall oak trees wisped from side to side.

"I heard this place is haunted," Julie said.

"Don't tell me you're scared?" Elsie asked, jokingly.

"I'm not a kid. I don't believe in ghosts."

"So what if you saw one with your own eyes?" Elsie asked. "Would you believe it then?"

"Ghosts don't exist, Elsie."

They walked through the parking lot, overgrown with weeds that broke through the cracked asphalt. They approached the rickety bridge and Elsie, who led the way, lifted the chain blocking off the bridge and stepped forward.

Cecilia approached the beginning of the bridge but she didn't go any farther. At one point Isaac pretended to chase Elsie. He soon stopped when he noticed that Cecilia wasn't following them.

"Come on Cecilia! The bridge is safe." Isaac jumped up and down on the rotted wood.

"Maybe she's the one who's scared?" Julie snickered.

Elsie rolled her eyes. "No one was talking to you." Her comment silenced Julie.

Cecilia examined the bridge's wooden surface before she took her first step. She noticed that several pieces of wood were moldy, in stark contrast to what Isaac said. She had never seen wood this old on a stable bridge.

"Come on, C!" Elsie motioned for her again. "This won't be any fun if you don't cross."

Cecilia stepped again and she heard the wood underneath her feet creak. She stopped.

"I'll get her." Isaac trotted over to Cecilia. He held out his hand and she grabbed it. "You won't fall through, I promise," he said. "I won't let you."

They walked with Cecilia taking baby steps. She kept her eyes glued to the wooden beams.

"We walked across it just yesterday." Isaac continued to reassure her.

Cecilia's baby steps morphed into a comfortable walk. Her eyes locked on the currents of the Minnesota River running beneath the bridge. The water crashed against the small rocks and a green soapy substance collected against its banks. The wind increased and the bridge gently swayed from side to side. She looked up and noticed that Elsie and Julie had already made it to the other end.

"Why would you hang out here?" Cecilia commented.

"I love it here," Isaac smiled. They heard another deafening sound beneath their feet and again Cecilia halted in her tracks.

"Once you reach the end, it's a piece of cake." Isaac took another step.

The breeze picked up, carrying a pungent odor of fish, as they reached the middle of the bridge. Cecilia curled her nose.

"Yeah, it kinda stinks down here but you'll get used to it." Isaac placed his hands around the rusted metal chain attached to the bridge's metal beams.

Cecilia gently pulled back the sleeve of his shirt to see his scars. She studied their abstract patterns, noticing that they were old. "Not to side with Julie but I have to admit. I'm curious about how you got those."

Isaac pulled down his sleeve. "It was a long time ago." He glanced over the edge. "The Minnesota and the Mississippi Rivers meet just up that way, near Fort Snelling." Changing the subject, Isaac began to explain the routes of the two rivers to Cecilia, telling her that the Minnesota River ran southeast and oddly enough it switched and then ran northeast. However, at Old Farmer's Road, the two rivers fought with each other for control. It made the underwater currents unpredictable and dangerous and since the bridge only stood a couple of feet above the river below, high tides made crossing it almost impossible. The moonlight glistened off the top of the dark, running water. She saw a faint image of themselves on the surface and she quickly moved away from the edge.

Elsie yelled from the edge of the bridge for them to pick up the pace.

They proceeded forward and with each step Cecilia grew more cautious. Isaac wrapped his arm around her waist while he guided her across. She heard the waves of water crash against the wooden beams of the bridge and felt the bridge move slightly from left to right. She tripped over an upturned piece of rotten wood, nearly falling to the ground, but Isaac strengthened his grip and held her steady.

Cecilia regained her footing and soon they reached the opposite end where Elsie and Julie waited.

"That wasn't so bad, was it?" Isaac smiled.

Cecilia regained her posture. No, it wasn't that bad, but the jealous glare she received from Julie made her feel uneasy.

They continued along. Tall trees blocked out the moonlight and the dirt path ahead led into darkness. Cecilia heard the sounds of crickets in the tall grass near the riverbed and felt a small pinch on her arm. She immediately slapped the area with her hand. "I hate mosquitoes." She rubbed the inflamed skin. This wasn't what I signed up for, she thought to herself. She had no choice but to follow them deeper into the inky woods.

Julie slowed her pace and soon Cecilia caught up to her. She dissected her with her eyes. "Do you like Isaac?" She asked in a whisper.

Taken aback Cecilia shook her head.

"Good." Julie smiled. "Because I like him. I've always liked him. He's mine."

The sound of leaves rustling and branches swinging broke the silence, making Cecilia turn her head to the left.

Startled, Julie also faced the noise. "What was that?" She adjusted her eyes and glared into the dark woods in an attempt to locate the noise. The wind grew still and the crickets increased their chirping, making it hard to hear the sound again.

Isaac placed his hand on Julie's shoulder. "It's just the wind."

Cecilia doubted it. She heard the faint sound of Elsie cursing and she looked forward, watching her lean against a tree. "There's a rock in my shoe." She slipped off her right shoe and began to shake the dirt free. She looked at Cecilia. "I guess this is your first time actually around nature."

"Not really." Cecilia looked ahead at the dark path. "Did anyone bring flashlights?"

Elsie put her shoe back on. She looked at Isaac. "We never bring flashlights down here. Don't need them."

"How can you see in the dark?" Julie asked.

"I can use the flashlight app on my phone." Cecilia searched her pockets. She pulled out her phone, searched for her app. Soon a bright white light revealed the path a couple of feet in front of them.

"If you makes you two feel safer." Elsie snarled.

At first the path seemed desolate. A small rabbit hopped across the trail in front of them and Cecilia jerked slightly, her body colliding with Isaac. Trees and thick bushes lined the path and their long branches began to curve above them, forming a nature made tunnel with no way out aside from turning back.

Small bushes replaced the trees and to the left Cecilia glanced at the largest rock cropping she had ever seen. The sandstone, heavily diluted with black water trails running down the side of its face, also revealed graffiti covering the lower portions of its surface.

Elsie cautiously approached it. She rubbed her hand along the surface, feeling the grimy, wet texture on her palms.

Cecilia approached the rock and scanned the multicolored images. A picture of a closed fist with its index finger pointing back to the bridge caught her eye. A phrase in bubbly black letters spelled out: "Go Back Now." To the right of the picture she saw another drawing of a closed fist but this time its index finger pointed down the path. Under the picture Cecilia read more writing; "Old Farmer. This way."

"That's a new one." Elsie pointed to the image of the closed fist.

"You've got to be kidding me," Isaac laughed.

"Old Farmer?" Julie read the bubbled words. "Like I said. I don't believe in ghosts."

"The Old Farmer isn't a ghost," Isaac replied.

"Then what is he?"

Elsie turned to face her. Her eyes widened and her face filled with excitement. "If you meet him tonight, you'll find out."

They walked deeper into the woods. Once again the shrubbery-lined route led the way. But as they continued walking, Cecilia noticed that taller trees began to replace them. The air grew thick and she found it difficult to breathe. She felt smothered by the greenery around her. The environment turned quiet and she no longer heard the crickets chirping. The only sound she heard were their footsteps crunching over the soil.

"So, where exactly are we going?"

"Yeah, were are we going?" Julie kissed Isaac's cheek.

"We're almost there," Isaac said. He looked at Elsie and she grinned, the left corner of her mouth lifting slightly.

"Are you sure?" Julie asked in a squeaking voice. "I mean, unless an old farmer really lives down here, I don't understand why you'd come out to this place. It stinks."

"Anything is possible."

"Yeah but a ghost?" She shrugged and laughed. "That's stupid."

"What's the story behind this old farmer?" Cecilia asked. Maybe a story ease the pain she felt from walking on the hard dirt path.

"He used to live here, down this road. Like over a hundred and fifty years ago."

"A hundred and fifty years?"

"Around the 1860s," Elsie replied. "During that time this area was just another small frontier town. He lived somewhere back here away from everyone with his children and their dog."

"The old farmer is an urban legend," Julie said, interrupting the conversation.

"I'm speaking." Elsie snapped at her. Julie quietly mouthed the word "sorry" and nodded for Elsie to continue.

"The people in the town thought the farmer and his family were devil worshippers. So when a woman from a prominent family went missing, they blamed him."

"So he didn't kill her?" Julie asked. "Because I heard that he did."

"Shut up and let me finish the story," Elsie blurted back. "So there was a witch who lived in town. She used magic to create a small clay figurine of the farmer. It was supposed to make him mortal, so he could be killed."

"Magic?" Julie mocked.

"Let her finish the story," Cecilia said, hushing Julie.

"So after the witch did that, the townspeople killed his dog and dragged the farmer to a nearby tree to string him up," Elsie continued. "They left his body swinging from that tree for months until his children cut him down and buried his decomposing body somewhere in the surrounding woods."

"How did his children escape from the mob?" Cecilia asked.

"They hid in the swamps," Elsie replied. "According to the legend, they're still alive today."

Julie exploded into laughter and quickly covered her mouth. "That's a stupid story. How can his kids still be alive today? They'd be over 150 years old."

Cecilia nodded her head in agreement with Julie's comment.

"Because he wasn't human and his children weren't human," Elsie replied. "They lived by eating the flesh of their victims."

"Eating their flesh, like...literally eating flesh?" Cecilia asked.

"What other way would you eat flesh, Cecilia?" Elsie brazenly answered her question.

In the distance they heard the sound of running water. The moonlight broke through the dense leaves and branches of the tree, revealing a turn up ahead. Cecilia turned off her phone app and placed it back in her pocket, having no need for its dim light. The turn was sharp and they approached the edge, staring down the steep embankment and the rushing waters of another river.

The river was wide and on the opposite side stood an old abandoned factory. Behind the light fog, Cecilia saw the downtown skyline of Minneapolis. A plane flew overhead and they caught another whiff of rotting fish. Cecilia immediately covered her nose and stepped back. An unnatural smell of rotting eggs also filled her nostrils.

The path turned and strayed away from the edge of the river. It ventured farther back into the woods and away from the fish filled air and the sound of moving water. A rustling sound echoed from the bushes ahead and they stopped. A brown and white cat jumped from the darkness, scurrying past Julie who screamed. The cat hissed and ran down the road until it disappeared in the darkness.

"It scratched me!" Julie examined her arm.

"It was just a cat." Elsie snorted while she still laughed.

Julie clenched her forearm and examined the small cuts bubbling with blood. "That's not funny." She sneered at Elsie. "Take me back. I want to go back now."

Elsie's laughter dwindled. "It's just a scratch. Relax."

Julie replied. "Don't tell me to relax."

The wind blew and Cecilia shivered. From her peripheral view she glanced at Julie rubbing her wound. The area had turned extremely dark and her eyes began to adjust to the environment.

"Isaac, I want to go back," Julie asked again.

"Maybe we should go back." Cecilia agreed.

"Stop being pussies," Elsie replied.

"What is it with you?" Julie's voice grew tense. "It's not safe out here, especially without any light. Why would you come down here without any flashlights or a freakin' phone?" She looked to Cecilia. "Take out your phone."

Cecilia gripped her phone and turned on the app again. In front of them they saw the remains of a disemboweled animal. Pieces of flesh, bone, as well as brown and white fur, were strewn across the dirt path. The ground underneath the cadaver was saturated with blood. Cecilia stepped forward and felt something squash underneath her. She lifted her foot, staring at what was left of what looked like a leg. They paused at the morbid picture.

Julie screamed and she held onto Isaac. "Please, let's go back."

Isaac pushed her away and he knelt near the remains. "Bite marks?" He stood up. The right paw of the animal, slightly disconnected from the rest of the remains, twitched intermittingly. "Cecilia, can you bring the light over here?"

Cecilia handed her phone to Isaac. The sight was disturbing. She'd never seen anything like this.

Isaac grabbed a stick from the road and began to poke at. "I think this was the cat that scratched Julie." He looked back.

"The cat that was back there?" Cecilia looked behind them. "But didn't it run this way?" Now frightened, she stepped back. "We should go back."

Isaac scanned the wooden area around them. "There are loose dogs around here."

"Are you blind?" Julie disagreed. "A dog can't do that."

Cecilia agreed with Julie, a dog wasn't capable of the carnage she saw before her. It had to be something larger.

"Stop whining," Elsie huffed at Julie's reply.

"Are you blind?" Julie raised her voice as her face turned beet red.

"We're in the woods Julie. There are animals everywhere." Elsie walked forward. "This isn't the first time."

"But it's the first time for me," Julie replied, "and I don't like it."

Ahead Cecilia noticed a small light flickered in the distance. She also realized that Elsie had disappeared into the darkness.

"Elsie!" Cecilia called out her name as she stepped forward, solely concentrated on the blinking enigma. The light seemed to dance in the distance and its glow was concentrated near the ground.

"There's something over there." Cecilia pointed to the light. They followed her gaze to the light down the road. The light pulsated and grew in size, becoming brighter by the second.

"It's nothing," Isaac said.

"I'm going back," Cecilia's voice cracked. She began to tire of Isaac's explanations. Something wasn't adding up and she didn't want to stand around to find out. "Something killed this cat." She pointed to the remains. "I don't know what that is and I don't want to find out."

The light became brighter and they heard the faint sound of leaves and dirt crunching in the distance. The wind picked up and the trees swayed from left to right. Small chunks of the dead cat tumbled across the path. A dog howled in the distance followed by snarling and barking.

Cecilia stepped back, feeling the need to run. She looked at Isaac for assurance but didn't see an ounce of fear in his eyes. Instead he stared straight ahead at the light quickly approaching.

"I'm leaving," Julie said, turning to Cecilia. "Are you coming or what?"

Cecilia nodded, and as she turned to speak to Isaac, he placed his hand on her shoulder. "Don't go." His eyes widened and a mischievous grin appeared on his face. "It won't hurt you because I told it not to."

Cecilia backed away. Butterflies ravaged her stomach and the air around her became thick and almost unbearable. "Julie, let's go."

Julie screeched in terror as she pointed at the darkness. With her eyes consumed with fear and her voice breaking the sound barrier, she spoke as her lips twitched. "Did you see it?"

Cecilia focused her sight but she saw nothing.

Julie turned and ran, however, Cecilia remained still, skeptical about what she saw. The light, now brighter, began to approach them, picking up speed.

"Isaac, we need to go," Cecilia said, starting to backtrack.

"Don't run," Isaac replied in a collected voice. "It'll chase you if you run."

Cecilia turned and ran. She felt her heartbeat increase and her lungs ache. Ahead she saw the outline of Julie running frantically. The growling they heard earlier grew louder followed by the sounds of an animal breathing heavily.

To her surprise, she saw the same light that was once behind her flare up in front of her. It made the tiny hairs on her arm tingle. She tried to stop in her tracks but she tripped over an upturned tree root and fell to the ground.

Cecilia felt a sharp burning sensation in her ankle. She looked down noticing she had twisted it and she couldn't run any farther. She lifted herself to her feet and began to limp, and she tripped again. Cecilia tried to get up again but this time the pain was too unbearable to stand. She began to drag herself forward, but as the light grew bright, illuminating everything around her, it stung her eyes and then disappeared.

In its place she saw a dog standing guard over her. Its glowing red eyes shot up at her and it snarled, showing its sharp canines. Its body was completely ravaged, with ribs half exposed, pieces of flesh caught in its sharp claws, and rotten skin dangling from its mouth. Its nose was hardly there at all. Cecilia screamed in pure fright but her voice was drowned out by the sound of Julie screaming ahead.

The dog now ran toward Julie, launching itself at her, sinking its teeth into her back. Julie fell. Cecilia raised her upper body, watching helplessly as the dog repeatedly attacked Julie. It nipped at her legs and arms before locking its teeth onto her neck. Behind her Cecilia heard footsteps closing in and she turned, seeing Isaac approaching her.

"Don't be scared," Isaac spoke, while watching the dog rip Julie to shreds.

Cecilia felt her mouth drop, disturbed by the sight of Julie's pending death. Isaac smiling at her just added to her confusion.

"Cecilia, this will be quick and painless." He reached into his pocket before he turned to speak to the dog. "Yes, I'm sure. I want to do this."

"Isaac, what's going on?" Cecilia caught wind of his strange behavior.

He continued to speak to the ravaged animal standing next to him. "Yes, I remember what happened to the other one. You keep reminding me...I know...I was wrong."

The dog growled at him.

"He wasn't our third...No, I'm not wrong about her! Stop insulting me!" He pulled out three small, smooth stones. "I'm doing this no matter what you say. It's my choice...Yes, I know what you'll do if I'm wrong, but I'm not wrong. Not this time."

Its deep growl got louder and Cecilia felt the dog's fetid breath on her leg. She closed her eyes, and thought about Glenn. Even memoires of her parents flooded her rattled mind.

"Yes, I'll look out for her. She's mine." He forced Cecilia's head back. "It won't hurt going down."

She felt one stone sliding down her tongue and to the back of her throat. It singed and her eyes began to water. She didn't feel the object enter her stomach, but she heard a scratchy voice. It came from the environment around her, carried by the mild wind.

Just one more.

One more.

As it spoke, it jiggled her brain, making her close her eyes.

Isaac leaned over Cecilia and his lips parted, forming a warm smile. "I chose you, Cecilia."

She closed her eyes, waiting for death to take her.

CHAPTER SEVEN
Miss Bernadette

Cecilia opened her eyes.

She focused, centering on the cracked ceiling of her bedroom. She raised her head slowly, glaring across the room at a bright blue light flashing from the bottom of her computer monitor. Her thoughts immediately turned to what happened at Old Farmer's Road. She remembered Isaac driving her there, walking across the bridge and into the depth of the swamp, and the dog. She couldn't forget the dog. However, everything else after that was too hazy and enigmatic to sort out. It all seemed to be part of a weird, psychotic dream. What she saw and experienced could never happen—ever. It just wasn't possible.

She saw the clothes she wore last night sprawled across the bedroom floor, including her pants splotched with dirt. As she climbed out of bed a sharp pain shot through her right shoulder and down her back. She gripped the area tightly as she opened the blinds, letting the sun's rays warm her skin.

She wrapped herself in her bath towel, opened her bedroom door, and peered out into the hallway. The sound coming from the television mixed with her parents' hoarse laughter. She tip-toed into the bathroom and closed the door behind her.

After dropping the towel on the bathroom floor, she stared at herself in the mirror, noticing grass clippings and dirt tangled in her brown hair. She splashed her face with water and peered back into her eyes. What the hell happened? A tingling in her gums made her lick the roof of her mouth. She pulled her lips back. The color of her gums looked darker than she remembered.

The hot water steamed her skin when she stepped into the shower. She heard her mother's heavy footsteps walk into the kitchen followed by the sounds of pots and pans clattering. Cecilia closed her eyes feeling the hot water soothe her aching shoulder. Just then a pain shot through her abdomen and settled in her stomach. With her arms wrapped around her waist, she hunched over in pain. She felt hungry but the wretched feeling didn't feel like hunger.

Soon the pain subsided and a voice called her name. At first it seemed to manifest around her, repeating itself over and over until she narrowed in, realizing it came from within her own mind.

Just one more.

One more.

It repeated her name and she felt her body fill with an uncomfortable desire to eat.

"Cecilia?" Her mother knocked on the bedroom door.

Cecilia opened her eyes.

"What are you doing in there?" her mother asked.

"What else would I be doing?" Cecilia replied in a saucy voice. She turned the shower knob and watched the dirty and soapy water swirl down the drain. After stepping out, she covered herself in a white bath towel. The sharp pain in her stomach returned and she tried her best to ignore it. She opened the bathroom door and she found herself standing face to face with her mother.

"You've been in there for a long time."

"No, I just woke up."

"I heard you and saw you walk into the bathroom over an hour ago." Her mother spoke. "Are you all right?"

It couldn't have been an hour. Cecilia looked at her wrinkled fingers. Could it have been an hour? "Yeah, I'm fine."

"What time did you get home last night?"

Cecilia hummed in thought. "Around one, maybe two in the morning. I wasn't paying attention."

"How can you not pay attention?" She placed her hands on her hips. "This is exactly—" Her mother paused and held her breath. Eventually her demeanor changed and she forced a widened smile on her face. "How was the party?"

Cecilia paused. "It was okay." Expecting her mother to be more upset, Cecilia shot her a puzzled look. "Are you okay?"

"Yeah, I'm fine. Why?"

"We're talking about the same party you didn't want me to go to, right?"

"Well," her mother folded her arms across her chest and she looked toward the ceiling, "after you left, your father and I had a long chat. We know that moving away from your friends was hard on you." Her eyes turned back to Cecilia. "You need your space. You're not a little girl anymore."

"Really?" Cecilia leaned against the bathroom wall, unable to decipher the point her mother tried to make.

"Is it that hard to understand?" Mrs. Richardson spoke. "You need your space."

Cecilia nodded, feeling the pain step up its attack. "Okay, I'll be out in a minute." She placed her wet stringy hair into a makeshift ponytail and turned back to the mirror.

Her mother gasped. "Cecilia what's that?"

"What?" Cecilia turned back to her mother.

"That! What's that on your back?"

"What? What's on my back?"

"Don't lie to me. I see it as plain as day." Mrs. Richardson placed her hands on Cecilia's shoulders and whisked her around so that her back faced the mirror. Cecilia looked over her right shoulder. Her mother was right. She saw a dark semi-circle with small black dots surrounding its circumference. It was a large tattoo and her skin was raised underneath it. Cecilia rubbed it, feeling the bumping texture. Befuddled, she looked at her mother in a wide-eyed stare.

"Just a party, huh?" Her mother bit her lower lip in frustration.

"I don't know how that got there." Cecilia panicked.

"So it just appeared?" She watched her mother squint and her lips suddenly crunch together.

Maybe it did just appear there, but Cecilia couldn't explain it to her mother. She didn't understand it herself.

"What were you thinking? Why would you do this to yourself?" Her mother raised her voice. "I'm trying to be reasonable, but how can I when you go out and do things like that?"

"I didn't do anything. I swear."

"Were you drinking last night?" Her mother asked.

"What?" Cecilia couldn't believe her mother's invading questions.

"You're going to explain this to your father." Mrs. Richardson stepped back out of the bathroom and she walked back to the kitchen.

Cecilia continued to gape at her new tattoo. She had to admit. She liked the design, but getting a tattoo wasn't something on her "to-do" list. She moved her back closer to the mirror, noticing small unique and hard to read lettering in the middle of it. Immediately she rushed back to her room and dressed herself. She wanted to go to Isaac's. Maybe he could tell her what was going on.

"Cecilia." She heard her father calling her from the living room. "Come here right now." He said in a rough voice.

Cecilia dressed herself in a long faded shirt and blue jeans cut off just above the knees. She walked into the living room, seeing her father sitting on the couch, clenching a pipe in his left hand. Her mother leaned against the wall. The way her father called her name meant only one thing. She readied herself for them to unleash an attack.

Mr. Richardson turned off the television and he tilted his head to the left. "So what's this about a tattoo?"

Cecilia remained silent.

Mrs. Richardson placed her hands on her hips with her eyes solely concentrated on her daughter. "Those two kids you met yesterday put you up to this, didn't they?"

"No." Cecilia blurted.

"So, you decided out of the blue to get a tattoo?"

"No."

"Then what Cecilia?" Her mother huffed. "What happened?"

"I don't know. It was just there when I woke up."

"Stop lying."

"I'm not lying." Cecilia narrowed her concentrated glare and her lips thinned. "It's not my problem that you don't believe me." Her voice dropped into a low rasp. "You'd never believe me anyway."

"Try us." Her father stood up from the couch.

Cecilia looked away and the voice in her head returned.

Just one more.

One more.

Trying to ignore it, she blinked and wiped her eyes.

"You're not allowed to hang out with those kids again. Do you understand me?"

"Their names are Isaac and Elsie."

"I don't care what their names are. You're not allowed to hang out with them again."

Cecilia's eyes darted from her father to her mother. "They didn't do this to me."

"Then who did?"

"I don't know." She headed for the kitchen. "If I did, I would tell you." She grabbed an apple and a carton of orange juice from the top shelf in the fridge.

"See, this is exactly why I didn't want her to go out." Her mother continued her complaint.

Cecilia poured herself a glass and the moment the liquid hit her lips, she felt her throat contract. She turned to the sink, spitting out the contents. "This is expired." She searched the carton for the expiration date.

"No it isn't. I bought it yesterday," her mother replied.

Cecilia made her way to the front door and left the house without looking back. She sat on the front steps of the house. The sunlight was bright and she rubbed her eye, feeling the sting of its effulgent light. She cursed under her breath and stared at Isaac's house next door, waiting for him to appear.

She hated arguing with her parents, especially her mother who always overreacted when it came to what she did. Even if she wanted to get a tattoo, Cecilia felt that it was her choice and not her mother's. She leaned her arms back, staring at the blue and partly clouded sky. A part of her wished for Glenn to be with her. He always comforted her during her family squabbles.

Asking Isaac about what happened last night proved to be harder than she expected. How could she ask the right questions when she didn't know what questions to ask? Sure, the tattoo was just one piece of evidence along with what happened at Old Farmer's Road, but what if he didn't have an answer?

She didn't feel comfortable in her own skin and her body ached, especially her stomach that continued to growl ferociously. She bit into the apple. It tasted raw and she spit the contents onto the pavement and tossed what remained of it in the front yard. She ran her tongue over her gums.

As she thought about Isaac, she saw the screen door to his home open. He stepped out, shirtless, wearing long baggy shorts. A smoldering cigarette dangled from his mouth. He shielded his eyes from the bright sunlight.

"Isaac." Cecilia stood up, noticing his flat and sculpted stomach. His skin was toned and while he walked toward her, she saw that his arms flexed sporadically. He was indeed attractive, and her cheeks flushed.

He looked to her. "You're up early." He walked to her and leaned against the railing, slightly standing over her. "How are you?"

She looked forward and briefly spoke. "What happened last night?"

He sat next to her. "What do you mean? We had a great time."

"I'm not talking about the party. I'm talking about that place you took me and Julie to."

"Oh, that." He removed his cigarette from his mouth, gripping it between his fingers. "Don't worry about it."

"Don't worry about it?" Cecilia repeated in astonishment. "I have a tattoo on my back."

"Don't scratch it," he said. "It'll heal wrong if you do."

"You know about it?" Cecilia extended her left arm behind her right shoulder.

"Of course I know about it. It's part of the process. It's normal."

"There's nothing normal about it." She stared at Isaac. "I expected to have a good time. I didn't expect to come home with a tattoo on my back."

Isaac reached out and gently grabbed her by the hand. "I'll tell you soon. Just take it easy until tonight."

Cecilia slipped her hand out of his grip. "Everything feels different." She rubbed her hand over her stomach. "And I feel like shit."

His smile withered from his face. "Like I said. You have to take it easy until tonight."

"And I heard this voice." Cecilia placed her hand on her head. "It keeps talking and it won't shut up." She looked at him. "Did you drug me last night?"

"Okay, hey-look." He grabbed her hand again. "Everything you're experiencing is perfectly normal. It's a lot, I know, but you'll get used to it."

"Used to what?" Cecilia exerted. She couldn't believe his reply. "I want to know what the hell is going on."

"I'll tell you tonight." He moved in closer to her. "Just promise me that you'll rest and take it easy."

Cecilia looked at him, confused.

The front door to her parent's house creaked open snapping Cecilia from her disturbed vision. She turned and saw her father with his golf bag draped over his shoulder. She stared at him for what felt like an eternity, expecting him to berate her about her tattoo. Instead he closed the door behind him.

"I'll be back in a few hours." He then thumbed at the door. "Give your mother some time to cool off."

Cecilia nodded suspiciously. "Okay."

Her father nodded to Isaac. "You must be Isaac."

"Yes sir." Isaac quickly hid his lit cigarette behind his back.

Mr. Richardson leaned over, kissed Cecilia on the forehead, , and he walked to the car. Cecilia nodded, suspecting that her father wasn't going to play a few holes. She waved at him as he threw his golf clubs in the back seat, started the car, and drove off.

Cecilia wiped the sweat from her forehead. "He's a better liar than I am."

"Your father?"

"He's doesn't golf," she replied.

"I knew a man like that." Isaac nodded and he yawned, reaching his hands above his head. "His wife caught him in the act." His upper body extended slightly and Cecilia was close enough to view every crease and any blemishes that were on his skin, including the scars on his forearm that still intrigued her. "Do you want to know what she did to him?"

Cecilia shook her head. "I don't care, Isaac." She took a deep breath.

"If your father is cheating, you should c-" He stopped midsentence and he turned his head to the left. They saw Miss Bernadette walking down the street in their direction. She waved at another neighbor trimming his flower bush across the street.

Isaac's lips curled in distaste. "I hate that woman."

The more Isaac talked about his dislike for her, the more Cecilia questioned why he hated her so much. He wasn't telling her everything about his connection with her. As Miss Bernadette approached, Cecilia eyed her white capris pants and her bright pink shirt with short sleeves. She was barefoot and she carried her white sandals in her left hand and her purse in the other. Her small, pug-nosed dog followed her, unleashed. When the dog made eye contact with Isaac, it began to bellow.

"Good morning," Cecilia said to her. Instead of replying, Miss Bernadette glared at her with wary eyes. Cecilia felt her forearms beginning to tingle. "My parents enjoyed the pound cake you brought the other day. Thanks." Still Miss Bernadette didn't speak as her dog continued to show its enmity toward Isaac.

Miss Bernadette snapped her fingers and the dog quickly hushed. "Did you have any of the pound cake?"

"No."

"Pity," she spoke. "I made it especially for you."

Cecilia took a deep breath. "I'm not a fan of pound cake."

"I didn't know that," she replied. "I'm sure you're not a fan of anything closely resembling food now."

Isaac snickered and he stood tall. "Go away old woman."

Miss Bernadette stepped forward and Isaac began to retreat. "You know I don't respond kindly to threats, especially when it comes from you." While she advanced, Isaac continued to back down. "For such a long life, you have had a short memory Isaac." Now standing inches from him, she jabbed her finger into his chest. "I know everything about you." She then moved back and turned around. "You don't think before you act because it's not in your nature to do so." She paced down the street and disappeared around the corner.

"What was that about?" Cecilia questioned Isaac.

He gathered his composure. "Stay away from her. She's dangerous." He turned and walked back to his house.

CHAPTER EIGHT

Impa

Throughout the day Cecilia remained in her room, laying in a fetal position with her bed covers over her head. The voice in her head continued in a never-ending loop, alone with the desire to eat. Any food she devoured tasted sour, including the tater tot casserole her mother cooked later that day. She tried simple foods, including fruits, but all that did was make her nauseated. The only thing that she didn't regurgitate was water, but only if she drank no more than a cup. None of it made sense.

She hid her sickness from her mother, who didn't pay attention anyway. Still angry at the tattoo situation, she ignored Cecilia and the vibe resonating through the household became acrid.

Cecilia's release from her pain came shortly before sunset as Isaac knocked on her bedroom window. "Let's go." He motioned for her to climb out.

"I can't. I don't feel so good."

Isaac smiled. "I know. We're going to find you some food."

"I can't eat anything, Isaac."

"This food is going to be different. It's what your body needs. Trust me."

Cecilia looked over her shoulder, contemplating the consequences if she snuck out to join him. The idea of finding something she could eat got the best of her. Quietly and quickly she dressed herself and climbed out of her bedroom window. Following Isaac, they crept to his car and she climbed into the passenger seat.

As he sped down the road, she found herself licking her gums, an annoying habit. As her stomach pain turned intense, she gripped her stomach and hunched forward in her seat. "Isaac, I'm so hungry." Her body rocked back and forth.

"I know. I'm hungry too." He swerved in an out of traffic. "But don't worry. We'll eat tonight."

Soon they made it to downtown Minneapolis. He pulled into the same super store parking lot where Cecilia met him and Elsie earlier, but he parked near the end and away from other cars.

"Why are we here?" Cecilia asked while she watched him get out of his car.

"Elsie said she'll be here as soon as she can." He slammed the driver side door shut and he walked around the car to open her door. He helped her out of the car.

"Why do we have to wait for her?" Cecilia leaned against the car and she looked up at the night sky.

"Because she knows exactly what type of food you need to stop the pain." He grabbed her arm gently. "Let's go."

As he led her toward Towley's, Cecilia felt her legs drag underneath her own weight. She wrapped her arm around Isaac, using his body as leverage. He continued to comfort her and she didn't understand the words that escaped his lips. His voice sounded jumbled and her hearing went in and out until the sound of his raised voice shattered her eardrums.

She pulled back from him and covered her ears. "Stop yelling." The multitude of sounds from car horns, streets spinning on the asphalt, people speaking and walking also made her lose control.

He studied her for a moment. "It's getting worse." Isaac opened the front door of the store. "I'm going to have to find you something if she doesn't get here soon." After he gently nudged her into the store, the sounds blasting her ears suddenly stopped. She dropped her hands and her eyes adjusted, watching customers, young and small, strolling up and down the aisles.

The shelves were not only stocked with materials such as perishables but there was a location of the store specifically cornered off for dollar items. Posters covered the walls. One customer in particular wore a dark business suit with a gray tie with long slacks bunched at his ankles and sleek shiny shoes. He picked up a knock off comic on the shelf and flipped through its pages before stuffing it underneath his arm. Cecilia saw Roger standing behind the counter.

"She's not here." Isaac scanned the entire store. A tall thin man wearing thick black rimmed glasses walked out from a door just behind Roger. He paused at the sight of Isaac. "Oh crap." Isaac turned his head to look away. "It's Mr. Towley."

The man who had unusually greased hair, stained yellow teeth, and an uneven moustache, hurried in their direction. "What did I tell you about coming in here?" He blared at Isaac as he removed his glasses.

"You said I could come in as long as I buy something," Isaac replied.

Rogers hastily walked over to them and before Mr. Towley could reply, he pushed Isaac and Cecilia toward the back of the store. "We'll go in the back." He tried to reassure his boss.

When they were out of Mr. Towley's eyesight, Roger dropped his hands. "Isaac, I told you he doesn't like it when you come here." They approached a metal door and Roger unlocked it. "He's been getting on me lately about that." He opened the door and he swiped his hand on the side of wall, flipping on the light switch. Cecilia caught a whiff of mildew lingering in the air.

"I don't care what he thinks," Isaac replied as he walked in.

Cecilia followed him in. Merchandise was stocked on the tall wooden shelves positioned against each wall of the rectangular room. Each shelf was packed with open boxes and stacks of merchandise.

"I care because I want to keep this job," Roger replied.

"Is Elsie here?" Isaac leaned against one of the shelves.

"No." Roger sighed. "Don't tell me she's also coming here."

Isaac lit a cigarette. "She was supposed to be here." His eyes moved about the cobwebs on the ceiling.

Roger laughed. "No, no, no. You guys can't be here. Not now."

"Stop worrying." Isaac elbowed Roger in the stomach and laughed.

Cecilia stood back and studied Roger's behavior carefully, picking up on small traits that she didn't notice during the first and second time she met him. Now he looked different...she dared to think in a delicious kind of way, and his scent soothed her nerves, calming the continuous pain she felt in her stomach for a brief moment. She snapped out of her ridiculous thought just as Roger turned back to the door.

"I'll be back. Just stay here and don't touch anything."

The moment he exited the room Isaac closed the door behind him and he leered at her. "He looks good, doesn't he?"

Cecilia didn't want to admit it, but he looked damn good.

She exhaled and took a moment to examine the stocked room. The silence that followed caused extreme uneasiness and she grew impatient waiting for Elsie to arrive. Hunger drove her and she wanted to break out and gulp down anything edible.

"I don't know why we have to wait for her." She returned to her unusual behavior of licking her gums. "I need to eat something...now."

"Smoking helps." He reached into his pocket and grabbed his cigarettes. "It curbs the hunger." He handed her a cigarette but she waved away his suggestion.

"I don't want a cigarette. I want to eat."

He inhaled again and looked at Cecilia for a brief moment without speaking. "We can't until Elsie gets here."

"Why?" Cecilia barked. "Does she tell you what you can and can't eat?"

"Simple food that you're used to isn't going to stop it. Having a bag of Cheetos isn't going to make it go away." Isaac scrunched his lips. "You need something else. You need something...human."

Confused, Cecilia stared back into Isaac's brown soothing eyes. She giggled at his sordid explanation.

Isaac looked back at her with an interested glare. "I'm serious." He leaned in closer and he rubbed his hand up her arm to her shoulder. "It's the only thing that'll stop it."

"Human?" Cecilia blinked rapidly. "Like, eating flesh?"

"Not flesh. Something better. The essence."

Cecilia didn't know what to believe. It would've been easy if he would have said nothing and ignored her complaints instead of mentioning something as crazy as that.

"Elsie can explain it better than I can," he said. "She's more well-rounded in the subject."

"Stop right there." Cecilia turned around to move herself away from the conversation. She started to think but even that became an issue as the pain in her stomach progressed. "That's crazy. I don't eat humans. I'm not a cannibal."

"Again, it's not the flesh that you need. It's the essence—the chi, the soul," he replied.

Their conversation was interrupted with noise coming from the front door. It flew open and Elsie stormed in followed by another woman Cecilia had never seen before. She was much older and looked to be in her twenties. She wore a brown pants suit and her black hair was tucked in a bun.

The woman paused in the doorway before gently closing the door behind her. "I thought I'd find you here Isaac," she said.

Isaac playfully raised his hands. "And good morning to you, Jan."

"I'm not playing." The woman jabbed her index finger into his forehead. "What did I tell you both about hanging out here?"

As good as it was to see Elsie, Cecilia couldn't keep her eyes off this woman. Like Roger, she looked edible and she smelled absolutely incredible.

Elsie sat on a wooden stool and she lit a cigarette. "You're not a cop. You're just some low grade private detective." Her short black skirt raised above her knees and she wore a bright purple short sleeve shirt. "So why should I care about what you say?"

"I personally know Mr. Towley, and he doesn't want you two here," Jan replied.

"What do you want?" Elsie whined. "To question me some more?"

"You know why I'm here Elsie. Don't play me for a fool." Jan stood in front of her and Elsie remained still, unwavered in her approach. "Fine. You wanna play silent with me?"

Elsie leaned back. "Why do you keep questioning me about what's his name?" she asked calmly. "I told you everything I know."

"Oh I'm going to keep questioning you until I find out what happened to Robert."

"This is harassment." Elsie placed her hand over her heart. "Look. I don't know what happened to Robert or your sister Allison."

"I don't believe you."

"I don't care if you do."

Jan honed in on Isaac. "Do you know why Robert kept going to Old Farmer's Road?"

Isaac shook his head. "Why would I know?" He flicked his cigarette and it landed by Jan's feet.

"Look, Jan. Isaac and I were affected by his disappearance too," Elsie spoke with a hint of sharpness in her voice as she stood to her feet. "We also want to know what happened to him. He's like a brother to us."

"Oh spare me the sarcasm," Jan quickly retorted. Her dark brown eyes moved to Cecilia. "Who's she?"

"Cecilia." Isaac positioned himself near Cecilia.

Jan turned around and headed back to the door. She took a look at Isaac and she waved her finger in his face and without saying another word, she gently closed the door behind her.

"Who was that?" Cecilia asked them.

"That is a thorn in my side. She thinks she's super special because she goes around, waving her plastic badge." Elsie rolled her eyes. "I want to eat her, so badly."

"Who's Robert?" Cecilia's question was followed by an eerie silence between them that she'd never witnessed before.

Usually quick to reply or agree with Elsie, this time Isaac didn't explain. Instead he turned to his sister. "Elsie," he said in a shy, low voice. "She's hungry."

Elsie turned and faced Cecilia. "I'm sure she is." She let out a girlish giggle and it extended into laughter.

"Elsie, this isn't a joke. She's hurting."

"Well you're the one who wanted her to be part of this. I warned you."

"Laughing at the situation isn't going to make her pain go away."

"You wanted your freedom." Elsie looked away. "I gave it to you, so she's your problem and not mine." Her body language suggested to Cecilia that she didn't care.

They saw the doorknob twist and the door open. "What did you guys do?" Roger faced them with a look of fright on his face.

"We didn't do anything," Elsie replied.

"Mr. Towley is calling the cops right now," Roger said. "You have to leave."

"Fine." Elsie walked to the door. She stopped and placed her hand on Roger's shoulder. "What're your plans tonight?"

"Why, is something going on?"

Elsie's eyes shifted to Cecilia. "We're hungry and we're about to get something to eat." Her eyes returned to Roger. "You want to come?"

Roger leaned back, nervously running his hands through his hair. "Yeah." He said almost immediately, but his body lowered slightly. "But my uncle is in town and we have a family dinner tonight."

Elsie's smile vanished. "Never mind." She pushed him away like an unwanted object.

"How about after?"

"No, we're going to eat now. Apparently this one can't wait." Elsie thumbed at Cecilia. She opened the door and walked out of storage room.

"Maybe tomorrow." Isaac suggested to Roger. He grabbed Cecilia's hand and let her out of the room. They followed Elsie outside just in time to witness her violently kick a waste can onto its side on her way to Isaac's car.

The atmosphere suddenly changed from excitement to annoyance. Isaac fumbled through the pocket of his jeans to find his keys. Cecilia gazed at him, wondering why everything felt like it had gone downhill. Her problem still persisted to the point that she felt she could eat anything, even human flesh, like Isaac mentioned earlier.

"What are we going to do?" Isaac asked his sister. "She needs to eat tonight."

Elsie stopped in her march and she briskly turned around. "I know that!"

Isaac stood down and only once did his eyes twitch to Cecilia who now felt obliged to speak.

"What's wrong with me?"

"I didn't do anything. He did." She quickly approached Cecilia. "So stop talking and let me think." She began to pace back and forth, rubbing her chin in thought.

"Maybe we should just take Roger anyway." Isaac suggested.

"Are you stupid?" Elsie ridiculed him. "We can't just take whoever we want whenever we want." She continued to pace. "I didn't think it'd be this quick. The others were never this quick." She turned abruptly and walked to the car. "Let's go. I think I have an idea."

Cecilia reluctantly climbed into the car and hunkered in the backseat. As soon as Isaac got in, Elsie gave him a direct order.

"Drive."

Isaac started his car. "Where?"

"Amber."

"Amber?" He pulled out of the parking lot and took a sharp left. "I thought you were going to wait?"

"I was but we can't, thanks to you." Elsie's raspy voice surprised Isaac.

"I think Roger is the better choice…"

"Would you shut up about Roger already," she interrupted him. "He's not an option, not now."

Isaac quickly silenced himself.

Elsie turned around in her seat and she snarled at Cecilia. "Look at her. She's weak and you know what happens to us if we get weak." She lifted her hands and covered Cecilia's eyes. Too weak to argue and fight back, Cecilia didn't object. She felt the car swerve from left to right.

"What are you going to do?" Isaac asked.

"I'm going to show her," Elsie replied.

"I wanted to show her."

"Well, you've given me no choice." Elsie turned her attention to Cecilia. "Because of my brother's stupid actions, I'm going to show you something. First, you better not scream or I swear I'll rip your throat out. Second, this will explain what you're experiencing, hearing, smelling...the whole freakin' caboodle. We have a lot of names: demons, soul eaters, but we prefer to be called Impa." She dropped her hands from Cecilia's face.

Cecilia screamed.

At first she thought she had hallucinated. What stared back at her wasn't the same person she'd seen just a few seconds earlier. The thing that looked at her had shriveled and gray skin. Its eyes had sunk back in their sockets and two large pointed fangs extended from the roof of its gums and past its bottom lip. Its nose had all but fossilized away, leaving two small holes and the smell of decomposing flesh permeated the air. Terrified, Cecilia jiggled the door handle to escape. Whatever this thing was that stared back at her didn't look human. It wasn't human.

"Why do they always scream the first time?" Its lips fluttered as it spoke. Cecilia recognized the voice immediately as belonging to Elsie, but the image still didn't fit. She pushed her body to the opposite side of the car to get away from the thing that latched its creepy hallowed eyes on her.

"I hate it when they scream." Suddenly its face began to change back before Cecilia's eyes. The skin tightened as the two large fangs retreated back and beneath its gums. As the eyes grew back to their normal size along with the nose, Elsie's face suddenly came back to life.

"What in the hell are you?" Still spooked, Cecilia continued to force herself back in the seat.

"I told you already. I'm Impa." Elsie returned back in her seat and she pulled down the passenger side mirror. "And so is Isaac and now, so are you." She began to fix her hair and check her face. "Get used to it."

"I'm not that...thing I just saw." Cecilia pointed at her and her eyes widened.

"Yes you are. The sooner you accept it, the sooner we can move onto more important things." Elsie closed the mirror. "Like finding you someone to eat." She clasped her hands together and like a little child. "I personally like Amber. She smells so sweet, almost like cotton candy."

CHAPTER NINE
Person of Interest

Jan Colfax placed her files in her locker and she closed the steel door. The electric clock on the wall read one thirty in the morning. She was tired and ready to go home.

Her workdays now consisted of ten to twelve hour shifts. The stack of files on her desk grew overnight and still she considered her sister's case her number one priority. It wasn't considered "cold" but thanks to her connections within the Minneapolis Police Department, she was constantly updated on the progress.

Although she also questioned Isaac's participation, she never doubted Elsie's. Witnesses placed a woman fitting her description near Old Farmer's Road the night that Robert and Allison disappeared. However, they also heard unusual howls coming from the area as well, which didn't make any sense. The police believed that Robert and her sister became victims of wolves that somehow made their way into the city. But when they found Robert's car the next day, speckled with nickel size blood, they quickly changed their minds. Still no bodies had been found. It was as if they had disappeared into thin air.

With each passing day the case became harder to solve. Not only did Jan have to deal with the possibility that her sister was dead, she also had to deal with the fact that Robert was the brother of her ex fiancé, Derek. She couldn't keep him out of the loop, even though it pained her to see his face. It was her sister who caught Derek cheating with Rosie, his next door neighbor.

The thought of making another trip out to Old Farmer's Road crossed Jan's mind. She needed something that would kick-start the case into high gear again. Questioning all of Robert and Allison's friends and their acquaintances got her nowhere. Elsie was the only one who made a significant blimp on her radar and she followed her suspicions. There was something odd about them and she couldn't place her finger on it. When she looked into their past, she didn't find anything relevant to the case. They both seemed to appear out of nowhere. They didn't go to school, and they lived with a distant relative who, when questioned, seemed to remain oblivious to their activities. The only hint of their criminal behavior was that they were both arrested for trespassing in the area during road construction a few years ago.

Jan walked through the nearly empty office, waving good-bye to a couple of local janitors, and stopped at the office of her boss and owner of I.S., Investigation Services, Gilliam. He didn't look up until she tapped the edge of his desk.

"Gilliam, I'm going home."

He lifted his head from a stack of papers on his desk. "You're still here? I thought you already left." He stood up from his desk and straightened his khaki colored shirt. Empty Styrofoam cups were scattered across his desk. "You need to get some sleep. You've been banging away at your sister's case nonstop, Jan. You know we have other cases, right?"

"Yeah, I know." Jan took a deep breath. "I just feel like I'm so close."

"Just don't get sidetracked," he replied.

She nodded. The first time she explained her idea to work on the case, Gilliam refused. He didn't want to step on the toes of the Police Department. But after a long chat and constant pressure from her, he trusted Jan to make the right decision.

He shuffled through the paperwork on his desk. "Did you make any progress with...what's her name again?"

"Elsie?"

"Yeah. How'd that go?"

"It's going." Jan sighed. She felt like sitting down and explaining her frustrations about how slow the case was progressing but she deterred her angst. He wasn't interested in knowing about her failures. He was only interested in her progress. He too believed that Elsie knew more than what she told everyone. "I know she was involved Gilliam. I just can't prove it. She's still confessing her innocence and her 'I don't know what happened but I feel sorry for the victim' attitude."

"Ahh, the sympathy speech?"

"Yes sir. The sympathy speech."

"Fact is Jan, you need something solid on her. I'm surprised she hasn't gone to the police and filed charges against you."

"Because she knows she's guilty and that's my leverage."

He rubbed his fingers through his gray streaked hair. "Still, you need to be careful."

"I made a promise to my parents and to Derek to find out what happened."

He nodded. "Speaking of which." He turned back to his desk. "He called the office today, wanting to speak with you. Is everything okay between you two?"

"If you call my continued hatred okay, then yeah. Things are fine."

Gilliam leaned back in his chair.

"I'll see you tomorrow." Jan turned and walked away. She grabbed her jacket off the coat rack. "Have a good night."

"Drive safe." Gilliam returned to his desk and she left the building.

High thin clouds partially blocked a bright, full moon that hung low in the sky. The agency was located on south 5th street in downtown Minneapolis, just shy of Hennepin Avenue. Jan hated working downtown. She preferred the quiet suburbs of White Bear Lake, the location of her apartment, to the downtown metropolitan area. She approached her car while she fumbled inside her purse, searching for her keys. She searched through random trinkets and things— pieces of paper, a lighter, pieces of loose gum, pen caps, and a small bottle of mace.

She heard a footsteps echo in the silent air and she immediately turned, expecting to see trash scuttling across the pavement. Instead she jumped slightly at Derek standing behind her. He stood with his hands in the pockets of his faded blue jeans and he wore a white shirt and a brown tuxedo jacket with black elbow pads. His greasy hair was slightly disheveled.

Waylaid by his approach, Jan placed her hand over her chest. "Derek, I thought I told you to stop doing that." She caught her breath and cleared her throat before speaking again. "What're you doing here?"

"Sorry for scaring you.' He quietly approached her.

"No. I was just...a little preoccupied."

A tired smile appeared on his face. "How are you doing?"

She glared at him. "I'm fine."

"Any new leads on the case?"

Jan knew where he wanted to take their conversation. Since the disappearances Derek had spent the majority of his free time scouring Old Farmer's Road for any clues, while drowning his sorrows about Robert in alcohol. He also wasn't the type to admit his mistakes, especially regarding his infidelity. However, he had an imagination that would put the kindergarten children to shame. He believed in a more supernatural reason behind the disappearances, and because of that, she pitied him.

"I'm working every angle that I can Derek," she replied. "I'm not a cop."

"I know, I know." His body tilted to the right. "You should be one." He placed his hand on the trunk of her car. "You're making more progress in the case, even if you don't think so."

As he talked Jan's nose picked up the smell of liquor filtering from his breath. He'd been drinking again. "Yeah, well it doesn't feel like it." She continued to search through her purse and she looked up briefly, watching him stare back at her. "I spent all day going through the evidence that I have—old interviews, crime scene photos. I talked to a person of interest..."

"A person of interest?"

Jan swallowed hard. She couldn't believe she let the information slip from her lips. Throughout the entire case, she never told him about Elsie's potential involvement.

"Who is it?" He asked indignantly.

"Derek, I got this." Jan plopped her purse on top of the car and she stood defiant with her hands resting firmly on her hips.

He nodded as if he agreed to her answer. "I know you do."

"It just takes time. Minneapolis has seen a spike in crime this summer, especially around that area." She located her keys and lifted them from her purse.

"But that's not what I asked you." He stepped uncomfortably close to her. "Why won't you tell me who this person is?"

"Because I know you, Derek."

"What do you think I'm going to do? Start my own manhunt?"

Jan stared silently at him until she found it within herself to reply. "Of course not." She smiled slightly. "But it's hard to confide in you since you, well..." She shook her head.

"Since you don't trust me anymore," he said, finishing her sentence.

"It's not that I don't trust you."

"You know I can help," Derek replied. "Another kid just went missing last week at that place. I'm sure of it."

"Let the cops handle it." She unlocked the car door and she tossed her purse in the driver seat.

"Just like they're handling this case, right?" He lowered his voice.

"Derek, stop hitting the bottle and get some sleep." Jan stepped into her car. "I'll call you tomorrow." She closed the door and started the engine. She looked back in her rear view mirror at Derek who watched her closely before driving away.

CHAPTER TEN
Something...human

Isaac's maniac driving only added to Cecilia's anxiety. Still unable to process what Elsie showed her, she remained huddled in the backseat out of fear that Elsie would release the monster inside her again.

Elsie continued to laugh at Cecilia's behavior while she revealed what she called "their secret to survive." According to Elsie, she had to pay close attention to the voice inside her head, which wasn't the worst revelation. What Cecilia paid the most attention to was how she could stop her stomach pain. The voice warned her that she had to feed on human flesh. She had to choose a victim and suck on their insides like a milkshake. If not, the pain would only grow over time, eventually making her unpredictable, which wasn't good for anyone.

The pain in her gums signaled that her fangs had formed. It all sounded too hard to believe. She had no fangs and she wasn't a killer, certainly not an Impa, whatever that meant. But the markings on her back told her otherwise. It marked her as one of them and it was the only way they could distinguish themselves from normal people. Elsie also claimed that she and Isaac were the only Impa in Minneapolis, however, there were more out there, somewhere. Their affliction ran in the family and if they had any children (Elsie hated kids,) they would inherit it as well. But in Cecilia's case, anyone could become one.

All this new information proved too much for her to fully absorb. She thought that maybe if she could somehow kick her memory into high gear, she would find a logical explanation.

"Old Farmer's Road has been our feeding ground for a long time," Elsie added.

Isaac pulled up to a large brick apartment building just minutes from downtown Minneapolis. He placed the car in park, honked his horn, and they waited. "You sure she's coming?" he asked Elsie.

"Yeah, she'll be here," Elsie replied.

A heavy set teenage girl with brown hair carrying a large leather purse exited the building and hastily made her way to the back seat.

Elsie forced a smile on her face. "Amber. Glad you could come out on such short notice."

Amber pulled out a large bottle of vodka from her purse. "Thanks for the invite." She touched Isaac on his shoulder. "You said you'd call me last night. What happened?"

Isaac put the car in gear, placed his foot on the gas, and the tires screeched. "I was busy." He began to drive.

Amber began to drink the contents from the bottle in large gulps and she passed it to Elsie. Cecilia cocked her head to the side, staring ardently at Amber. The worst thing she could do was to head back there, but the proclivity within her, that she couldn't explain or understand, wanted badly to accompany them. Her speech stammered whenever she opened her mouth.

When they finally arrived at Old Farmer's Road, Isaac parked next to a large tree lying on its side next to the river embankment. He killed the lights and looked to Cecilia. "It's almost time." He turned off the car.

Elsie handed Amber the bottle of vodka and told her to finish it. Without hesitating Amber gulped the rest of it with no signs of stopping. They watched her as she devoured the last drops and handed the empty bottle back to Elsie.

"Wow." Impressed, Elsie tossed the bottle out the window.

Amber opened the door and staggered to her feet. Her body slightly swayed back and forth and she wrapped her hand around Isaac's waist for support.

"Drunk, already?" Isaac said to her. "You should've taken it slow."

Cecilia had never known anyone to down a bottle of vodka without thinking about the consequences. While they walked toward the bridge, Isaac held onto her as Amber rubbed her hands over his chest and up to his neck. She burped loudly and excused herself with a loud laugh. This shouldn't have bothered Cecilia. She wasn't interested in Isaac like that but still, something inside her wanted to push Amber down the embankment and into the raging waters of the Mississippi.

"I'm sure that Isaac told you about smoking. It helps curb the hunger."

Cecilia heard Elsie speak as she approached her. Elsie grabbed the pack of cigarettes from her pocket and handed them to her. "You've been quiet the entire ride." Elsie stood next to her.

Cecilia moved away. "What do you expect me to say after what I just saw?"

"Relax C." Elsie handed her a cigarette.

"We're going to kill her, aren't we?" Cecilia lowered her voice.

"No." Elsie placed her arm around Cecilia. "You are." She nodded in the direction of Isaac and Amber who now stood at the edge of the bridge. "Isaac likes to use his charm to subdue his victims. Me? I like brute force."

"I'm not going to kill her," Cecilia replied in a snarky tone.

"I guess you don't want to eat." Elsie trekked down to the bridge, meeting up with Isaac and Amber. Cecilia didn't want to follow but something inside her, perhaps the hunger that Elsie spoke about, pushed her forward. She flicked her unlit cigarette into a nearby bush and agreed, for now, to ignore her frenzied state and to follow them.

A cool breeze came across the bridge from the east, fluffing up Amber's long red skirt just enough to show the bottom of her buttocks. They crossed the bridge. With each step she took, Cecilia eyed the raging whirly river currents through the cracks in the wooden boards beneath their feet. They reached the end and continued, passing the rocky outcrop, until they were deep into woods and they could no longer see Isaac's car.

Amber, still locked onto Isaac's arm, suddenly stopped and planted a wet kiss on his cheek.

Isaac immediately jumped back and rubbed his cheek.

"Kiss me." Amber puckered her lips again.

Isaac placed his hand over her mouth. "How about later."

Amber smiled weakly and she looked to Isaac. "Okay."

They continued to walk, passing the very same spot where Cecilia had seen the light bearing down on her and Julie the night before. She slowed her steps and the wind picked up, tingling her arms. But they continued on until they came upon an empty spot surrounded by tall trees and thick bushes. The grass was cut lower than the other grass surrounding the area. The moon above was partially crowded by thick clouds, lighting the area in a zig zag pattern.

Cecilia glanced in awe. This place wasn't here last night. Isaac spun Amber around and planted his lips on hers. They began to kiss passionately as they moved to the middle of the area. Cecilia huffed, watching their display of affection as Elsie walked off to the right, examining the area. She stopped briefly and watched Isaac lift Amber's shirt over her head, tossing it behind his back.

At that moment, Elsie walked over to her. "This is the part that I hate," she whispered. Cecilia didn't bother to entertain her response but that didn't stop Elsie from talking. "But he's so good at it."

The pain continued its assault and Cecilia grasped her stomach.

"Go over to them," Elsie said.

"No. I'm not going to do this."

"The only reason I'm being patient with you is because Isaac wants me to," Elsie continued. "You will go over there and you will kill her and you will eat." She positioned herself behind

Cecilia. "Believe me, it'll be the best decision you've ever made in your useless existence." Gently she pushed Cecilia toward Isaac. "Look at her," Elsie whispered in her ear. "Smell her. Imagine the thought of having her, feeling her soul replenishing you."

The more Elsie began to coach her, the more that Cecilia felt frozen in her gaze. She began to see Amber as not a person, but something that she craved and needed. Isaac gently pulled Amber to the ground where they continued their passionate kissing, distracting her. His eyes moved in her direction and he smiled briefly.

"This is it C," Elsie whispered. "Ready?"

"Yes..." Cecilia heard the low sound of flesh being pulled apart followed by a small pinch in her gums. She felt something hard and cool brush the bottom of her lip and when she went to touch them, she felt sharp canines. Quickly, she covered her face.

Sensing Cecilia's nervousness, Elsie stood in front of her. "Stop hesitating and do it." She forcefully removed Cecilia's hands from her face.

"I can't." Breathing erratically, Cecilia shuffled back.

"How do you think we've survived after all this time?" Elsie began to hound her. "You think this is just for show? You think we're lying to you?" As her rage grew, Cecilia saw her face transform into the hideous creature revealed to her in Isaac's car.

She attempted to move back but something stopped her from doing so. Her feet felt glued to the earth and her body turned rigid. The air drew quiet and the voice inside her head returned.

Just one more.

One more.

This was what had happened at Old Farmer's Road. This was exactly what she couldn't remember about last night and it terrified her. Her memory came back to her: the voice, the dog—all of it had actually happened!

"I can't Elsie," Cecilia spoke in a panicked whisper.

Isaac stood to his feet. "What's taking so long?"

"She's chickening out." Elsie snapped at him.

Unaware of the commotion, Amber turned around and lay on her back, staring at the sky.

"Don't get on my bad side, C." Elsie grabbed Cecilia's arm and pulled her forward against her will.

Just one more

One more.

The voice inside Cecilia's head continued, filling her body with new feelings that overwhelmed her. Desire replaced fear.

Amber raised herself from the ground. "What's going on?" Her eyes quickly turned to Cecilia and she let out a terrifying scream. The noise echoed through treetops and the dark frosty air. Cecilia launched herself at her, pushing her back to the ground. Amber squirmed underneath Cecilia's weight.

With Elsie and Isaac helping, they managed to pin Amber to the dirt. Amber's eyes widened further. Tears streamed down her dirty face and in her last breath she mouthed the phrase "help me" but her plea didn't make them move an inch. In one quick motion Cecilia nested her fangs into the soft flesh of Amber's stomach. Blood spurted from her wound but Cecilia didn't stop. She suckled gently and quietly. She felt warmth fill her body and her hunger subsided and faded away along with the voice inside her head.

Amber's body began to convulse and her eyes rolled into the back of her head. Then there was silence. Her blood began to pool underneath her body, spreading out toward their feet.

A thick string of blood hung from Cecilia's lower lip. "Oh God, oh God." She scurried on her back, away from Amber's motionless body. She wanted to scream, to lash out at Elsie and Isaac for making her do something as despicable as taking the life of another person. Panic overtook her again but as she licked Amber's blood from her bottom lip, her craving for more soon replaced her revulsion. The corner of her lip curved into a half snicker as Amber's essence began to fill her body.

Isaac knelt beside her and wiped the remaining blood from Cecilia's mouth. "Feels good, doesn't it?"

Cecilia closed her eyes and her body swayed from side to side. "It's fucking fantastic."

Isaac planted his lips on Cecilia's cheek, tasting her sweat. "I told you she could do it." He said to his sister as he rubbed his fingers through Cecilia's hair.

"It's still too early to tell," Elsie replied as she shrugged. "I do know one thing though."

"What?"

"She's greedy. She didn't leave us any." Elsie turned and walked away.

Still unsure of what had just happened, Cecilia closed her eyes and bathed in the aftertaste.

CHAPTER ELEVEN

Something evil down there...

Derek pressed on the brakes as his car came to a screeching halt at a red light. He looked to his right and to his left. There were no cars around, yet the light had turned. He sighed. The streets of Minneapolis were vacant, deserted. The city was usually quiet until the early morning when commuters from the surrounding suburbs drove into the city in their SUVs and small compacts to go to work in the bustling downtown area. In a decade, the population of Minneapolis increased from a little under a thousand to well over four thousand. It was the place where the state raked in the money.

But for now he enjoyed the peace and quiet. It allowed him to think and his thoughts still centered on the conversation he had with Jan. He didn't want to believe that she wasn't doing enough to solve his brother's case, however, he believed that she hesitated in going down avenues she didn't understand.

When his brother disappeared he felt that the world had crashed all around him. His alcohol consumption grew along with his need to escape the heartbreak. Still, to this day, he believed he and Jan could reconcile, even if the disappearances seemed to be the only thing they had in common.

The light turned green and he stepped on the gas pedal. The car screeched and he drove toward the freeway entrance. He drove by Loring Park and the Walker Arts Center, noticing several groups of homeless people walking down the street. He was in no hurry to get home. There was no one to welcome him except for his three cats and even they didn't appear half the time he walked through the door. Before he left his apartment he filled their food and water bowls to their brims and he left the window open for them. The only person who'd wait up for him was Rosie, and only if she was in the mood.

He pressed on the gas pedal and the car jerked as it entered onto the freeway ramp. The freeway itself was desolate except for a few cars speeding by. He leaned his elbow on the car door. He remembered the route to Old Farmer's Road like the back of his hand, only because he had sped down this way numerous times when his mother worried about Robert's whereabouts.

Derek remembered the day Robert mentioned Old Farmer's Road to him. He listened intently as Robert talked about the Old Farmer and his death. Derek remembered how ridiculous the story sounded. He didn't believe in life after death, spirits, and demons. However, Robert complained about the voices in his head and the hunger pains that grew worse over time.

Derek remembered the last time he saw Robert. He'd stopped by the apartment and they spoke for hours about Robert's plan to attend college out of state. He remembered his brother's happiness about finally leaving Minnesota. He said that something evil existed at Old Farmer's Road and he unwillingly had become part of it. He had to devour the souls of innocent people to stay alive. He talked about the ferocious dog that protected the area from unwanted visitors and sometimes participated in their evil deeds if necessary. He showed Derek the branding on his shoulder blade and talked about leading innocent people to that area, only to kill them.

Through all this Derek took the stories with a grain of salt. He couldn't believe every word his brother said. Robert wasn't a murderer and he damn well wasn't some supernatural entity that ate human flesh to survive.

At the last minute Derek swerved his car to the right, taking the off ramp. He took another sharp turn around the corner and sped down the street. He then turned off his car lights when he approached the dead end street leading to Old Farmer's Road.

Up ahead, he noticed a car parked on the side of the road. He slowed down, pulled over, and turned off his car. He rolled down the window, feeling the slight breeze brush up against his skin which made the prickly hairs on the back of his neck stand straight up. He stared down the road, pass the chain divider which swung back and forth. The area hadn't changed since the last time he'd been here. He then heard the sound of gravel crunching underneath feet and distant laughter.

He opened his door and quietly stepped out. He stood ready and waiting as his eyes froze on the darkness in front of him. The outline of a figure materialized followed by two more people. Derek felt his mouth fall open when he finally saw the female figure appear out of the shadows followed by a taller male and a female with curly brown hair. They continued to walk toward him, unaware that he stood in the dark, watching their every movement. Finally Derek cleared his throat and the first female he saw stopped in her tracks and squinted her eyes at him with the other two slowing their pace.

"What are you guys doing down here?" Derek asked them.

The female looked oddly familiar to him, but he couldn't place her. He stepped forward, trying to get a better look when she spoke.

"Derek!" She pointed at him then turned slightly to face the other male. She cupped her hand over her mouth and whispered in his ear. The other male reacted by suddenly stepping behind the other female, partially hiding himself. The sight of Derek didn't seem to disturb the teenage female. Instead it made her more curious. She continued to walk toward him, coaching the other two to follow her.

"Derek!" she said again. "You're Robert's brother, right?"

Derek felt like he knew her too and he searched his mind, trying to find the answer. The teen male lifted his keys from his pocket and electronically unlocked the doors. Suddenly Derek understood why she looked familiar. He'd seen her standing outside his parent's house a few days before Robert disappeared.

"You're Robert's friend," Derek said to her. "Elsie." He looked her over and while thinking about what Robert told him about her, he couldn't believe that she was the ringleader of their fragile group.

The other male open the back door and leaned his arms on the roof of the car. "Let's go."

"Yeah, yeah in a minute," she replied back to him.

"And you're Isaac." Derek's eyes moved toward the other male. However, it was the other quiet girl that he didn't recognize.

Elsie placed her hands on her hips. "I'm surprised to see you here. Robert used to tell us that you hated this place."

"I still do." Derek watched as the other girl climbed into the back seat of the car. He quickly glanced at the car's license plate. "What are you all doing here?"

"Stargazing, walking, eating...you know. Enjoying the night," Elsie replied.

Isaac called out again. "Let's go!" He opened the driver side door.

Elsie walked around the car to the passenger side door. "I hope to see you around." She opened the door. "Oh and again, sorry about your brother. I really miss him. We really miss him."

Her apology sounded empty to Derek. He watched as the car started but before the boy drove off, he rolled down the window and Elsie leaned over to him.

"Oh and I wouldn't go down there if I were you," Elsie said to Derek with a wide snicker plastered on her face. "There's something evil down there."

Isaac revved the engine. Derek watched the car speed off with tires screeching and they disappeared around the corner. He waved the brown cloud of dust from the air around him and turned back to Old Farmer's Road.

Evil? He stood there contemplating why Robert's friends liked to hang around the forested area of Old Farmer's Road when they knew about the murders and disappearances.

He heard the water in the distance and the sounds of leaves rustling in the wind. In the distance he caught a brief pulsing light just shy of the trees, which made his body jump.

He squinted, watching the white light continue to pulsate. He rubbed his eyes and stared again, still seeing the light. "Hello?" He called out to it but got no response.

The light suddenly vanished.

Derek looked back at his car. He had a reason to go down there to investigate but now the area gave him goose bumps. He began to doubt his dismissal of Old Farmer's Road, and all of the stories he'd heard. Perhaps there was something to the supernatural things that Robert had told him.

Robert had feared Elsie. He said that she was ruthless but it was Isaac that he held accountable for turning him into a monster. Both had deep dark secrets and connections with the area that went back hundreds of years.

Elsie had to be the prime suspect Jan mentioned. He knew it. He felt it in his gut. It was the same feeling he'd always felt when he knew he was onto something.

He was sure of it.

****

"Cecilia. Wake up."

Cecilia opened her eyes slowly. Her vision took a little while to come into focus and when it did, she saw Isaac sitting next to her, carefully stroking her hair.

"Did you know that you snore?" He stood up with a smile beaming across his face.

Cecilia blinked the harden crust on her eyelids away. Her legs throbbed and she felt weak and tired. "What time is it?" she moaned.

"It's a little after noon."

Cecilia grabbed the pillow and placed it over her head.

"The cops found Julie's body this morning."

Cecilia quickly tossed her pillow to the floor and she raised herself up, looking wide eyed at her. All at once the notion of Old Farmer's Road came back to her. "Where?"

"Where do you think?"

As soon as memories of last night came back to her, sorrow, disbelief, and fear returned. Everything that she forgot about the night Julie died pummeled her memory along with the events of last night. She jumped out of bed and felt her heart beginning to palpitate.

"It's okay," Isaac said.

"It's not okay." They deserved the worst that could happen to any murderer. Murderer! The word itself made her cringe. How could she let this happen? How could she kill anyone? Cecilia wanted to ball herself up on the floor and wail but she knew that wouldn't do any good.

"You feel better though, right?"

In fact she felt better than before but that still didn't help her fragile state. She scratched her disheveled hair and glanced around the cluttered room, realizing that she wasn't home. Clothes littered the floor and in the middle of the room she saw a green sleeping bag with two black hooded jackets. On a computer desk a large wad of cash, held together with a large rubber band, sat undisturbed.

"I know this is a lot to take in, but you'll get used to it in time."

Cecilia felt the corners of her dry mouth crack as she opened her mouth to speak. "Is that supposed to make me feel any better?" Raving, she slapped his arm. "I didn't want this. I never agreed to it."

Isaac's face filled with doubt.

She didn't know what to do and it didn't help that she would soon be wanted for murder. Her only option was to stay calm and leave so she could go to the police, but no one would believe her, especially anyone in a right mind. There were no such things as Impa.

"I have to go home." Cecilia wiped the sleep from her eyes and she straightened her hair. She dragged her feet as she walked out of the room.

Cecilia scanned the small home. There was a sliding glass window that opened up to an outside deck. Dishes cluttered the kitchen counters along with empty bottles of vodka. A small broken bookcase stood in the corner, leaning to the side. Old Christmas lights hung from the ceiling and a fake Christmas tree, complete with decorations, leaned against the corner of the room.

Elsie sat on a two-seated couch in front of the television. In the kitchen Cecilia saw an older woman with dirty blonde hair pulled back into a weak ponytail standing near the stove. She smiled at the woman who didn't return the gesture. The wrinkles on her forehead moved and she bit her lower lip. She looked tired and out of touch with what was going on around her.

"You're up." Elsie said to Cecilia. "Look at this crap." She pointed to the television. "They said the F.B.I. might get involved." She folded her legs.

Hanging on the wall to her left near a sliding glass door that led to the backyard was a picture of Isaac with the woman she saw in the kitchen. In the picture Isaac smiled back at the camera, however, the woman looked uncomfortable.

Cecilia turned back to the television. What Isaac said earlier proved to be true. Human remains belonging to a female had been found a few miles south of Old Farmer's Road, wrapped in seaweed on the banks of the Mississippi River.

While the report continued Elsie cursed low under her breath. "This is the worst news report I've ever seen in my life." She grabbed the remote and turned off the television. "And I've seen many."

"Are you hungry?" Finally the older woman spoke to Cecilia. "I can make you something." She reached for the cabinet when Elsie quickly snapped at her.

"We don't eat that crap, remember!"

The woman shivered at Elsie's voice and shuffled off into the corner of the kitchen. "Oh, I didn't know she was like you."

"Well now you do." Elsie turned around in the couch to face her. "Unless, you're offering."

"No. I'm sorry. I'm sorry." The woman repeated.

The tension in the room thickened and the woman lowered her gaze.

"It's okay." Cecilia said to the woman. "Thanks for the offer." She felt the need to make the woman more comfortable. She smiled again. "I'm Cecilia. It's nice to meet you."

"She's our cousin." Isaac walked into the kitchen. "I keep forgetting her name." He turned toward her. "What's your name again?"

"Who cares?" Elsie stood up from the couch.

"Maybe you should. She's your family."

Elsie laughed at Cecilia's comment. Their family dynamics didn't make any sense. Cecilia didn't want to stir the pot any further. She already had too many questions that didn't have answers.

"I'm going home." She walked toward the door.

"Already?" Isaac followed her.

Cecilia took a deep breath. "I don't know what happened last night and I'd rather not know." She grabbed the knob and in one quick movement Elsie hurried to her and placed her body in front of the door.

"You gonna tell your mommy and daddy?" she said in a low voice.

"Why do you always feel the need to threaten people?"

"Because it's fun." Elsie's eyes gazed into her and it made Cecilia feel uneasy. She opened the door and she stepped aside. "Keep your mouth shut."

Cecilia walked out and she heard Isaac behind her. She stood on the top step. The bright sun blasted her face and the hot morning air blew through her hair, making her tuck the loose strands behind her ear.

Isaac pulled out a cigarette, lit in, and inhaled. "By tonight, you'll be hungry again."

Unexpectedly he embraced her in a tight hug.

"I have to go." She pushed herself away from him and she began to walk the short distance to her house.

"We're going out again—tonight."

"Have fun."

"Cecilia, you can't ignore this." Isaac called out after her. She stopped. "Watch me try."

"It won't do you any good."

She looked over her shoulder. "We committed murder last night Isaac."

"I understand the way you feel," he replied. "Elsie and I have been through it. But you'll get over it. You shouldn't feel sorry for what you have to do."

"Any normal person in the world would regret what we did last night." She faced him.

"We aren't normal." Isaac lowered his voice.

"Oh right. We're Impa now," Cecilia replied sarcastically. She grew tired of hearing the name. "We eat souls. What else do we do? Can we fly? Do we live forever?" She turned away.

"No, we can't fly." Isaac jumped to the bottom step. "We don't live forever. We age slower than normal people."

She couldn't believe his answer and she shook her head, trying to make some sense of the conversation. "You know what? I just want to get as far away from both of you as possible." She continued on her short trek home.

"I'm serious, Cecilia. You can't walk away from this."

She ignored him.

"When the pain and the voice in your head returns, you'll know what you have to do."

"Just shut up, Isaac," Cecilia said, raising her voice. She had grown tired of his remarks and his lack of sympathy. "Just leave me alone."

Cecilia didn't feel special and she didn't feel important. She felt like a killer, and the image of Amber's dead body at their feet would never leave her brain. She promised herself that she wouldn't end up like Elsie or Isaac, two people who seemed incapable of remorse for their actions.

Again she thought about going to the cops and telling them everything she'd seen at Old Farmer's Road, but the idea didn't feel right. The new part of her loved the taste and the way she felt after she fed from Amber. It scared her.

"Why would you do this to anyone?" she asked. "Why would you turn someone into this...thing?"

"I didn't just choose anyone, Cecilia. I chose you," he replied. "And regardless of how you feel, it's who you are now."

She didn't want to admit it, but Isaac was right. If the hunger returned again, she couldn't ignore it.

CHAPTER TWELVE
Never Enough

Jan watched the forensic investigator lifted the white sheet from the body. She gazed at the bloated body of the deceased female with its eyes half eaten away, and her purple tongue protruding from her swollen mouth. Her stomach was cut opened and her intestines rested on the ground next to her. The rotten, musty smell overcame her nostrils and she placed her hand over her nose.

The investigator smiled as he looked back to her. "Ahh, I do love the smell of decomposing flesh in the morning." He acted a little too entertained by her reaction. Not everyone could inspect a bloated corpse and comment on its unique odor. Yet she didn't complain. It was because of her contacts within the Minneapolis police that she wasn't standing behind the yellow tape with the news crew, watching from a distance.

"It's not Robert Ellsy?" She said in a mumbled voice.

"Nope. This one is a female."

Jan swallowed hard. Her next question escaped her lips in a slow stutter. "Allison?"

"No. I don't think so."

"Are you sure? How can you tell?"

The investigator closely eyed the body. "At this stage of decomposition I'd probably say her time of death was a few days ago. It's not your sister."

"Oh, thank God."

"Water does amazing things to a human body." He continued to pull back the sheet, revealing more of the victim's chest, also ripped into shreds. The body's upper frame was more decomposed with the rib cage clearly visible. "The body was in the river for a few days." A leech had latched itself above what was left of her belly button. He pointed to the remnants of the stomach. "Looks like bite marks on her stomach."

Jan took a few steps back and she placed her hand on her chest in comfort. Whoever did this had no remorse and no shame. She'd seen some badly decomposed bodies in the morgue but nothing to this extreme. She didn't want to imagine what her sister's body would look like if they found it today.

She turned back at the crowd standing behind the yellow police tape, which had grown in size since this morning. She expected they would be there until midnight, trying to interview anyone assigned to the case. While she was looking she saw Derek squeeze his way toward the front. Their eyes met and he quickly motioned for her to come to him. She felt reluctant but she owed it to him. She wanted badly to apologize for her rude behavior the previous night.

She approached him and soon found herself bombarded by news reporters who pushed their microphones in her face. She lifted the tape and allowed Derek to walk through unscathed.

"How'd you manage to get on the other side of the tape?" he whispered to her as they walked away from the crowd.

"I told you. I know people." She noticed he was poorly dressed, wearing only a short red and black flannel jacket, a faded white t-shirt, and ripped blue jeans. Again she smelled alcohol on his breath and his skin and before she had the chance to tell him, he gently grabbed her wrist, pulling her even farther away from the gawkers.

When they were alone but still in sight of the crime scene, news reporters, and cameras, Derek released his grip and lowered his voice to a whisper. "Is it him?"

"No. It's a female"

"Allison?"

"No, it's not her."

He looked away, disgusted. "Another kid?"

"The body is badly decomposed." She sighed. "It'll probably take a few days before they have an I.D. on the victim."

Derek stood back and stared into her brown eyes. He didn't have to say anything to her. She already knew what crossed his mind.

"Derek, I don't want to hear anything about the old farmer." She looked off into space.

"I know it sounds unbelievable but it fits perfectly," he said.

Jan didn't like the sound of his voice and she placed her hand on his shoulder to comfort him. She wanted to somehow make him understand that there were no such things as the supernatural.

He wiped his head in frustration. "It's just like the old cases I told you to skim through. The Barker case, the Johanesen case. Remember that John Doe from last year?"

She remembered those cases as clear as day. All of the victims were found either near the riverbanks a few miles from Old Farmer's Road. All of the bodies had been badly mutilated with their stomachs cut wide open. "Yes, I went through them a few times," she answered.

He looked up at her. "And you saw the resemblance between all the cases, right?"

She held up her hand to stop him. "What do you want me to do Derek? Do you want me to admit that there's something supernatural going on?"

"I want you to be open minded," he said.

"If you told anyone what you told me about the old farmer, they'd consider you a nutcase."

"I'd rather be a nutcase than say nothing," he replied. "Wouldn't you?"

Jan stood back, surprised by Derek's comment.

"All I'm saying is...just be open minded about things, Jan." He placed his hands in the pockets of his flannel jacket.

She held up her hands again in defiance and he stopped his rant in mid-sentence. She glared at him, making the same face she always gave him when he crossed the line. He stopped, but only for a moment, before starting back up again.

"I came down here last night." He looked away briefly. "I stood a few feet from where we're standing now." He took a deep breath. "I saw something."

Jan's eyes widened. "What did you see?"

"Two of Robert's friends; Elsie and Isaac," Derek said in a monotone voice. "They were with some girl."

"Are you sure it was Robert's friends?"

"I know what I saw," Derek replied. "We talked for a little bit and they drove off." He lifted his arm and pointed down the dirt path. "I also saw a blinking light over that way, in those trees. There was someone or something else down there." He dropped his hand.

Jan buried her face in her hands. He was pushing the conversation back to the paranormal and she had enough. "Derek, go home and I'll call you."

"I'm not lying about what I saw." His lips drooped in despair.

"I believe that you believe it."

"No. You don't."

"Derek." She reached out to him. "Just, go home."

He stepped back from her. "This isn't going to be solved with shoddy police work and a prayer." He started to pace back and forth. "Those kids know what's going on. That girl, Elsie, knows what's happening in those woods."

"Just because she was the last person to see him alive doesn't mean she's involved," she finally admitted to him. "As far as I know there's no physical evidence linking her to the crime."

"She frequents this place often. That should be enough." He discontinued his pacing and lowered his hands.

"Now, go home." She grabbed his wrist gently. "I'll call you later, okay?"

"Yeah, yeah."

She patted the top of his hand before letting it go. They both walked back to the crowd.

"Jan, could you do one more thing for me?"

"Yeah. What is it?"

"Check the body. There might be a tattoo or a marking on the left or right shoulder blade." He lifted the yellow police tape, looked over his shoulder, and flashed her a quick smile before he melted into the crowd.

Jan stood in thought. Maybe blaming the disappearances and murders on ghosts was easier than dealing with the truth. The sun's rays blazed on her forehead and she shielded her eyes, returning to the crime scene.

She approached the forensic investigator again who stood up from the body and wiped his forehead with his forearm. "Do me a favor." She placed her hand on his shoulder and she leaned close to his ear. "Can you see any visible tattoo on the victim's shoulder?"

"Can't tell," he answered. "If there was one it's probably gone now."

"Can the medical examiner search the back for tattoos?"

"Oh, the M.E —he does that all the time. It's standard procedure." He smiled. "I'll let you know as soon as he finds something."

$$****$$

Staring at the stucco ceiling, Cecilia found herself lost amidst the small protruding pebbles caught underneath the white plaster. The cushion of her bed pressed hard underneath her back and she moved her body up, positioning her butt just above a deep indentation in her mattress.

When she opened the front door to her parent's home, she found the inside vacant and quiet. Realizing that she was alone, she made her way into the bedroom. She waited for her mother to barge into her room, questioning her about where she had gone last night, but that didn't happen. But that wasn't the only thing on her mind.

With each passing thought about Amber and Julie, she shivered in disgust. She couldn't burn the ghoulish image of Elsie from her thoughts. The appalling attacks tore her mind into pieces and what she saw, witnessed, and experienced—it couldn't be true. She wanted no part of it.

She also couldn't explain why Old Farmer's Road had such an appeal to her. What person in their right mind would want to go back to a disastrous place like that? Maybe the pull she experienced wasn't natural, and that thought made her shiver again, and draw her pillow closer to her stomach. She closed her eyes, trying to sink into the darkness when a voice brightened her murky vision.

Roger.

The voice seemed to come from all around her. It spoke again and the vision of an old shack settled deep in the forest suddenly came into view. She saw its withered frame and a path overrun with decaying leaves leading to it. A tall, dark and gloomy figure stood to the right of the shack with its back toward her. She saw it drop to its knees near a pile of dirt.

Just one more.

One more.

Her stomach began to ache.

"Who are you?" Cecilia said out loud. "What do you want with me?"

Just one more.

One more.

She covered her ears, trying to block out the voice but it continued in her head along with the return of her hunger pains. The urge to eat began to drive her and she desperately wanted it to stop. "Get out of my head!" She rocked back and forth.

Just one more.

One more.

"Stop it!" She screamed again. "Stop it! Stop it!"

The voice suddenly stopped and she heard the sound of her phone buzzing, snapping her back into reality. She opened her eyes and wiped the sweat from her drenched body. The phone buzzed again and she grabbed it off the lamp stand, staring at Glenn's name.

She placed the phone up to her ear. "Hello."

"Hey baby."

She exhaled, feeling relieved to hear Glenn's warm voice. "I'm so glad to hear you."

"How are you?"

She couldn't tell him the truth. "I'm good. You?"

"Great. I just miss you," he replied. "Did you get my message?"

"Yeah." Cecilia cleared her throat and paused. "Wait. What message?" A brief pause interrupted their conversation.

"I left a message on your voicemail. Did you get it?" Glenn asked her.

"Really?" Cecilia sat up in bed. "No, I haven't checked my messages this morning." She heard commotion in the background mingled with male voices. "What's going on?"

"I'm helping my roommate set up for a party tonight," he replied. "But yeah, I left you a message. I was thinking about going up there to visit you."

"Visit me?" The pain subsided for a brief moment before returning its hellish attack. She bent over, grunted, and gripped her stomach in pain.

"Cecilia, are you okay?" Glenn's worried voice echoed over the phone.

Just one more.

One more.

The voice spoke loudly and she thought she heard it coming from the phone. It dropped from her hand and landed on her bed.

"Cecilia? Hello! Cecilia!"

She picked it up and placed it gently against her ear. "Sorry." She closed her eyes, praying that the voice would go away and take the pain with it. "I think I have a stomach bug." Her vision began to blur. "Glenn, did you hear that?"

"Hear what?"

She paused. I'm going crazy. "Nothing. I thought I heard something," she replied. "How about I call you tomorrow?"

"Cecilia, are you sure you're okay?"

"I'm fine. Really. Enjoy the party."

"You didn't tell me your opinion about me coming out to visit you."

"Can we talk about that later? I have to go." Cecilia hung up her phone and she grasped it in her hand. With her mind heavily distorted, she stood up from the bed, glaring at it.

Roger.

Her chest felt heavy and her thoughts began to sway. The voice rattled her brain and at first, she thought she was imagining it. "Roger?" She said out loud. "What about Roger?"

Just one more.

One more.

"What does this have to do with Roger?" Now she strongly believed that she had gone crazy, responding to voices that no one else could hear. But it remained persistent along with her mania to the point that all she could think about was him.

Without a second thought she hurried from her bedroom, grabbed her keys, and left the house. A presence drew her down the street in the direction of downtown Minneapolis and she began to walk. The sun was near the horizon, giving the sky a yellow orange glow. The humidity made her shirt bond to her sticky skin, and the absence of wind couldn't help with the heat. Cecilia covered her eyes from the sun, obeying the alien momentum that toyed with her, yanking her, and filling her head with fiendish thoughts. Her body obeyed it, even though her mind told her to fight against it.

Her footsteps slowed as she passed by Miss Bernadette's home. Thanks to the red curtains raised slightly, she was able to gaze through the front windows, finding the inside to be quaint. Small roses decorated the front yard next to the freshly cut grass. She placed her hands on the white wooden fence surrounding the property and lifted her head, taking in the smell of daffodils. Eerily enough, she found herself sympathetic to everything Isaac told her about the woman. Now she didn't trust

Miss Bernadette either and she found the old woman to be a threat, but she didn't know why. She had no reason to hate her.

Cecilia heard the front door unlock and it opened. Miss Bernadette stood in the doorway, wearing a long white ruffled dress and a pink blouse with her silver necklace dangling from around her neck. It caught the sunlight, blinding Cecilia for a quick second. Her dog ran from out of the house, between her legs, and straight to Cecilia. It growled and barked viciously at her and Cecilia jumped back from the fence.

"Puggy can be a little over protective." Miss Bernadette looked fixedly on Cecilia and walked out of her house. She snapped her fingers and the dog ran back to her. "Especially if the person she's barking at isn't a person at all." She wiped her hands on her flower pattern apron, leaving brown streaks.

"Excuse me?" Cecilia nervously placed her hands in her pocket.

Miss Bernadette moved forward and now she stood on the second step. "Don't worry my dear. I'm not here to out you. I can help you."

Cecilia nodded. "I'm fine."

"Your face shows otherwise." Again she moved forward and this time she stood on the sidewalk. She rubbed her hands together and small flakes of what looked like dried clay to Cecilia fell to the ground. Miss Bernadette inched forward. "If you ever want to talk, you can talk to me."

Cecilia smiled, finding her statement odd yet refreshing. "Thanks but I don't talk to people I don't know about my problems."

"But I know your problem and I can help you solve it." By now Miss Bernadette stood near the fence. "I know what's inside you, dear. I know what's troubling you."

Cecilia replied in a suspicious tone. "I doubt that." She began to walk backwards along the fence.

"I can help with the voices and the craving." She walked along the perimeter of the fence, toward her. "All you have to do is just give me something in return."

She held out her clay-covered hand and finding her advance peculiar, Cecilia jumped back. She knew about the voices, but how? This had to be some kind of test. Maybe Miss Bernadette was just like her, Elsie, and Isaac. Maybe she was also an Impa.

Cecilia squashed the idea. Whatever was happening wasn't mythological in anyway. Isaac and Elsie were murderers, plain and simple, and she helped in their killing spree.

She played dumb. "I don't know what you're talking about. I have to go."

"You've already went through the change but it's still not too late for you," Miss Bernadette continued. "Don't let it take control of you. Stand up to it. Ignore the voice."

Cecilia picked up her pace.

"It'll always tell you that you need just one more, but it'll never be enough."

Cecilia's pace turned into a jog. She stopped just around the corner, catching her breath.

Scared that Miss Bernadette would see her fear and concern, Cecilia didn't dare look back.

CHAPTER THIRTEEN
Hunger

Cecilia didn't stop until she had made her way to downtown Minneapolis. The walk took her under an hour and the entire time she felt conflicted between what pulled her to Towley's and how she could let anything of that magnitude control her.

She walked into Towley's, bumping into the owner himself who stood just inside the entrance, straightening a shelf full of magazines. She didn't break her stride and headed toward Roger who stood behind the counter, attending to a customer. Before she caught his attention, she felt Mr. Towley's heavy hand on her shoulder.

"I thought I told you that you ain't supposed to be here." He barked with the smell of old hot tobacco on his breath.

He towered over her and she pulled away from him. "I just need to talk to Roger."

"Not on my time, you don't."

"Just a minute, that's all." She extracted herself from their confrontation and made her way up to the counter. As soon as Roger finished with his customer, she tapped the counter to grab his attention.

"What are you doing here?" He lowered his voice. "Are Elsie and Isaac with you?"

"No. I need to talk to you."

"Come back in thirty minutes."

"Now, Roger." Any other day she would've felt obligated to respect his wishes but now she knew there wasn't any time for this. She grabbed him by his wrist and dragged him from being the counter to the back room.

"Cecilia, I have to work." He tugged at her.

"It'll be quick. Promise." She opened the door and shoved him inside. Her own actions stunned her but she didn't waste any time. She had him alone, right where she wanted him.

"I'm going to lose my job." Roger turned on the light and the stock room came into focus. The air smelled of wet boxes, mild mold, and lingering cigarette smoke.

"It's only for the summer, right? You'll find another one." She closed the door behind her and leaned up against it. Holding her head back, she took a deep breath. "What do you know about Old Farmer's Road?"

"What everyone else knows." Roger thought for a moment. "Is this why you're here? Why don't you ask Elsie or Isaac? They go there all the time."

"I'm asking you, Roger." She cocked her head to the side, finding herself oddly immersed in him. The urge of wanting to feed gradually rose inside her. She felt at any moment that she'd lose control and do to him what she did to Amber.

"Old Farmer's Road is just a place to hang out."

"What about the murders?"

Roger stood in thought. "What about them?"

"How many people were murdered there?"

Roger eyed her briefly. "I don't know. Maybe ten— hundreds."

Cecilia paused. "Hundreds?"

"The area is supposedly cursed." Roger shrugged. "I don't believe in it."

"What if I told you that the place is cursed?" Cecilia reached into her pocket and pulled out a cigarette.

"There's no such thing." He stuttered his answer. "All that stuff Isaac and Elsie say about the old farmer isn't true. They just say it to scare people away from the area."

"No. It's true." She lit her cigarette. Realizing that Roger knew nothing about the horrors and that he was as dumb as a bag of rocks, she inhaled. The smoke curled in her throat and she released it in perfect round donut circles. It eased her hunger for now.

Roger smiled. "They put you up to this, didn't they?"

"What?"

"Elsie and Isaac." His face flushed with excitement. "They told you to play a trick on me, didn't they?"

"This isn't a joke Roger. I'm being serious."

Taken back, Roger lapsed. "You really believe that the old farmer exists?" His smile disappeared.

The door rattled from the outside and it burst open. Mr. Towley stood in the entryway, thumbing back at the counter. "Roger. Go back to work." He pointed at Cecilia. "You. Leave. Now."

Glancing behind him, Cecilia saw Elsie and Isaac. Their timing couldn't have been more disturbingly perfect. Elsie slipped by him and into the room, grabbing onto Cecilia's wrist.

"Don't worry. We're leaving." The stern look on her face made Cecilia feel uneasy and she didn't stop Elsie from pulling her out of the room.

Mr. Towley straightened his shirt. "If I see you kids here again, I'm calling the cops."

Elsie gently guided Cecilia to Isaac and she turned back to Mr. Towley. "Go ahead. Call them." Now a crooked smile appeared on her stylish face. "You think the cops scare us?"

Trying to ease the situation, Cecilia spoke. "Sorry, Mr. Towley. You won't see us here again."

Elsie winked at Roger. "See you tonight?"

"You're going tonight?" He nodded and smiled. "Yeah. See you there!"

Isaac wrapped his arm around Cecilia and they walked to the exit. Her nose picked up the smell of strong cologne resonating from his neck. "You can't do that here. Not in front of people." He said to her in a whisper.

Cecilia looked at Isaac with awkward eyes. "I'm hungry."

Elsie soon joined up with them. When they reached the parking lot she quickly turned around she began to snarl at Cecilia. "You must be stupid!"

"I wasn't going to kill him."

"Then why did you come here?"

Cecilia paused. With their eyes locked on her, they waited for an explanation.

"I don't know why I came here. I just had to."

"You're lying." Elsie's eyes darted to Isaac. "She's your responsibility. Why weren't you watching her?"

Isaac held her close. "She's hungry Elsie." He ran his hand over her hair.

Elsie moved in closer. "I don't care if she's starving. She has to know that she can't just run off and eat someone in front of humans."

Cecilia pulled away from Isaac. "You and Isaac did this to me, remember? This isn't my fault."

"Isaac did this to you, not me," she quickly replied. "I would've rather eaten you instead."

Quickly Isaac interjected. "Cecilia, we aren't saying it's your fault. She's saying that you can't run off like this."

"That's why we go to Old Farmer's Road," Elsie added. "We go there because it's the safest place. We're protected there."

"Who protects us there? The old farmer?" Cecilia's question brought an eerie silence to their conversation. Isaac's eyes connected with Elsie's and they remained quiet. They were hiding something and Cecilia wanted to know.

"You haven't told me everything, have you?" she asked them. "Was he like us?"

Elsie chuckled. "No. He was better." Feeling that she won the argument, she huffed. "Get your act together C." She jabbed her finger into Cecilia's chest. "Now, because of you, we have to take Roger tonight." She opened the passenger side door to Isaac's car. "We eat together." She climbed in. "We share our meals." She slammed the door shut.

Cecilia looked to Isaac for support but instead he let out a long sigh and he laced his fingers on the back of his head.

"Isaac, I…"

"She's right, Cecilia," he interrupted her. "That's how we survive."

"You call this surviving?" She couldn't believe his tone of voice.

"Yeah, I do," he replied. "We've been doing this for a long time. This isn't new to us but this is new to you." She grabbed her by her shoulders and began to plead with her. "Listen to my sister. She knows what she's talking about."

"Whatever this voice is, that pushes me, wanted me to be here," Cecilia said as she tapped the side of her head. "It won't stop until I eat and I don't want to kill anyone."

"And you'll soon know how to control it," he replied. "You're new at this so it's hard for you. I understand that. But Elsie is telling you the truth. If it wasn't for her, I would've died decades ago."

Decades? She didn't know what he meant.

"This is more than just urges and fulfilling them," he said. "It's about living, surviving. If anyone finds out who we are, that's the end of us Cecilia. Do you understand that?" He shook her. "We can die."

Sensing his growing nervousness, she nodded quickly. Isaac dropped his hands and his body relaxed. "Promise me that you won't do that again."

"I promise." Cecilia bit her lower lip and she watched as now satisfied, Isaac smiled at her. Something foreign stirring inside her helped to open her eyes. She had to accept the abnormal feelings coursing through her body, drawing her closer to Isaac and her ability to accept her new life as this evil thing.

For now, she has to tread carefully. Regardless of how Elsie reacted to her, she didn't want to be far from Old Farmer's Road. Only there did she feel safe.

****

Cecilia had no choice but to sit in the back seat of Isaac's car and wait with them until Roger got off from work. Those two

hours felt like eternity to her and when they saw the lights inside
the store dim, her entire body perked up at the thought that soon
her hunger would be satisfied.

As Roger gleefully ran to the car, she held her head low to
avoid eye contact. I should warn him, she thought to herself.

Elsie jumped out of the vehicle. "Sit in the front." She told
Roger as she climbed into the back.

Roger didn't question. Isaac sped off and they headed to Old
Farmer's Road.

"You didn't have to wait for me." Roger said as his eyes
remained on the road. Isaac continued to drive without so much
as a flinch at his question.

Elsie, sitting directly behind Roger, playfully slapped Roger
on his arm. "Why not? We didn't want you to miss it."

Cecilia didn't say anything. Instead her fingers fidgeted in
her lap, like two wounded birds. Warning him about his
impending death crossed her mind.

Roger adjusted himself in the front seat. "I can't wait."

Elsie chuckled quietly. "I can't wait either." She slapped the
back of his seat. "I think you'll love it there." She elbowed
Cecilia gently. "Don't you think he'll like it there?"

Cecilia looked at her clammy hands as if they weren't hers.
The murders along with the cravings had traumatized her. What
had happened still didn't feel real. It never would. She thought
that soon she'd wake up from her horrible nightmare and
everything would turn back to the way it was. No Isaac, no
Elsie, no Old Farmer's Road, no voice, and no hunger.

"Isaac you're driving like my grandma!" Elsie laughed.
"Speed up for your darling Cecilia. Did you forget that she's
hungry!"

"You're mocking me again." Isaac pressed his foot on the gas
pedal. The car jerked forward and immediately picked up speed.
He gripped the steering wheel as the car swerved in and out of
traffic.

Roger turned around and said to Cecilia, "You should've
seen Mr. Towley's face after you guys left. He wasn't happy at
all."

"Would you be if you were him?" Cecilia asked.

"Who cares about him," Elsie interrupted. "He can't do anything to us."

"I wish I could find another job." Roger turned back to the front. "Good thing it's only temporary."

Cecilia ignored the rest of the conversation about Roger's boss and turned her eyes to the passing scenery. When the subject of the conversation changed to Miss Bernadette she felt her stomach gurgle and her throat crack.

"She threatened me the other day." Isaac said.

"Why didn't you tell me? I would've gone over there and ended her." Elsie's rude statement caused Isaac to burst out in laughter.

"Yep, just like the other time when she threatened you."

"Now you're mocking me Isaac."

"I'm just saying."

"Well don't say anything."

Suddenly Cecilia spoke. "Why do you hate her so much? Is it because she knows about us?" Her comment made Elsie snap her head in Cecilia's direction.

"Knows about us?" No longer laughing, Elsie's face hardened.

"She knows," Cecilia said.

"She doesn't know anything," Elsie said.

"She knows, Elsie."

Elsie eyed Cecilia before she said. "And how do you know this?"

Cecilia's eyes met Isaac's the rear view mirror. He had now tuned entirely to the conversation to the point that his driving became more erratic, scaring Roger.

"She told me," Cecilia answered. "She said she could help."

"You spoke to her?" Elsie turned her entire upper body in Cecilia's direction. Isaac swerved the car to the left, avoiding a slower car in the middle lane.

Roger grabbed onto the dashboard and his eyes widened. "Slow down," he said in trembling voice.

"Why would you even look at her C?"

"Because I believe her," Cecilia answered. "I think she really wants to help. And please, stop calling me 'C'."

"Oh, so now you're giving me orders?" Elsie scorned her. "She's the enemy C, if you haven't noticed already."

Enemy? Cecilia retreated and looked away. Still she saw from the corner of her eye that Elsie hadn't taken her eyes off her.

"She doesn't want to help us, idiot. She wants to kill us."

Startled, Roger asked Elsie about Miss Bernadette. Instead of answering, Elsie quickly hushed him and told him to stay out of the conversation. "Isaac, you need to educate your girl before I do it my way."

Cecilia felt a bubbling urge inside her throat and she tried to contain the need to vomit. The acidic liquid settled but then she felt it regurgitate again. She immediately covered her mouth, trying to contain the liquid swimming up her throat.

Elsie whispered low enough to avoid Roger's prying ears. "We should let you starve and send you back to her." Her eyes revealed her anger and rage. "She'll kill you just like she killed all the others."

"Hey, Cecilia doesn't look so good." Roger tapped Isaac on his shoulder. "Pull over."

"No," Elsie objected. "Keep driving."

Panicked, Cecilia slapped the back of Isaac's seat. "Pull over."

Isaac swerved the car quickly to the right and came to a screeching halt. Cecilia immediately opened the car door and leaned her head over the side, watching a yellowy liquid expel from her mouth. Isaac ran over to her and he gripped Cecilia's hair to pull it back as he heard the vomit hit the ground in a deafening splat.

"Are you alright?" He kneeled next to her.

Cecilia lifted her head and stared into his eyes. "I feel dizzy. This can't be normal."

"Let her starve." Elsie leaned back and sneered at the spectacle.

"You know what'll happen to her if we do that," Isaac replied in a whisper.

"Why do you still think I care? She should have thought about that before she went to that witch."

She felt Isaac's hand rub her back. "We're almost there. Just a little further."

Cecilia wiped the remaining puke from the corners of her mouth with the back of her hand. She raised herself up, wiping the wild strand of her hair away from her face.

"She isn't the one Isaac," Elsie said. "You were wrong...again. Just like with Robert."

"She is the one. Just give it time," Isaac said.

"You also said that about Robert." Elsie huffed. "You're track record isn't that great."

Quieted, they stared at each other. For the first time Cecilia felt fearful for her life. Even Isaac stood down and nervously looked away from Elsie. He turned and walked back to the car. Cecilia closed the door and soon Isaac sped down the freeway.

With each bump the car ran over, Cecilia felt her stomach act up. They all remained quiet and Isaac periodically looked back at her through the rear view mirror, flashing a weak smile. He mouthed to her that things were going to be okay. It was a phrase that Cecilia grew tired of hearing.

CHAPTER FOURTEEN

Home

When they arrived, Isaac pulled over on the dirt road and turned off the car. Elsie immediately jumped out and stretched her arms into the air.

Cecilia crept out from the vehicle, followed by Roger. She glanced around the area. The wind blew slightly and mist formed collectively in the distance, blocking out her view of downtown Minneapolis in the distance. She shivered slightly from the wind and felt Isaac's arms wrap around her from behind.

"I'm sorry about Elsie. She can be a headache sometimes." He whispered gently in her ear.

"Headache? Your sister is crazy."

Immediately he placed his finger over her mouth. "Shhh…she'll hear you." He then removed it. "Don't say that."

Stumped, she inspected him. "You're scared of her, aren't you?"

"Terrified." His lips curled slightly in his response.

Cecilia remained cautious of her surroundings. She didn't want to go any farther into the woods fearing what would happen next but the pain…it proved too much for her to not want to go. She heard the gravel crushing underneath Elsie's feet as they passed the chained barrier and began to walk toward the bridge.

"So the old farmer lived here?" Roger asked in awe.

"That's the story," Elsie replied.

"Cecilia believes he did. Do you?"

Elsie shrugged. "Anything's possible."

Cecilia looked back at Isaac. His eyes were impervious to each and every move that Roger made.

"There's a place to rest after the bridge." Isaac pointed. "Cecilia, we could stop there if you're still feeling weak."

"Yeah, Cecilia. We could stop there." Elsie mimicked Issac's voice.

Cecilia slowed her pace and waited for Isaac to catch up to her. "What will happen to me if I don't feed?"

"Don't worry about it. You're going to eat."

"But I want to know."

Isaac rubbed his hands over Cecilia's upper arms in an attempt to warm her chilled body. "First, you feel the pain and hear the voice."

"What is that voice? I mean, is it a ghost?"

"No, it's the hunger. The voice warns us that we need to eat. It's like your stomach growling when you're hungry. We don't have that like normal people."

"And where does throwing up fit on this list?"

"That's the second part," he replied. "If you continue to ignore the pain and the voice, you throw up. After that your mind starts to play tricks on you. You forget things and you become rabid."

Her eyelids failed to blink while she stared back into his eyes. "And after that?"

He saw her confusion and instigation. "You start to age...rapidly. You grow weaker—you can hardly sustain yourself. In a few days' time, you'll die." He grabbed onto her tightly and they began to walk across the rickety bridge. As he opened himself up to her, she wanted to inundate him with as many questions as possible before they reached the end.

"Is there any other way we can die?"

He shook his head. "We're pretty invincible. I mean, we can feel pain like normal people, but we heal quickly, as long as we eat."

"So the scars on your arm? What happened with that?"

"Oh, those." He looked at his forearm. "It happened a long time ago, shortly after my father died."

"How did he die?"

"You already know," he replied.

Cecilia thought for a moment. "Your father was the old farmer?" She slowed in her footsteps.

"Yeah," he answered. "He wasn't a bad man Cecilia. He had to kill people—not because he wanted to, but because he had to. We were a happy family. We were strong and careful as long as we remained together and the witch knew that." He looked back at her. "Miss Bernadette is a descendent of the witch who helped those idiots kill our father. That's why you can't go to her for help. That's why Elsie said she's the enemy. She will break us if we aren't careful."

Cecilia didn't understand and she didn't want to believe his story. Still, if something like what she was existed, any other supernatural thing was possible. "She said she could help us."

"Elsie may act overbearing but she's right when it comes to that woman," he replied. "She'll pretend to help you but her goal is to destroy you. Our father thought that witch could help us get rid of what he called 'the devil's disease.' Instead she made these little clay figures in our image. She called them figurines. She tricked my father, telling him that she could trap the evil inside of them but in order to do it, she needed something from us to bind to it. She needed a strand of my father's hair and he gave it to her. That's all it took."

"Like a voodoo doll?"

"Something like that, but it's made out of clay. Once she had my father's hair, she bonded him to it and somehow she made him weak enough so the townspeople could kill him."

Cecilia quickly remembered the dried clay she saw on Miss Bernadette's hands. It couldn't be a coincidence. "But that happened over a hundred years ago."

He looked at her. "Like I said, we age slowly. We're a lot older than we look. The more we feed, the stronger we are."

"Is that why you're afraid of Elsie? Because she's stronger than you?"

"Elsie has never stopped feeding since she started," Isaac said. "I've had my moments, like you, when I refused to eat, and each time I found myself returning to what I knew best."

They had reached the middle of the bridge and Cecilia began to remember the first time she went to Old Farmer's Road. The memories of the dark trail up ahead and how Julie had her arms wrapped around Isaac flooded her mind.

"When the townspeople came, they chased us. They almost got me." He rubbed his scars. "But Elsie saved me and she never lets me forget it."

"So why did you chose me?"

"You took Robert's place."

"Why did you choose him?"

"Cecilia, please don't ask me that," he whispered to her.

"I think I have the right to know. Why did you do to him what you did to me? Why did you kill him?"

"I didn't kill him. Elsie did." His face twitched and his lips began to tremble. "I don't want anything bad to happen to you and I don't want you to be on Elsie's bad side. Stay away from Miss Bernadette and don't become my sister's enemy."

Cecilia believed him. However, one question remained. If he didn't like what had happened around him, why didn't he find a way to stop it? There had to be a way, and she refused to think otherwise. When confronted with her question, Isaac immediately attempted to move away from the conversation, but Cecilia wouldn't let him go that easily.

He spoke in a raised voice. "I won't abandon my sister." His answer traveled and Elsie and Roger, who stood on the other end of the bridge, took notice.

"No, I'm not saying that." Cecilia lowered her voice. "I'm saying that there has to be something that can stop this; that can make us normal."

"Maybe for you, but not us. Elsie and I were born this way," he replied, defeated.

"After all these years, you haven't tried to look for a cure or for something to help stop the killing?"

"There is no light at the end of the tunnel for us. We are who we are."

When they reached the rock cropping her memory jumped again. She recalled the strange writings pointing in the direction to the narrow path that she'd seen before. Everything began to make sense, thanks to Isaac's historical knowledge.

Elsie grabbed Isaac by the arm and pulled him violently toward her. She questioned him about the conversation but he remained quiet.

Roger slapped his arm. "Something just bit me."

"A mosquito." Cecilia replied. She stood in the middle of the dirtied pathway, observing the darkness in front of her. Her mind remained indecisive about continuing but Elsie and Roger trekked forward, leaving her with no other choice.

Their shadows on the dirt road grew long and distorted in the moon's unearthly glow. The path now seemed long and the darkness ahead swallowed the tree branches. The night that once scared her now welcomed her, and she felt that someone or something waited for them at the end. This force grew in strength, squashing her hunger and focusing all of her undivided attention on what was to come.

"You still think the old farmer lives down here?" Roger asked her.

"Yes," Cecilia said, turning to Elsie, who drew a blank face at her answer. Her lips had slightly parted with the right corner of her mouth flinching in short spats.

Roger stopped in his tracks. "I heard his house is still down here, somewhere."

"I wouldn't doubt it," Cecilia said, gripping onto the sleeves of her jacket, feeling that the air had cooled a few degrees. Now walking ahead, her eyes moved from left to right across the darkness. This time there were no lighters to brighten their surroundings. It was just them, and the trees.

Elsie caught up to her. "What are you doing to my brother?"

"I'm not doing anything."

"You're up to something and I won't let it continue," she whispered.

"Elsie, I'm hungry and I want to get this over with." Cecilia forced a smile on her face. "I'm not trying to fight it anymore. I just want to eat."

"That's exactly what Robert said before he tried to get Isaac to turn on me." Elsie replied with a demonic giggle.

"I'm not Robert."

Elsie forced her to stop walking by placing her hands on her shoulder. "You're just like him. All you normal born people are."

Cecilia moved away from her. "Sorry if I don't bow down to you like your brother."

Elsie gazed into Cecilia's eyes. Cecilia tried to look away but Elsie placed her hand underneath Cecilia's chin, moving her head back in her direction. "No one in this world will break the connection I have with my brother. Not even you."

"Maybe he sees in me what he's never been able to have," Cecilia replied, "someone who doesn't order him around like a slave." She slapped Elsie's hand away from her chin.

Suddenly Elsie's face warped, returning to the foul and ugly thing she'd seen days ago in Isaac's car, but this time she didn't hide her true face. She grasped tightly onto Cecilia's neck. Agitated, Elsie growled and the ragged noise bellowed through the air, like a pack leader calling out to its servants.

The loud noise made Roger cover his ears. A small white light appeared ahead of them and it moved in unison to Elsie's howl, fluttering rapidly. Cecilia felt her throat contract and she gasped for air. She felt a smoldering sensation on her back coming from her tattoo. The wretched voice returned and it called out to all of them: *Just one more.*

Isaac wrapped his arm around Roger's throat and began to choke him. Roger fought hard against his attack but soon Cecilia saw his legs go limp followed by his eyes rolling into the back of his head.

Elsie then let Cecilia go.

She stumbled back, rubbing her sore throat, and with clenched teeth she uttered in despair, "You tried to kill me!"

"If I wanted you dead, you would be dead already." Elsie clacked her long fangs together.

Cecilia turned to run, but seeing Roger stopped her. Her mouth felt heavy and she couldn't speak. She felt her lips contort and her jaw suddenly snap shut. She placed her hand underneath her jaw in an attempt to pry it open. She tried moving her legs but they stood in place. Standing aghast at the situation, she knew what she had to do.

Isaac picked up Roger's body with ease, and he draped it over his shoulder. He then continued along the path in the direction of the blinking light. Cecilia didn't want to follow but again she felt her legs tense up as they began to move. Ahead, small twigs and branches partially blocked their way. As the three of them approached the clearing, they began to twitch and retract themselves, revealing a dark shape up ahead.

The moonlight shined on a shack tilted slightly to the right with worn brown shingles curled from being exposed to the weather. Two empty square orifices with broken glass replaced the spot where windows used to be. Along with the shack, many of the front deck's boards were tilted and rotted through. The land surrounding it was just as decrepit and fell victim to Mother Nature's abuse. The dirt was free of grass and brown sandy dirt swirled in mini typhoons along the dry earth.

Elsie approached the shack and climbed the steps. She opened the aged door. It swung back and squeaked. She looked back at her friends for a final time before walking in and disappearing into the shack's darkness.

"Home," Isaac said, heading forward.

The shack's inside appearance didn't stimulate Cecilia's amnesia and it didn't do anything for her zombie like stature. She found the inside new and mysterious. Her feelings of remorse for what happened to Roger went away, replaced with a need to finally get what she came there for.

She placed her foot on the bottom step and felt the wood bend underneath her weight. The interior smelled of old mildew and rotten wood. The shack was extremely small with only one living room and a small room in the back exposing the kitchen. The wood continued to squeak as they walked, passing by the stone fireplace covered with dirt, engulfed in cobwebs. A round broken mirror hung on the wall by a thin rusted chain and a bent nail. A heavily scratched desk sat in the corner, covered with years of accumulated dust motes.

They walked through the doorway and into the kitchen. A porcelain sink, that still gleamed white underneath a layer of dirt, was fastened to a wooden stand next to another broken window. Hanging near the low ceiling were cabinets with their doors barely attached at the hinges.

Elsie continued to walk toward the back and stepped outside. She opened two storm cellar doors slightly upraised in the earth's surface, revealing worn stairs leading down into darkness. Isaac pushed Roger's body down the stairs and he rolled until his body rested on the final landing.

Elsie was the first to descend down the stairs. Cecilia peeked into the dark void. The air seeping from the cellar was hot and stuffy. She felt Isaac's soft touch on her shoulder, giving her the confidence to move forward.

The flickering candles stationed on wooden shelves lining the entire space came into view. Cecilia heard a whimper but for some odd reason the noise didn't move her to look for its source. She watched Isaac grab a handful of candles and place them on the floor in a perfect round circle around Roger's body. Cecilia watched as Roger lifted his head as blood streamed from a cut on the side of his face.

Elsie ripped off Roger's shirt. He opened his mouth and began to snuffle what sounded like garbled words but he instantly went silent when Elsie kicked him in his side.

"Isaac didn't tell you everything about our father." She traced her fingers around Roger's lips. "The witch and the humans did terrible things to him." She kissed Roger's cheek. "Witches killed our mother when we were just babies. They tracked our family down with their magic and incantations."

Roger's watered eyes circled the cellar. Cecilia had never seen someone so scared before.

"By killing him the witch thought she had destroyed our power and made us weaker. But what she didn't know was that his soul remained trapped here, forever." She smiled seductively at Cecilia. "He still feeds. He will always be hungry." She walked to the edge of the circle and raised her head to look at the ceiling. "Father. Are you here?" She called out.

The candles began to shake and the tiny flames flickered.

Isaac smiled in absolute delight. "He's here."

Cecilia frantically eyed the environment around them, waiting for their father to manifest in front of their eyes. Power surged through her veins, her bones, her skin and it possessed every inch of her body. She wanted to cut it out of her. The ground underneath them began to tremble and her shoulder began to ache. She reached around to feel her back, discovering that the skin around her branding had grown hot.

"Father. We brought you sustenance." Elsie's words seemed phantasmal.

What Cecilia saw manifesting itself before her eyes would've scared her into complete silence if she wasn't silent already. Thick white smoke suddenly appeared in thin air above Roger. It swirled gradually around the perimeter of the circle until it condensed and gradually began to form the outline of a spectral body. The smoky manifestation then hovered over Roger and what looked like small slivers extended from the location of its mouth.

It began to feed, sucking the essence from Roger. It continued and Roger's body began to convulse. Just then Cecilia felt herself release. She felt freed from her zombie stature.

Isaac motioned to her. "Eat."

But Cecilia stepped back, giving herself time to process the carnage in front of her. Now up against the wall, she slid her body toward the stairs leading up and out of the cellar.

"You need to eat Cecilia," Isaac said again.

Just one more.

One more.

This time the voice came from the white smoke. It wisped around and blocked Cecilia from the exit.

Isaac held out his hand to her. "You know what will happen if you don't eat."

Cecilia moved her body forward and as Elsie stepped away from Roger, she accepted her nature. She fed, feeling the warmth fill her cold body, silencing her pains. She didn't stop until she had absorbed every drop that was inside him.

Roger's body began to deteriorate. It wilted and his skin sank, revealing the outline of his bones. His eyes dried and his eyelids sank further into his head. His mouth dropped open and his tongue protruded, withering into a small pencil shaped husk. The smoky figure blocking the exit curled and evaporated into thin air.

Cecilia staggered back onto the floor. The feeling of euphoria settled into her and she leaned back, feeling full and satisfied.

Isaac marched over to her. "You should feel better now." He cradled Cecilia in his arms.

"Why did you let her eat your portion?" Elsie replied angrily.

Isaac rolled his eyes at her. "She needs it more than me."

In his care, Cecilia lowered her body to the ground. She felt that she could do this again. She had to if she wanted to live. She closed her eyes and drifted into darkness.

CHAPTER FIFTEEN
Aftertaste

"You look good," Jan said, as she stood up from the booth and greeted Derek with a warm hug.

Derek scanned the room. The small diner only had ten seating booths and a long counter. Before Jan broke off their engagement, they would make the long trek to the diner daily before sunrise. While what they ordered changed, their daily routine remained the same. They claimed the booth at the far end. They ordered their pot of coffee. Sometimes he'd order hash brown with scrambled eggs and oatmeal and she'd order oatmeal with extra brown sugar.

The electric clock on the wall read 11:45 p.m. in bright red. Derek couldn't sleep and he called her to meet, hoping that she had new information about the body discovered earlier that day. He couldn't get his mind off who the victim was and if the body was connected to Robert's friends. It also didn't help that Rosie complained to him all night about her friend, Julie, who had gone missing.

Derek sat across from Jan and picked up the two-sided menu from the table.

"I told the waitress we didn't need it." Jan sipped her coffee. "But I think she's new and doesn't know better."

Derek nodded and still scanned the items on the menu. "I think I'll try something different." He pointed to the Morning Special: two eggs, two pieces of ham, and buttered toast. He placed the menu near the edge of the table and he held an empty porcelain cup in front of him. "You didn't get me any coffee."

"Well, I know how you like your coffee," Jan answered. "Half coffee, half vodka."

"I've been cutting back on the vodka." Derek leaned back in the seat. He rubbed his chin, realizing that he was overdue for a shave. The prickly hairs stung his fingers, so he placed his hands on the table. "I'm sorry if I was hard on you earlier today."

"It's fine," Jan replied.

"I'm really sorry." He waited for her to accept his apology. Acknowledging his wrongs were the first steps in mending their broken friendship. He didn't want Old Farmer's Road to be the only thing they had in common. He missed her, and deep down, he wanted everything to go back to the way it was. Wishful thinking.

"Derek, it's okay," she replied.

"I've just been...these past few days have just been difficult for me."

"I know, but you have to understand that I'm working as hard as I can on this."

Derek nodded. "Yes, but sometimes it feels like we're the only ones who are."

"Believe me, we aren't." Jan rubbed her forehead in thought.

The waitress approached their table and pulled out a white pad from the back pocket of her black jeans. Her name tag, which sat lopsided on her chest read "Sara" and her dark hair was buzzed short. "What'll it be?" Her words slurred together.

"Morning Special: eggs scrambled. White toast and some coffee."

The waitress turned to Jan.

"Just the coffee."

The waitress nodded and walked away.

"Derek, I'll make this quick. The M.E. checked and he didn't find any noticeable tattoos on the body." She lowered her voice.

"But the body is so badly decomposed that it was hard to tell. The victim could've had a tattoo."

The waitress returned with a pot of coffee.

"Please, leave the pot." Derek spoke. As soon as she left, he continued. "I was up all night, trying to figure out why Elsie and her friends were at Old Farmer's Road." He reached into the pocket of his pants, pulling out a crumpled piece of paper. "I remembered what Robert said about the place and about what he saw. I found this in his belongings at my apartment." He handed the paper to Jan. "He drew it for me a week before he died."

Jan opened the ragged piece of paper and stared at the pencil drawn image of a withered face with deep eyes and long sharp fangs extending from the roof of its mouth. She looked up at Derek. "What's this?"

"Robert told me that this creature is responsible for the deaths."

Jan slid the paper back to Derek. "This isn't evidence Derek."

Derek leaned in closer to Jan. "It's the best lead we have."

She sighed and lowered herself in the booth. "Derek, a picture of some hideous creature doesn't help."

"I believe that he saw this thing at Old Farmer's Road." He took a deep breath. "I know you'll never believe me so I've decided that I'm going to show you." Derek stood up from his booth. "I'm going to get to the bottom of this." He stuffed the piece of paper in his pocket. "I'm going to find this thing, whatever it is."

"Derek, don't do anything stupid." Jan stood up, surprised.

"I'm not."

"Let's talk about this," she pleaded. "You just ordered your food. We have all the time in the world to discuss this."

"I'm not hungry."

"Derek..."

"It's not going to wait. It's going to keep killing."

"Sit down. Please."

He paused, realizing that he had overstepped his bounds as he always did when it came to Old Farmer's Road. He lowered himself back in his seat.

"I know you think you're doing what's best but you have to realize," she pointed to the piece of paper, "this doesn't exist. We're not looking for a creature. The killer is human, Derek."

"A human couldn't have done this." He shook his head. "No."

****

No mention of Roger crossed their lips. Like Amber and Julie, his name became unspeakable including everything that happened that night. What didn't disappear was the hunger that grew stronger within her. It became unbearable.

The next night they killed Sara, a college student with an addictive love of marijuana. Like Julie, Isaac lured her to Old Farmer's Road. After choking her into unconsciousness, he dragged her to the cellar of the old shack. Elsie got first taste and when she became full, Isaac allowed Cecilia to feed. He ate whatever remained.

The next night Elsie brought Kevin, Sara's feeble-minded boyfriend who had no idea that he too was chosen to suffer his girlfriend's fate. That time Isaac didn't feed at all. Instead he gave his portion to Cecilia, which angered Elsie.

After Kevin, Cecilia finally thought she had some control over her hunger as the pain began to withdraw from her body. For the first night since her transformation, she didn't feel the need to kill and eat. She felt freed from her ravenous state and convinced herself that now she had the opportunity to find a reason to end the atrocities. She needed Isaac's help to do so.

The following night after Kevin's death, she asked Isaac to go with her to the movies. Worried that Elsie would squash the invitation, Cecilia made sure to explain her reason thoroughly. She pretended to go along with the notion of being an Impa. She faked her interest in it to the point that she lied about a teenage boy who worked at the theater and how delectable he looked. Knowing that Isaac cut back on his feeding for her, this boy was to be her "thank you" gift to him. After hearing her explanation,

Elsie barely agreed and with a push from Isaac, she let the issue go.

As soon as Cecilia and Isaac drove down the street, Cecilia didn't waste any time in telling him the truth. She made him pull over just down the street.

"Why are we stopping?" he asked.

"Isaac." She turned to face them. "There isn't any boy."

He looked at her with wounded eyes. "What?"

"There isn't any boy. I just wanted to get you away from your sister."

He put the car in park and leaned back in his seat. "Then why did you bring me out here?"

"I'm going to go to Miss Bernadette and ask for her help."

His eyes widened. "I already told you, she will kill us!"

"We have to try, right?"

"Cecilia, there is no trying with her. She will kill you."

Cecilia heaved in desperation. "I thought that maybe you'd like to come with me."

He looked forward. "I'm not going anywhere near that witch."

Cecilia opened the passenger door. "Fine. You can wait here." She stepped out and slammed the door shut. She walked down the street. She didn't forget what Isaac had told her about Miss Bernadette and it remained fresh in her mind. If Miss Bernadette had a way to end the murders, Cecilia wanted to help her in any way possible.

She ventured forward until hearing the sound of snapping twigs behind her and on her left. She paused and looked over her shoulder, seeing Isaac approaching.

"Cecilia, stop." He walked up to her.

"You don't have to go with me."

"If you're doing this because you're angry with me, I'm sorry."

"I'm not angry with you." She sighed loudly. "I just want all of this to end."

"You're angry with me because if you weren't, you wouldn't be going there." He moved in front of her. "I told you, Cecilia. She's the enemy."

"And I told you that we need all the help we can get," she replied.

"Did you not listen to anything I said about her!" he blurted out. "She can't and won't help you." He ran his fingers through his hair. "I'm trying to protect you. That's all I've been doing these past few days. I was serious when I said I don't want anything to happen to you." He gently grabbed her arm. "This isn't a smart thing to do."

"Like I said, you don't have to come with me." She walked around him and picked up her pace down the street.

"Wait!" Isaac called out after her. He jogged, catching up with her again.

"Have you ever thought about all the people you've killed throughout your life and those who you will kill? Has that ever crossed your mind?"

"Yes, all the time," he replied.

"Any person with a conscious would want to stop that." She grew tired of his excuses and his 'what ifs.' He reminded Cecilia of her father when they lived in California. He always had excuses for cheating on her mother, and the clues he left around the house that pointed to his infidelity. One night, after he came home smelling of lilac perfume, which lingered in the hallway for days, he blamed the scent on the secretary, knowing that wasn't the case.

"If Elsie finds out she'll kill us both."

"And that's why we have to find a way to stop it. Not just for you but also for your crazy sister."

"Stop calling her that. She isn't crazy."

"You're scared of her, Isaac. Why don't you stand up to her?"

"She's family."

"You said the witches' magic made your father vulnerable, right? Maybe they could do the same for to her so that she has no choice but to stop." She said to him in a coarse whisper.

"Miss Bernadette would stop her all right," he replied. "By killing her."

Cecilia looked up at the thick cloudy sky and he followed her gaze. To the north she saw the sky lit up briefly with rumbles of thunder. It was midsummer and the humid nights were starting to become unbearable. She smelled the moist air as she continued to walk.

"Did you forget that part?" Isaac lowered his gaze. His eyes locked onto her face and for a brief moment, he smiled. "You're different from the others, Cecilia." He raised his hand and his warm palm brushed her cheek. "I don't know why. You just are."

Feeling trapped, she stepped away from him. "How many were there before me?"

Isaac shoved his hands into the pockets of his jeans. "Too many to count."

"And you did nothing to protect them?"

"I did everything I could," he replied. "They just...they didn't fit. They didn't understand or want to accept it."

"Can you blame them? You're killing people every day. Do the math, Isaac. That's a lot of killing. Why would you want to change people into something like you and Elsie? Because you feel incomplete? You're not strong enough? Bored?"

He quickly turned away. "Stop it."

"No, I won't. Don't you get it? You'll never have this complete family that you want. No one in their right mind would enjoy killing people on a daily basis."

"You're wrong."

"How am I wrong?"

"So far you have been the only person who's enjoyed it," he replied.

Cecilia immediately stopped walking.

"You're the only person who actually enjoys the after taste," Isaac said. "Not Robert or anyone else. Just you."

CHAPTER SIXTEEN
Soul Eaters

Miss Bernadette's house sat eerily quiet. Isaac, who stood next to Cecilia, flinched at the sight and stepped back. "We shouldn't be here," he whispered.

For the second time Cecilia saw his fear and dread about her, fresh and out in the open. He shivered slightly and sulked so low to the ground that she thought he might lie on the pavement.

She opened the gate and stepped into the front yard. The wind picked up, tingling her arms and the back of her neck. With each step she took, the cold wind brushed against her body. The wind dissipated when she reached the front steps and the smell of incense and rose water filled the air. Cecilia raised her hand and pressed it forward. It connected with an invisible wall and she looked back at Isaac, mystified.

What she experienced made Isaac scurry back farther from the home. The invisible wall felt liquefied as if droplets of water were the glue that held it all together. It exuded a peaceful, tingling sensation that traveled throughout her body.

The front door to the home opened but no one stood at the entryway to greet her. Cecilia stared back into the darkness, unable to move until the barrier dropped unexpectedly. Now free, she climbed the steps and up to the porch.

"Cecilia." Isaac rushed into the front yard and she looked back just in time to see his body connected with the barrier that had now moved to the gate. He slammed into the invisible force and unable to move any further, his eyes billowed in horror.

"I'll be fine." She mouthed her words to him before she stepped inside. The door closed behind her on its own, the interior of Miss Bernadette's home lighting up, coming to life. Potted plants hung from hooks embedded in the ceiling. A small table next to the front window held several small plants all arranged in a row, from smallest to largest. Near the back, in the living room, she saw an altar on a large table draped in a white cloth. The table itself was decorated with a small black metal bowl, cone incense, and books.

The home gave off a mellow atmosphere that Cecilia didn't expect. It wasn't the dark and dreary home she expected it to be. There weren't any voodoo dolls or large cauldrons. The floor creaked beneath her feet as she stood in the living room. Finally Miss Bernadette appeared from a back room. Wearing a long flowing black dress, she made her way to Cecilia.

"Welcome. I'm glad you could come." Miss Bernadette grabbed a cushion on her brown leather couch, fluffed it, and placed it back. "I haven't had a chance to clean up the place."

"Is that magic?" Cecilia thumbed behind her and toward the front door.

"Just a little barrier protection spell."

"You have a..." Cecilia searched her mind for the right word to say. "...you have a nice home."

"You know what they say. Home is where the heart is." She walked into the dining room, standing just to the right of her altar. It grabbed Cecilia's full attention and she didn't know what to make of it. Above it, she saw the image of a large silver pentacle nailed to the wall, which made her temporarily rethink her decision to come in. Next to it stood a large black bookcase filled with a variety of ancient texts. However the pentacle and the altar were the least of her worries.

"The barrier is necessary. It keeps out anything not human."

"Not human?"

"Yes, like Elsie, Isaac, and you."

Cecilia didn't know why she felt obligated to defend the way Miss Bernadette described her. She still thought of herself as human but when her memories moved to the people she helped killed, any courage to do so quickly disappeared.

"You said you could help me." She cautiously walked over to her. "Can you?"

"Yes, I can." Miss Bernadette motioned for her to come closer.

"Without killing anyone, right?"

"I hope so."

"I'm serious." Cecilia iterated her stance. "I don't want anyone else to die, and that includes Elsie and Isaac."

"I don't want any innocent people to die as well." Miss Bernadette reached for a book on the bookcase. "Long before our ancestors wrote down their myths, there were legends about creatures who ate the flesh of humans and their blood in order to survive and stay young. A vampire is just one example."

"Vampires don't exist."

"Are you sure about that?" She winked at Cecilia. "Just because you've never seen one doesn't mean they don't exist." She pulled a large book from the shelf and returned to her altar. "Ahh, here it is." She opened the book. "Have you heard of Ammut?"

Cecilia shrugged. "No."

"In Egyptian mythology, Ammut was a female demon who ate souls." She flipped through the pages, stopping at the image of a colorful creature Cecilia never seen before.

"Ammut or as some called this demon, Ammit, had the head of a crocodile and a body of a hippopotamus and lion. She weighed the heart of humans against the weight of a feather. If the heart wasn't pure, she would devour it." Miss Bernadette laughed gently. "It's amazing how much creativity and talent went into these drawings."

"What does this have to do with an Impa?"

"So, they told you what you are?" She eyed Cecilia. "They have many names. The Choctaw called them 'Shadow People.'

In Scotland, they call the females 'Selkies'. My people simply call them 'soul eaters.'"

"Look, I'm not here to talk about goddesses, demons, and mythology. I want to know how you can help me..." she said, catching her breath, "I mean, help us."

"You, I can help. However they cannot be helped."

"Why not?"

"They can't suppress who they are. It's like asking me to change your eye color. They were born with it. It's part of them."

"But you can stop it, right? You can make it easier to control the hunger?"

"They are children of Ammut. You can't change a demon's seed." Miss Bernadette placed her hands on Cecilia's shoulders, turning her around. She pulled down her shirt and gazed at Cecilia's branding. "This was given to you, like an unwanted but curable disease." She dropped her hands and turned to face her altar. "You have a choice. You can be saved." She began to search her altar. "Like I was saying, there are different types of Impa."

Cecilia repositioned her shirt. "So what type are Elsie and Isaac?"

"The rarest." Miss Bernadette grabbed a small brown leather pouch from the counter and opened a drawer underneath the table. "Their kind is nearly extinct, thanks to my people. They are related to a type of creature that my ancestors, the Hausa, have been battling since they revealed their horrid ways." She opened the pouch, pulling out three smooth stones. "It's said that some of them can transform into ravaged dogs at will."

Cecilia immediately thought about the dog she saw on her first night at Old Farmer's Road.

"Together, they can be extremely powerful and harder to kill. While it is easy to spread their condition onto others, like yourself, it is much harder to keep the newly transformed victims in line with their treacherous ways. This is why the ones they do choose don't last long. Their hunger generates from the stones they keep locked away in their stomachs. It is said that if they regurgitate a stone and a normal person, like you, devours it, then you become one. It's where their hunger comes from."

Stones? Cecilia folded her arms across her chest and searched her mind for anything she could remember during her first time at Old Farmer's Road. She remembered Isaac holding stones in his hands, but if she believed what Miss Bernadette told her, that meant that sometime, during that night, she had swallowed one.

"I don't remember eating a stone."

"Swallowed, Cecilia. You swallowed a stone," Miss Bernadette replied. "You just don't remember. Once it is inside your body, the stone separates into three more. Now you too can also inflict the curse on another poor soul."

"Swallow, eat…regardless, I would remember something as strange as that."

"That's what all the victims say when I tell them," she replied. "You aren't the first and you won't be the last. You could've avoided this if your body was prepared for it." She smiled. "If you had eaten the lemon pound cake I gave to your mother, you wouldn't have been affected."

"Wait a minute." Cecilia paused the conversation in order to give herself time to process the new information. "You put something in the cake so I wouldn't have been affected?"

Miss Bernadette nodded.

"So who do those stone belong to?" Cecilia looked at the stones in her hand.

"These particular stones belonged to their father." She closed her hand. "Like every Impa my ancestors have killed, their stones are taken and kept safe so that they can't be used on another unsuspecting victim." She placed the stones back on the table. "Once they are removed, the Impa will die." She pulled from her pocket a small grayish object, made out of clay that stood about six inches tall. It had dots for eyes, no mouth, no nose, and no limbs. Its head was covered in scraggly gray human hair. "In order for my ancestor to kill their father, she needed something which belonged to him. His hair."

"Figurines." Cecilia stepped away from her. "Isaac told me about how one was used to kill his father." She looked up at

Miss Bernadette. "He was right. You don't want to help them. You want to kill them."

"Killing them is the only way to help them and it's the only way to help you," she replied. "Their hunger will never stop, but for you Cecilia, I can't relieve your body from this dreaded trait. With my help I can suppress the hunger so that you can live a normal life." She turned to her shelves on her right. "Don't you want to be freed from this?" She grabbed a small box and placed it on the table.

"I do but not at the expense of Isaac's life."

"He isn't as innocent as he seems to be." She opened the box, revealing two old and weathered figurines—a male and a female that looked like Elsie and Isaac, and another that resembled her. "You have not seen his true face yet, have you? He is far more dangerous than his sister."

"I've seen Elsie's real face." Cecilia picked up the object made in her image and studied its features. Angered, she threw it back in the box. "Why did you make one of me?"

"As a precaution." Miss Bernadette placed the book aside. "It is my duty, as a descendent, to make sure that this evil doesn't spread. You don't understand how violent they can be once they are backed into a corner. In this case, Elsie is much more violent than her brother. She is the reason why I have a barrier spell in place." Miss Bernadette began to attend to her altar. "However, Isaac is more insidious when it comes to his tactics—beware." She grabbed other leaves and spices from nearby shelves, and placed them in a black metal bowl. She grabbed a small mixing spoon and began to crush the ingredients down to a greenish yellow paste. The smell of old leaves and what Cecilia thought was ginger, filled the air. After she finished she forced Cecilia to turn around and lift up her shirt.

"What are you doing?"

"This might sting at first." She applied the paste over Cecilia's branding. "It is the first step in freeing you from the voice."

"The voice tells me when I'm hungry." Cecilia felt the cold lumpy paste turn warm the moment it touched her skin. She reached to scratch it but Miss Bernadette slapped her hand away.

"Don't touch it." She lowered Cecilia's shirt. "As I've said, it will stop the voice. If you do what I say then killing won't be a priority for you." Again Miss Bernadette grabbed what looked like small leaves from the counters around the altar. Cecilia watched, noticing that the burning pain from her tattoo began to subside. Instead of mixing these ingredients in her black bowl, Miss Bernadette placed the items in the small brown leathery pouch. "Like their friend Robert, he also came to me for help and they killed him for it. But I didn't give him a charm bag to ward off evil. This will protect you...for now."

"What's in there?" Cecilia asked.

"Sage, agrimony to ward off evil influence, some lavender for luck," she replied, "and other things." She closed the small bag, tying it, and she handed it to Cecilia. "Put this in your pocket. I can't stress this enough. Don't lose it and don't let them know you have it."

Cecilia grabbed the pouch and examined it before placing it in her pocket. "So as long as I have this, I won't have the need to kill and to eat? But if I don't eat, I will die."

"If you don't want to die, you must get me what I need." She walked into the living room. "Strands of their hair will do."

Cecilia didn't have any clue on how to get what Miss Bernadette needed without signaling Isaac and Elsie of her betrayal. She also didn't want to help the witch kill them, especially Isaac who she saw as a pawn following Elsie's orders.

"And what if I decide not to do it?" Cecilia's eyes widened and she gazed at Miss Bernadette.

"Oh, you will do it if you want to live." She extended her arm forward, holding onto something so small that Cecilia had to squint to see. When her eyesight narrowed in, she saw a long piece of hair hanging from between Miss Bernadette's forefinger and thumb.

"Is that mine?" Cecilia gripped her hair. "How did you..." her question freezing on her lips as she realized that Miss

Bernadette had what she needed to combine her with the figurine she made in her likeness. "This is not what I came here for. You said you would help me." She looked out the window, seeing Isaac standing on the sidewalk. She walked to the front door and before she left, she turned around. "You're not giving me any choice."

"I am giving you a choice," she said. "Either you help me to stop them or you can die with them."

CHAPTER SEVENTEEN
The Truth

As soon as Cecilia stepped out onto the porch, she heard the sound of the door creaking and finally closing behind her. Realizing that she wasn't harmed, Isaac embraced her tightly and his arm skimmed over her shoulder and along her branding. She grunted and immediately caught herself as to not give away what Miss Bernadette had done to her.

"Are you okay?" He moved back and looked her over. "What did she say to you? Did she threaten you?"

He bombarded her with questions. She cleared her throat. "I'm fine Isaac. We should head back." She paced down the sidewalk with her head low.

He didn't take his eyes off of her. "She had to say something, didn't she?" He looked back at the house. "What did she tell you?"

Cecilia didn't want to tell him. She had no way to summon the courage to do that. Was Isaac as cunning as Miss Bernadette made him out to be? Was he the real threat and not Elsie? All she wanted to do was go home and think, but Isaac wouldn't let it go that easily.

He took a deep breath. "Why won't you tell me? She wanted you to kill us, didn't she?"

Cecilia refused to meet his stare and answer his questions.

"She still has those figurines of us," he said as he nodded to his own statement. "Did you see them?"

Cecilia glanced over at the cars parked down the side of the street. "Yes, I saw the ones she had of you, Elsie, and your father." She revealed only the half-truth to him.

At the mention of his father, Isaac's composure changed. "I told you Cecilia. You can't trust her." He pounded his right fist into his left hand.

"That's ironic coming from you," she replied. "I learned a lot more from her about what you did to me and to others before me."

He stopped pounding his hand and dropped his arms to the side. "You don't believe her, do you?"

"Honestly, I don't know what to believe anymore."

"You believe what she told you?"

"She was spot on, Isaac." She looked at him. "Why didn't you tell me about the stones? Why didn't you mention that the people you turn don't last long?"

He fell silent.

"Exactly. You didn't want to because you know I would've run to her for help the first night." She argued back. "She made a figurine in my image and she has my hair. If I don't help her, she will kill me along with you and your sister."

"How did she get your hair?" He bustled in front of her with his arms stretched out to stop her forward trudge. "Cecilia, we have to get it back as soon as possible."

"It's too late."

"We need to go back—kill her tonight."

"No." She smacked his arms away from her. "I'm tired of all this killing." She raised her hands in the air. "All of this, what we do, it has to stop." She pointed her finger in his face. "It can't go on forever and you know it."

"What do you want to do?" He stared at her finger. "There isn't any peaceful resolution when it comes to that witch, not as long as she has what she needs to kill you."

"I'm not killing her." Cecilia giggled unexpectedly at the situation. "Even if I agreed to go back and kill her, there's no way we can just walk straight through that barrier. It's there to keep things like us out."

He walked forward and his chest met her finger. "I'll do anything. Just tell me what you want me to do."

"You can start with not feeding."

"I've tried but all it does is make me sick and delirious." He continued to move forward, making Cecilia step back. "But if you really want me to, I'll stop for as long as you like." His face began to warp in front of her eyes, revealing scraggly skin, furrowed eyes, and sharp elongated fangs. His features matched Elsie's true face but his appeared much deeper and dangerous than her own.

"This thing is what I am and I don't want to be this anymore." His face transformed back and his eyes showed a hint of remorse. "But Elsie won't let me stop it. She's too controlling and I can't stand up to her...not on my own anyway."

Quickly he embraced her in a tight hug. Cecilia let her head rest against his chest and she heard his rapid heartbeat.

"I won't let that witch hurt you. I mean it." Gently he caressed her head. "We have to get those figurines from her. It's the only way."

Cecilia began to tell him about the charm bag. When she mentioned the yellow ointment Miss Bernadette rubbed on her tattoo, he halted and turned to her.

"She did the same thing to Robert. Elsie found out about his visit with the witch and she killed him."

"So don't tell her."

"I won't."

They walked back to the car and within seconds Isaac parked in front of her house. They silently approached the front door to her home and she unlocked it quietly to avoid waking up her parents. His eyelids dropped and she felt that he didn't want her to leave him.

Their attention was adverted by a dark colored car parked at the end of the block on the opposite side of the street underneath a dim street light. Cecilia squinted, seeing slight movement of someone in the front seat. Isaac followed her gaze and he stared at the vehicle.

"Who's that?" she asked him.

"Probably a neighbor." He looked back into her eyes and without a thought he kissed her gently on the cheek. "Good night, Cecilia."

She placed her hand on her cheek as if her palm could absorb his kiss.

****

"What do you want baby?"

Her breath smelled of cigarettes and cheap wine. Her sweat soaked skin rubbed up against Derek's back and still deep in sleep, he grunted and moved away from her.

Rosie rubbed her hands on his chest and they moved up to his neck and back down just beneath his caved belly button. "Derrrrek." She called in an annoying whisper. "What do you want baby? What do you want me to do?"

Derek opened his eyes slightly, feeling the sharp pain tug from the crust in his eyes. He rubbed it away and blinked a couple of times. Sunlight seeped through the yellow stained curtains, lighting the room and the filth all around him. He reached for the open bottle of vodka on his lamp stand, knocking over a picture frame that fell to the floor.

Rosie giggled and covered her mouth as if embarrassed. She saw Derek's dark brown eyes turn to her and she rubbed the side of his face. "You're ignoring me." She huffed.

"I'm tired, Rosie."

"I'm sure you are. You left early in the morning and you came home late last night. Where did you go all day?"

He repositioned himself in his bed and turned his back slightly to her. He examined the mess on the floor. Vodka had spilled over the edge of his bed sheets and over a stack of disheveled papers. He reached and picked up the picture, setting it back on the nightstand. The quaint graduation photo of Robert, in his exquisite cap and gown, stared back at him. Wine had seeped through the cracked glass and covered the picture in a reddish bubble. He placed the picture face down, knowing it was useless to try and save it. There were other pictures of him, packed in boxes in his closet and underneath his bed. Those pictures were far better.

"I was following up on a few things."

"Like what?"

"Robert's friends. I wanted to see where they lived." Derek spoke through tight lips. He felt Rosie's small hands slide down to his chest and she began to rub him gently. He closed his eyes, enjoying the sensation, until she spoke up again.

"You're stalking them?"

Derek replied but his thoughts went in the opposite direction. He had watched Elsie and her two friends from the shadows but had yet to catch any of them in the act. He couldn't prove his accusations against them to Jan, and he had to, if he wanted to see justice served. He began to accept the terrible realization that Robert's disappearance would remain a mystery and the case files would never leave the dingy basement of the downtown Minneapolis precinct. He feared the worse, which made him want to do more.

Rosie slithered her body on top of Derek and yanked back the covers. Her breasts bounced and she began to sway her body back and forth in a grinding motion. Derek placed his arms on her narrow hips, feeling the jutting bones against his fingers. She closed her eyes and began to moan in a way that he had never heard before. It made him open his eyes and he stared at her emaciated frame.

"Do you want me to keep going?" Rosie asked, biting her lower lip.

He nodded.

She worked him harder until he felt her tailbone digging into his inner legs with each bounce. Her stringy hair flopped and she tilted her head back, her moaning growing louder. Soon her thumping gradually halted and she looked back at him with a smile gleaming on her face

"How was that?" she asked.

He pushed her off and moved to the edge of the bed with his head in his hands. A pungent odor of sex drifted to his nose. He wiped the sweat from his head and felt Rosie's arms wrap around his body.

"What's wrong?" Her question sounded more like a whine.

"You're smothering me." He moved his shoulders, breaking her hold.

Rosie plopped back on the bed and draped the covers over her legs. "Well excuse me for caring." She rolled her eyes.

Derek raised his head from his hands. There was a time for Rosie and now was not it. She was overextending her welcome and he desperately wanted her to leave. She craved attention. The need to be wanted sometimes blurred her actions and her choices. That was what got him in trouble in the first place.

"Have you heard from Julie?" Derek asked out of the blue.

"Nope." Rosie answered. "I'm beginning to think that she's never coming back. Maybe she found some other young kid to rock her world. You know she's a cougar."

"She still likes going to those high school parties, doesn't she?"

"Yep. If you ask me that's a jail sentence waiting to happen."

Derek chuckled under his breath. Obviously Rosie forgot about how she too would frequent these teenage parties. She had found her last boyfriend at one and eventually he went a few rounds on her face, roughing her up good. She was all talk and he didn't stop her from continuing on her tangent. However he knew the truth about her. He knew everything about her.

The first time they met, she threw herself at him. For days he snuck out of the place he stayed with Jan so that he could see her and talk to her. She liked to dress scantily, offering him drinks, and talk to him about her life story. She found solace in knowing that she still had what it took to seduce any man.

"Have you thought about filing a missing person's report?" he asked her.

"Why?" Rosie quickly replied. "Do you think any cop would bend over backwards for someone like her?"

"I can talk to Jan if you'd like."

"You know she hates me for what we did. I don't blame her."

"I don't have to mention your name."

"Isn't she working on Robert's case?" she repeated. "How's that going by the way?"

Shitty, was the first word that popped into his feeble mind.

"Nothing, huh?" Rosie answered her own question. "I told you, cops in this city don't care about you unless you're rich or powerful. You and I, we're just part of the poor population who live in this hell hole."

Derek stood up from his bed and walked to the middle of his room. He felt his feet sticking to the floor and he raised them slightly to see that the substance was dried soda. He wiped his foot on his leg and turned back to Rosie. "It's time for you to go."

Rosie shot him an awkward glance. "I'll never understand you." She rolled out of bed, stark naked. "You're weird sometimes." She began to rummage through a pile of clothes on the floor near the end of the bed. She picked up her white bra, a black leather mini skirt, and a white wife beater and began to dress. "First you want me to come over," she put on her bra and slipped on her mini skirt, "and the moment you start thinking about your brother, you want me to go. You're a weird asshole, you know that." As soon as she put on her shirt she left the apartment, slamming the door behind her.

He placed his hands on his hips. He was getting impatient and needed answers soon. He had to follow Elsie and the others more closely. He assured himself that from now on he was going to be a thorn in their side.

CHAPTER EIGHTEEN
Obsessed

Isaac shifted his head to the right and heard a loud snap. A sharp pain shot from his neck to his shoulder blade. His body felt as if it had been run over by a semi, and he moaned, feeling his jaw crack open. He blinked, letting his surroundings around him come into view. Through the blinds he saw the horizon meshed in a bluish hue with the few stars that littered the sky.

Realizing he had slept the entire day away, he repositioned his body to the left, facing his bedroom wall where his eyes met Elsie's. His sister's unexpected presence made him quickly pull back his bed sheets and jump to his feet.

"What's wrong?" The fact that he stood in front of her naked didn't trouble him. They had both seen each other unclothed— the first time when they hid in the trees as the townspeople killed their father. However this time something didn't feel right. The way her eyes studied his face, moving from head to toe, suggested some sense of urgency.

"I thought you fed last night." Wearing a long white shirt and white socks, Elsie lowered herself on the edge of his bed as she rubbed her hand over the sheets.

He thought about the trip to Miss Bernadette's house and his promise to Cecilia that he'd keep it a secret. He wasn't going to change his mind and it wasn't as if he hadn't kept secrets from his sister before. "She wasn't hungry." He felt his whole body drop as he lied.

"I'm not talking about her. I'm talking about you."

He shrugged. "I wasn't hungry either."

Elsie sighed. "You're becoming obsessed with her, Isaac."

He stretched his arms above his head. "No, I'm not." Again he heard his bones popping and a searing pain traveled from his wrists to his shoulders. The soreness he felt perplexed him.

"You were never like this with the others," Elsie said. "Not Robert, not the one before him; no one since you've been on this silly campaign to make another one like us."

"She's the one." He circled his room in search for clothing to wear.

"No, she's not." Elsie stood to her feet. "Look at you! You've been acting different since you first saw her."

"And that concerns you, why?" He replied as he picked up a blue shirt from the floor.

"Oh you know why, Isaac."

"So you're bothered because I'm doing something different for a change?" He sniffed the shirt and finding it suitable, put it on. "The world isn't the same world we grew up in—things change. It can't remain just you and me forever."

"You're lying to me." She approached him.

"Elsie, it's too early for this." As Isaac walked a sharp pain shot through his right knee. He stumbled, and placed his hand on his bed to stop his fall. His eyes sluggishly drifted to her and she placed her hands on her hips.

"You don't know how much damage she's doing to you," Elsie said in a monotone voice.

He stood up straight and scratched his disheveled hair. "Afraid that she'll take your place?" He knew where his sister wanted to take the conversation. The topic wasn't unfamiliar. They had dealt with it before. Elsie always feared the moment when he'd realize that he wouldn't need to rely on her for support and survival and that soon he would break free from the hold she had on him. She didn't want to be alone and anyone who came in between them she saw as a threat.

He dreamed of a day when they had a way out all of it—the "a-ha" moment that meant that he wouldn't have to hold back anymore. He had grown tired of Old Farmer's Road, their connection to it, and the outdated rules their father had forced upon them as children. He had enough of the voice, the threat of witches, and the private detective snooping into their lives. In Cecilia, he saw a way to find a cure for these problems. Not only did she fulfill that role, she fulfilled him.

Being the oldest, their father gave Elsie all the tools they needed to survive. Isaac couldn't remember a time that his father actually let him figure things out on his own. He constantly held Isaac back, fearing that his son would lose control. After his death Elsie stuck closely to these teachings. She carefully selected victims who wouldn't be missed, just like their father taught, while Isaac preferred to choose anyone who looked edible. He wanted to embrace all the qualities of being an Impa, including the mischievousness and their humble way of life. All she cared about was power and making sure she stayed in the top spot of their warped little pack. It pushed Isaac farther away from her.

"Don't start with that again Elsie. It won't work this time."

"Cecilia is going to be the death of you." She placed her hand on his left cheek. "She can't care for you like I can. You have to remain focused."

"I haven't been more focused in my entire life."

"I wouldn't be so sure about that." She dropped her hand and rolled her eyes. "Why do you always do this to yourself? Why do you always go against what father taught us?"

"I'm trying to do what's right."

"By what? Losing control?" Her eyes went in and out of focus as she stared at his face, making Isaac nervous. "I'm doing this, all of this, for you. I'm the only one who can protect you from you."

They heard soft, slow footsteps approaching the bedroom door. Elsie snapped her head in its direction and revealed her quick temper. "We're talking!" Her voice shattered Isaac's ears and he covered them, baffled as to why his hearing had turned so sensitive.

They heard Margaret's voice from the other side of the door. "Isaac has a phone call. It's your friend, Cecilia. She needs you to come over as soon as you can."

"Tell her he's not coming!"

Isaac moved around Elsie and he opened the bedroom door. He looked back at Margaret who covered her mouth in fright.

"No. Tell her I'll be there as soon as I can." He forced himself to smile at her.

"Are you okay, Isaac? You look sick." Margaret stuttered.

Suddenly Elsie slammed the door in her face.

"Why did you do that?" Isaac asked. Angered, he pushed Elsie aside.

"You're not going over there."

Isaac shook his head. "See. This is exactly what I'm talking about" He grabbed a pair of blue jeans on the floor next to his bed. "You're not shielding me, Elsie. All you want is to control me." Again he felt his body ache.

Her eyes blinked uncontrollably. "You're so quick to run to your precious Cecilia, that you haven't realized that something is wrong with you."

Isaac's eyes skinned Elsie from head to toe. "I'm fine."

"That girl isn't some delicate flower Isaac." Elsie's harsh voice filled his ears. "You don't have to drop everything to protect her. She won't help you like I can."

"I'm responsible for looking after her."

"And I'm responsible for looking after you." She brushed her hand through his hair. "You need to eat. You're aging Isaac." He saw grey strands of his hair connected to bits of his flesh resting on her palm.

At first he didn't understand what she meant yet, when he took the time to process it, his mouth dropped in utter shock.

He walked out of his bedroom and down the hall. Taking a sharp left he headed into the bathroom, turned on the light, and stared at himself in the mirror. What Elsie said was true. He noticed the gray strands in his hair and wrinkles around the edges of his mouth. He saw exhaustion hiding behind his eyes in the dim bathroom light. He blinked, hoping that what he saw had to be a part of his imagination. But it was still there—an aging image of himself. He examined his timeworn face, touching his skin. The rough texture startled him and he looked away

"You're life is more important to me than her." Standing behind him, Elsie leaned against the wall with her hands folded and an "I-told-you-so" look on her face.

There was an immediate cure for this—feeding. But he had made a promise to Cecilia that he wouldn't revert to that. He wanted to keep his vow but he also wanted to live. Isaac stormed out of the bathroom and headed back to his room. With his hands on his head, he began to pace irritably back and forth, thinking of what to do next.

Elsie stood near the side of his bed, watching his every moment. He glanced at her expression, seeing her obvious concern for his well being. Still it wouldn't be enough to stop him from his plan of action.

"You and I both know that it won't last long," she said. "You'll die before the end of the week."

"I'll last as long as I have to." He began to dress himself. "She needs me." He left and walked into the living room.

Elsie followed close behind. "You're too weak to help her."

Before he reached the front door, he pushed her away from him. "You're just afraid of what I might do."

She grabbed onto his shoulders in desperation. "I'm more afraid of what I might have to do to you if you don't stop this." She lowered her voice. Isaac turned to unlock the door but she slammed her hand against the wood, shutting it back into place.

"If you're going to kill me, then take your best shot," he said, as he glared back at her.

"Why do you always think that I want to kill you?" After a couple of seconds of silence she spoke again. "That's the last thing I would ever want to do." She narrowed her eyes at him. "You're up to something. What are you planning and what does it have to do with her?"

He remained reticent. She continued to question him until finally, he snapped.

"Newsflash, Elsie, I'm not like you and I'm not like Dad," he retorted. "I have no desire to suppress who I am anymore and you can't hold me back."

He pulled his body forward, almost colliding with her. His threatening stance made her drop slightly back and away from him. For the first time she gazed back at him in fear and he liked it.

Eventually Elsie gathered her poise and spoke again. "She won't help you with what you need."

"You don't know that."

"Oh I don't?" Elsie snickered. "Should I remind you of all the others you made that I had to kill because of you? Remember that little redhead, Jessica, you met at the speakeasy in Chicago? You were all over her, saying that she was the one who would complete you; that she understood you; and what did she do in the end? She ran back to her family in Chicago and you were too tormented to chase her. I had to kill her because she would've revealed us to those humans."

He felt a pressure rising in his chest.

"Oh, and Mickey Johanesen. The only thing you had in common with that boy was that you desired the same type of victims. He tried to kill you and you almost let him. I had to stop him by ripping out his stones. Remember that?"

"Stop, Elsie," his voice grating and deep.

"And how could I forget Robert? He's the reason why Jan is all over me, not you. I had to kill him because you told him that he could leave." She snickered. "You know damn well that no one can leave."

"I'm done listening to you."

"And now we have Cecilia. What to do about her?" Elsie drummed her fingers together. "I'm going to have to kill her too."

"If you do, I'll kill you—and you know I will." He watched her snicker wilt from her face at his reply.

Margaret, now totally tuned in on their conversation, carefully approached, and she began to plead with them. "Please, don't fight."

"Stay out of this." Elsie warned her as she turned back to Isaac. "Would you really kill me for her? Is she more important than your own flesh and blood?"

Once again Isaac moved to open the front door but Elsie stopped him by pushing her hand up against it.

"This is exactly why father trusted me more than he trusted you," she said. "You don't know how to handle yourself Isaac. You'll never learn."

Again Margaret pleaded with them to stop bickering and this time, Isaac reacted.

He grabbed her by the neck and began to squeeze with all his might. He directed all his anger toward his father and his sister. Elsie latched onto his forearm to stop him, but he pushed her with such force that she stumbled and almost fell onto her back.

"Isaac, stop it." She screamed out to him, but he didn't listen.

"You're right." He barked at Elsie. "I don't know how to handle myself." He felt his facial bones contort and transform. His fangs slithered from his gums and he bit down into Margaret's arm. He lost himself in his frenzy, letting his true nature take over for the first time in over a hundred years—no regrets and no remorse. He sucked hard and violently, while staring back into the face of his sister glaring back at him in concern. When he finished, he tossed Margaret's body to the side and leaned against the door, feeling his insides tingle in exuberance.

Elsie stared at Margaret's pruned body with wide eyes. "What have you done?"

"I was hungry." He felt his blood rush to his face, leaving it pale and gray. Malevolent energy grew rapidly inside him, making him pulse with excitement.

"Not like this." She quaked in her stance. "You're letting it control you."

"That's exactly what I want." He closed his eyes and took a deep breath. He felt his features revert back to normal. He had enough energy to hide some of the changes to his body, thanks to Margaret, but he needed more.

"I've done everything in my power to protect you." Elsie stood down and took a step back. "I've looked after you. I've placed my own life in danger to make sure that you would be safe. Brother, this is not like you."

"I'm not your experiment," he said in a hushed voice. "You don't know what I am because you and father have never allowed me to be what I am."

"So now you just want to run rampant and do what you want?" She argued back. "You think Cecilia will help you do that? I can tell you that she won't, Isaac. She's not the answer to your problem."

"For me, she is." He opened the door. "If you really want to protect me sister, then do something about that private detective." He closed the door behind him.

****

Mr. and Mrs. Richardson sat at the kitchen table, their eyes focused on the woman that Cecilia saw interrogating Elsie at Towley's a few days ago. She introduced herself as Jan Colfax, a private investigator at I.S. Investigations who just wanted a little bit of their time.

Cecilia listened quietly as Jan spoke to her parents about several disappearances at Old Farmer's Road. She assured them that their daughter wasn't involved, but had been frequenting the place with Elsie and Isaac, who lived next door to them.

Her mother looked at Cecilia in disapproval. "I thought I told you to stay away from those kids."

"Isaac and Elsie. Their names are Isaac and Elsie." Cecilia leaned against the wall with her hands folded across her chest. Her eyes moved periodically from them to the door as she waited for Isaac to arrive. Besides Elsie, he was the only one who knew how to handle Jan. She didn't want to say anything that would confirm the accusations about their involvement.

"Mr. and Mrs. Richardson. I don't want to scare you," Jan said. "However, I think it's important that you both know about the area."

"Oh no, I'm grateful that you're here to tell us." Mrs. Richardson replied. "There's something about those kids next door that doesn't feel right."

"I want to make sure you understand that Elsie and Isaac haven't been connected to the murders or the disappearances. Their frequent visits to the area, however, are a little unusual."

They heard the screen to the front door open, followed by a knock. Cecilia hastily opened the door and she smiled briefly at Isaac before she noticed his unique change in appearance. She saw a hint of grey in his hair and wrinkles around his mouth and the corner of his eyes. He looked substantially older and immediately she connected what she saw to his lack of nourishment.

"Are you okay?" she whispered to him.

"Yeah. I'm fine." He groaned and placed his hand on the doorframe for support.

The last thing she wanted was to expose his change to Jan and her parents. "No, you look horrible. Go home. I'll call you later."

He glanced over her shoulder. "I'm fine. Really." He smiled.

Upon seeing him, Jan stood up from the chair. "Isaac. I'm surprised to see you here." Glancing at his appearance, her eyes widened. "You look sick. Did you catch a bug or something?"

"Just a little under the weather." Isaac smiled at Cecilia's parents. "Good morning Mr. and Mrs. Richardson." Cecilia stood aside as he pushed the door open and walked in.

Mrs. Richardson stared at Isaac, her eyes darting back to her daughter. "This is the last time you're hanging out with him? Do you understand me?" She stood up and stormed into the kitchen.

"Whitney, don't take it out on her," Mr. Richardson spoke.

"Are you serious? Your daughter sneaks out every night to this horrible place and you're telling me that I'm taking it out on her."

"I don't go there every night," Cecilia said, looking away.

"You won't go there ever again. Do you hear me?" Her mother wiped her hands on her apron and stood firm with her feet planted to the ground.

Jan stood up from the table. "May I speak to your daughter for a moment?"

Cecilia's mother sighed and released her rigid posture.

"Cecilia, I just have a couple of questions." Jan straightened her gray dress slacks and white shirt before she spoke up again. "You're not in any trouble. I'm not here to arrest you."

Cecilia's eyes darted to Jan. "You're a private detective. You can't arrest me."

"Obviously," Isaac said.

Mrs. Richardson folded her hands across her chest. "Isaac, you need to go."

"No, he doesn't." Cecilia's sudden reply startled even her. She then turned back to Jan. "So what do you want to ask me? I already told you I was with Isaac and Elsie at their place a few nights ago."

Jan cleared her throat. "I'm interested in your whereabouts for last week."

"I was with Isaac."

"Can anyone besides Isaac verify this?"

"I was also with Elsie," Cecilia replied.

"All those nights?"

"Yeah? Why?" Cecilia stared back, motionless. She tried to think of something to say that wouldn't place herself in Jan's suspect pool.

"Could you come down to my office?" Jan turned to Isaac. "You too Isaac, if you don't mind."

"Why?" Isaac questioned.

"Your friend Roger was reported missing a couple of days ago," she spoke. "I wanted to question him but it's obvious now that I can't. You both knew him right?"

"Yeah. Last time I saw Roger he was working," Isaac answered.

Mrs. Richardson sat down at the kitchen table. She covered her face with her hands and shook her head in distress.

Noticing her frustration, Jan tried to comfort her. "Your daughter is not a suspect. This is strictly voluntary."

"If it'll help you understand that I have nothing to do with it, then fine, I'll go," Cecilia replied.

"I'll go too," Isaac added.

A slight smile appeared on the Jan's face. "You both wouldn't mind if I got your statements on paper, would you?"

Cecilia pouted but quickly changed her demeanor. "Nope."

"Just a statement, right?" Mr. Richardson asked. "How long will this take?"

"It shouldn't take that long," Jan replied. "I promise you. I'll have your daughter in and out in no time."

CHAPTER NINETEEN
Those Kids

On their way to downtown Minneapolis, the voice and the hunger returned. This time it slammed into Cecilia with more force than before. She gripped tightly on the charm bag Miss Bernadette gave her but it didn't seem to work. Even the ointment she applied on her branding wasn't having any effect.

The voice grew louder and became more forceful to the point that she placed her hands over her ears and lowered her head to silence it. Noticing her weird behavior, Isaac placed his hand on her leg in comfort.

"You okay?"

Cecilia nodded. "Just a headache." Old Farmer's Road still remained a harbinger in her disheveled mind. A force full of invincibility, power, and carnage wanted her to go back there. "Are you sure you don't want me to drive?"

"I'm sure." He placed both hands on the steering wheel and leaned forward. "I may be older than you but I can still see."

"We'll figure this out soon. Don't worry."

Isaac pulled up in front of I.S. Investigations and turned off the car. "Cecilia, I have to tell you something." He took a deep breath. "Elsie will never see things our way, you understand that right? She won't change. Not for me and definitely not for you."

"I know."

"No, Cecilia. You don't. When she gets desperate, she acts out. Right now her main target is you and with the way I am, I can't stop her if she wants to hurt you."

Cecilia stepped out of the car and Isaac followed.

"I think this time, she's gone off the deep end." He pulled out a pack of cigarettes from his pocket. "She won't stop with you."

"I'll be careful."

"That won't help," Isaac replied. "I think I know what I have to do now."

She gently placed her hand on his arm. "What are you saying?"

"I'm going to have to kill her." His eyes remained low to the ground. "I don't want to, but she won't let me go...I can't be freed from her unless I do this."

Cecilia searched her mind for the right words to say in order to comfort him. The thought of erasing Elsie from her life had crossed her mind, but not her death. In Isaac she saw his turmoil with what he planned to do, and in any other circumstance, she'd talk him out of it. However, it was Elsie and if she had to go, she had to go.

"She will kill your mother and your father," he said. "She'll kill everyone in your extended family just to see me hurt. She knows I care about you and that scares her." He crossed his arms over his chest and rocked his body from front to back. "I'm sorry that I forced this on you."

"It's okay, we'll deal with it." She patted his shoulder. "If we have to go back to the way she wants it, for now, then that's what we'll do. If that'll keep my parents safe."

She walked into the building, not expecting her interview with Jan to last long. Her stomach continued to twist into knots, and at the same time she felt torn between how she could avoid telling Jan the truth and still protect her parents from Elsie's wrath. Tack boards filled with missing animal posters, referrals for lawyers, and assistance for spousal abuse littered the walls of the hallways. The old building had a tall ceiling with fluorescent lights positioned every few feet.

"This way." Jan motioned for them to follow her and before Cecilia could take another step, Isaac placed his hand on Cecilia's shoulder.

"Let her ask her questions but please, don't tell her anything."

Cecilia nodded to his advice.

"Isaac, wait there." Jan pointed to a wooden bench.

Cecilia continued to follow Jan down the hall and into a small, dank office space cornered off by a huge brick wall and lengthy windows. Cecilia walked in first and Jan closed the door behind them.

"I thought you were a private investigator?" Cecilia asked. "Since when do private investigators have offices like this?"

"I.S. Investigations is bigger than most private detective companies." Jan walked to the opposite side of the desk. "We're highly regarded as one of the best in the United States."

"Are you the only company looking into the murders?"

"No." She sat down. "Let's get started."

"Look," Cecilia said, as she lowered herself in the chair across from Jan. "I don't know anything. I don't know what happened to Roger. I don't know why you think that I might." She continued to spew lies and each time Jan shot holes in her stories. Cecilia was sure that Jan would find out the truth by catching her in a lie. That would be easier than blurting out what really happened at Old Farmer's Road. She had to find a sway to get Jan's full attention away from her and Isaac. She thought about turning Jan's attention to Elsie. Perhaps that would give her some time to think about how she could protect her parents and for Isaac to get what Miss Bernadette needed—strands of Elsie's hair.

"Cecilia, how did you meet Roger?"

"I met him through Isaac and Elsie." Cecilia watched Jan pulled out a notepad and begin to scribble something incoherent on the paper.

"Where did you meet him?"

"Towley's."

She tapped her pen on the desk. "How did you meet Isaac and Elsie?"

"Near Towley's."

"Have you seen anything suspicious at Old Farmer's Road?"

"No. Nothing."

"And you know that people have gone missing there?"

"Yes and no." It was a half-truth.

"Care to explain?"

"I heard about Robert, but that's pretty much it."

"Did Elsie and Isaac mention him to you?"

"Yeah, right after I saw you at Towley's. After we left I asked them why you were there and who you were. Then they told me about Robert."

"They both knew him." Jan paused. "He was last seen with Elsie near Old Farmer's Road."

"Well, Elsie did mention something else."

Jan's eyes narrowed in on her. "What did she say?"

"Just that he pissed her off and she was glad that he was gone. That's it."

"Are you sure?"

Cecilia nodded. "Yes, I'm sure," she said, hoping that her lie would put a nail in Elsie's coffin.

"What about Isaac? Did he say anything about Robert?" Jan continued to scribble on her notepad.

"He wants to know what happened to him." Cecilia sighed and she felt her body sinking into the uncomfortable metal chair. She looked around Jan's small office. Certificates lined the walls, sealed behind glass frames. Her desk was cluttered with loose paperwork, old coffee cups, and a broken stapler that teetered on the edge of the desk.

Jan scrunched her lips. "Are you sure? Think hard now."

"Yes." Cecilia raised her voice. "Look, we don't know anything, okay. Can I go now?"

Jan leaned back in her chair. "Not just yet."

Cecilia remained silent for a few moments. "I'm leaving." She stood up.

"Sit down." Jan demanded in a strong voice and Cecilia retook her seat.

"Elsie and Robert were known to frequent that area along with Robert. Before your family moved to Minneapolis, they were also suspects in the disappearance of a little girl whose body was never found."

Cecilia looked at her fingernails and nervously began to dig the dirt from underneath them. Her mind wandered and she desperately wanted to get out of the office. "What does this have to do with me?"

"I think you're covering for Isaac."

"Why would I do that?"

"Because Elsie covers for him as well, which makes me think that Isaac is more involved than his sister." Jan sighed and she gripped her pen between her hands. "Tell me if I'm wrong."

"Isaac would never hurt anyone."

"People are capable of anything. Both of them are delinquents with a rap sheet longer than any I've seen, even from a hardened criminal."

Cecilia laughed under breath. She knew Jan was feeding her fluff.

"They both have been arrested numerous times for disorderly conduct, stealing…you name it. But each time Elsie is the one who takes the blame."

"Are we done?" Cecilia blurted out.

Jan leaned back in her chair and she studied Cecilia. "Just a couple more questions. We found a body of a woman, a Jane Doe, a few weeks ago, several miles down the way from Old Farmer's Road."

Cecilia shrugged. Her eyes moved to a picture of Jan and another older man standing on a beach that hung on the wall. The male looked oddly familiar. She squinted and her eyes narrowed in on him. His round oval face, his disheveled black beard and the deep indentations underneath his eyes. She'd seen him at Old Farmer's Road.

"Who's he?" she questioned, pointing to the picture.

Jan looked at the picture. "Derek. He's my...let's just say he's my friend. He's also Robert's older brother."

Cecilia stood up and walked over to the picture. Everything made perfect sense. She now knew why Jan was so interested in Robert. "He was there at Old Farmer's Road a few nights ago."

"He told me," Jan replied.

At that moment Cecilia heard her phone buzzing in the pocket of her jeans. She looked at her phone and a warm feeling overcame her. It was Glenn. She answered it, hoping that whatever he was about to say would calm her shaky nerves.

"Hey, baby."

"Glenn. I miss you."

"Miss you, too baby," he replied. "How are you?"

"Good. You?" Cecilia thought. She had never lied to Glenn but she didn't want him to get involved fearing that if he knew too much, he would end up another bloated corpse the cops would have to pull from the Mississippi River.

"I'm here, in Minneapolis," he spoke.

"You're here?" Cecilia's eyes widened. "Since when?"

"I arrived this morning," he replied. "I left a message on your phone telling you I was coming. You didn't get it?"

Cecilia slapped her forehead. "I don't have any messages, Glenn."

"Your friend didn't tell you?"

"Friend?"

Elsie! She paused and her eyes began to tear. When did she answer my phone?

"Glenn, where are you?"

"I'm staying at the Stoneybrook Motel at Park and Nicollet."

"I'll be there in under an hour."

"I can come to you Cecilia."

"No. I'll come to you. Just stay there and um...if anyone stops by, don't let them in."

"Is everything okay?"

"Yeah. I'll call you when I'm on my way." Without saying good-bye she hung up the phone. She then turned around to find herself facing Jan. "I have to go."

"Something wrong?"

"Are we done here?"

"We're not done here."

"Oh, I'm done," Cecilia quickly replied. "And so is Isaac. We came willingly so you can't keep us here."

"Wait." Jan pulled her card from her breast pocket. "Take this. You might need it."

Cecilia snatched the card from her grasp and rushed to the front door of the precinct. She didn't say a word as she walked hastily toward Isaac. He stood to his feet and followed her out of the building to the street where he saw Cecilia, hunched over with her hands resting on her knees.

"What happened?" he asked her.

"Elsie." Cecilia stood up straight. "What is she up to?"

Isaac shrugged. "I don't know what you're talking about."

"Don't lie to me, Isaac." She pushed him. "You told me that she's going to hurt the ones I love. My boyfriend from California is here, now, in Minneapolis."

"I honestly don't know," he said with a hint of concern in his voice.

"Would she?" Cecilia couldn't imagine what devious plans Elsie had.

"Kill him?" Isaac finished her sentence. "Yeah, she would." He stared at her with a strong gaze.

"I have to warn him." Cecilia eyed the pavement, thinking that if she could close her eyes, for just a second, maybe the situation would go away.

"I'll drive you." Isaac volunteered himself and Cecilia immediately disagreed.

"No. You need to make sure Elsie doesn't do anything to my parents, okay?" She put her faith in him, although, his change in behavior made her doubt if he wanted to intervene.

"If she tries to do something to them, I can't stop her in this condition. I have to feed." His brown eyes darted back and forth. "In the meantime, take this." He reached his hand into his pocket and placed one long piece of curly brown hair in her palm. "It's some of Elsie's hair. I would go back to that witch with you but I can't. You have to do it."

Cecilia briefly looked at the strand in her hand. "Isaac, are you sure?"

He placed his hands on her cheek and kissed her forehead. Cecilia opened her mouth. She wanted to choose her words carefully but her mind went blank. He turned abruptly and walked toward his car. She followed him quietly. He started the car, and stared down at his trembling fingers, resting in his lap.

"I still think you should go to Miss Bernadette as soon as you can," he said, and then drove down the street, with his hands gripping on the steering wheel tight.

"I need to make sure Glenn is okay." She had to find a way to warn Glenn and to help Isaac before things spiraled further out of control. For once in her life she felt herself being torn in opposite directions. She didn't have time to do both. Lost in "what ifs" and "how to," she paid little attention to Isaac as he spoke to her.

"It's a bad idea." His voice echoed over a commercial on the car radio.

Cecilia jumped, startled, and quickly looked at him. "If you don't want to take me then drop me off at the corner. I'll take the bus."

"What if Elsie is already there?"

"Isaac, listen to me." She raised her voice to silence him. "I'm going there regardless. So, either shut up and drive me there or drop me off."

****

Cecilia's excuses replayed through Jan's head. She hoped having Cecilia alone and away from the others would open her up. Instead, Cecilia seemed more agitated.

Jan didn't bother to chase after Isaac as he followed Cecilia out the front door. She couldn't keep them any longer if she wanted to. Still, she had an idea about Cecilia's involvement.

Cecilia was gullible enough to defend Isaac. Her friendship with him blinded her.

Jan went through her notes and searched through the evidence gathered at Old Farmer's Road. A few hours later she stared at the front door, waiting for Derek to arrive. Finally, he appeared, wearing a large brim hat pulled low to cover his eyes and a long trench coat that she found ridiculous for the hot and humid summer weather.

He lowered his head in an attempt to hide his appearance from her boss who sat near the far back. When he walked into her office, he closed the door behind him and checked the lock.

Jan leaned back in her chair, twirling a pencil between her fingers. She wanted to chuckle at his unnecessary and almost comical approach.

"I got here as soon as I could." He checked the lock again. Satisfied, he pulled down the blinds.

"You didn't drive?"

"No. I didn't want to make myself visible." He twisted the handle and watched the blinds swing shut. He pulled off his hat and placed it on the chair.

"You look...exhausted." She watched him run his fingers through his hair.

"I haven't been sleeping all that well." Derek took off his trench coat and draped it on the back of the chair. He breathed deeply and licked his dry, cracked lips.

Jan caught a whiff of alcohol on his breath. The urge to bring up his extensive drinking passed over her and she decided to ignore it. Besides looking tired he smelled like he hadn't showered in days. The blue and green striped polo shirt and the blue jeans he wore were splotched with yellow and orange stains.

"So, you interviewed the other girl today?"

"Yes. I talked to her. Elsie's brother, Isaac, was also here but they left before I could talk to him." She leaned forward in her chair, intrigued.

"And did you find out anything?"

She sighed. "Nope. Nothing."

"It has to be those kids. I've told you Jan, they know what happened down there."

"The girl, Cecilia, is placing the blame on Elsie." Jan sat straight up in her chair. "But I think she's covering for Isaac."

"I don't know what those kids do at that place, but they're doing something back there, something." He slammed his hand on the desk. "And it's not normal."

"Derek, that's enough." She cut him off. "I don't want to hear about creatures and blinking lights and demons." She felt her body rush with anticipation. His alcoholism had strained their relationship, making him unreliable. It saddened her to see that nothing had changed.

"Frankly, there's still no evidence that can place any of them there at the time of the murders. Give me something Derek, anything that'll stick, and I swear I will follow it through."

"But I've already told you."

A tap on her office door interrupted their conversation. Gilliam pointed at Jan and he signaled to her that she had a phone call.

"Hold that thought." She stood up from her chair. "I'll be right back." She walked out of her office and followed Gilliam to the counter.

"What is he doing here?" he whispered to her.

"I called him."

"Why?"

"I wanted to update him. Who's on the phone?"

"I don't know, but the caller said it's urgent."

They approached the counter and he handed the phone to her. "The caller also said they have information about Robert's disappearance."

Jan placed the phone to her ear and immediately she heard the sound of a female whimpering.

"This is Jan Colfax. How can I help you?"

"Help me." The voice whispered.

"Hello? Who's this?"

"They're making me to do it. They're going to kill me."

"Wait, what—who's going to kill you?"

"Elsie and Isaac."

Jan paused. "Cecilia?"

"I need to meet you somewhere safe."

"Cecilia, wait. Where are you?"

"We need to talk. Can you meet me?"

"Yeah. Where?"

"34th and Portland. In the back of the grocery store on the corner."

"I'll call the police."

"No. You. I need to talk to you."

The phone clicked.

"Hello?" Jan called into the phone. Delighted at the good news, she rushed back to her office to tell Derek, but he wasn't there. Her eyes turned to her desk and on the tablet, scribbled on a notepad, he had written a message:

If you want evidence, then meet me at Old Farmer's Road before midnight. It has to be before midnight. Before they get there.

-Derek

CHAPTER TWENTY
Glenn

Isaac dropped his speed as the car pulled up in front of Stoneyard Motel, a small one-story motel straight out of a horror movie. He remained quiet, up to the point when Cecilia got out of the car. Before she closed the door, he leaned over and grabbed her by the wrist.

"Are you sure about this?" He looked worried.

To calm his nerves, she patted the top of his hand.

"At least let me walk you to the front door."

"If your sister is here, and I don't think she is, I'll scream for you." Cecilia pulled away from him and closed the door. She walked to Room 105, glancing behind her every so often, watching Isaac who refused to take his eyes off of her. She also scoured the area for any signs of Elsie. Relieved to find nothing, she straightened her shirt and black capri pants and glanced at herself through the window, making sure that her appearance was suitable for Glenn. She cupped her hand over her mouth to check her breath and before she finished she heard the door click and open slightly.

She saw Glenn, bare-chested, his lips whitened by toothpaste. She smelled the strong pasty odor of mint as he wiped his mouth with the back of his hand. He swallowed and immediately wrapped his arms around her.

He looked better than ever. She didn't think that he'd look any different, but it felt like a lifetime had passed since she left California and when she felt his rock hard body pressing against her chest, her body grew warm, a tingling sensation running down her spine.

She walked in and he closed the door behind her. The room was dull—the walls brown, the ceiling a stucco white stained by years of cigarette smoke. There was only one bed with brown and white sheets and a small television set reminiscent of the 1980s.

He set his toothbrush by the bathroom sink and dried his mouth with a towel hanging from the frame of the bathroom door. He turned and faced Cecilia, wearing only black gym shorts with his university's logo and hugged her again.

"I've missed you."

Cecilia gently kissed him on his cheek. "I've missed you too." She sat on the bed, finding it hard and stiff.

He sat next to her. "Did your Mom drop you off?"

"Yes." She lied to his face, but only to keep him safe. "Did anyone stop by?"

"No, just you." He continued to smile at her.

"Oh, thank God." She just wanted to rest in his arms and stay there until the next morning, but she couldn't.

"Is something going on?" His hazel eyes washed over her.

"I've done some bad things, Glenn."

"Bad things. Like what?"

Cecilia smiled back and leaned over to kiss him. Their lips met and for a moment, she found herself lost in translation. "It's not safe for you here." She kissed him again and this time he held on tightly while their tongues swirled passionately around one another.

He pulled back. "Are you in trouble?"

"No, it's just not safe for you here."

He hugged her tightly and his eyes moved to her upper back. "What's that on your shoulder?" He pulled back from their embrace.

She closed her eyes, wishing that he hadn't seen her tattoo. He tugged at her shirt to reveal the entire brand and she stopped him.

"It's nothing."

"It smells awful. When did you get it? What in the hell are you putting on it?"

Cecilia looked forward.

"Is that the bad thing you did?" He laughed softly.

"Glenn, this isn't funny. I'm being serious."

"Okay, okay. Sorry." Cecilia slid toward him and she laid her head in his chest. "I'm sorry." He kissed her forehead. "I just want to know who's been stenciling on my girlfriend."

"Stenciling?" Cecilia found herself giggling.

"Yeah. You belong to me," he replied lovingly. "You're my girl."

Although his words sweetly tickled her ear Cecilia couldn't help but think that if knew what she'd done, he wouldn't feel the same way. She couldn't hold onto him until she took care of her Impa issue. She needed to leave so she could give Miss Bernadette Elsie's hair before sunrise—before things got worse. She pulled herself away from him and shot him a glance.

"Cecilia, what's wrong?" He looked back at her with concern.

"I want to be with you so much," she replied. "I just...I just can't right now."

"Can't what?"

"The longer I stay here, the more dangerous it is for you." She rubbed her forehead. "She'll come for me." She fell into his arms. "You can't be here when she comes."

"Who'll come for you?"

She closed her eyes. "I'm just so tired of this. I'm tired of all of this."

"Get some rest." He cleared off his bed.

"No, I can't." She sat straight up. "I have to get you out of here."

"I'm not going anywhere until you get some sleep." He gently pushed her back onto the bed. "We can talk about it when you wake up." He pulled the covers over her and she sulked under them. He tucked the cold sheets around her neck and shoulders.

He walked away and Cecilia closed her eyes. But something was missing and she reopened them, focusing on Glenn walking into the bathroom.

"Glenn." She called out.

Glenn turned. "What is it babe?" He hurried over to her.

She pulled back her covers. "Lie with me."

Glenn nodded and got into bed. He pulled the cover over them and he draped his hand over her side, pulling her in close. "I'm here baby." He kissed her gently on the back of her neck. "And I promise, nothing's going to happen to you."

****

Just one more.

One more.

The whispers drew Cecilia further into the abyss, ripe with the smell of river water and sewage. She felt something slap against her face which made her hold her hands out in front of her, feeling for something–anything–that could give a sense of her surroundings. Instead a hand reached out to her.

Just one more.

The full moon brightened the sky, illuminating the swamp around her. When the mist cleared, Isaac stood in front of her. It took her a few moments before she noticed that he didn't look old and fragile. Instead he looked like himself—like he had just fed.

Cecilia jumped, yet oddly enough, she felt relieved. *Am I dreaming?*

He pulled her from the mist and placed his index finger over mouth. "I don't have much time. I need to show you something." Isaac's sorrowful eyes blinked.

"How are you doing this? How are you making me dream about you?"

Isaac placed his hand underneath her chin and he lifted it slightly. "You need to let him go." He stepped aside.

"Glenn?"

"He's holding you back."

A few feet in front of them Cecilia saw Glenn on his knees with Elsie standing behind him. Her distorted face stared back at them as a dark haze swirled around her.

Bewildered, Cecilia covered her mouth as Elsie placed a blindfold over Glenn's eyes and gagged his mouth.

"She's going to kill him and I can't stop her."

Cecilia quickly turned to face Isaac. "You have to stop her." Worried, she tried to run to his side but Isaac held her back.

"He's not as important as you are."

Elsie's sharp fangs pierced the back of Glenn's neck. She began to feed on him and he tried to fight back, but she overpowered him. Cecilia ran at them and again Isaac held her back. With his hands digging deep into her shoulders, he began to shake her.

"Wake up, Cecilia! You need to wake up!"

Cecilia opened her eyes to a loud knock coming from the front door of the motel room. Sitting at the only table in the room near the front of the room, Glenn looked at her. "About time. I called over an hour ago."

"Don't answer it," Cecilia whispered, still reeling from her dream.

They heard the knock again.

He approached the door "Room service at this place is horrible." He unlocked it.

Before Cecilia could speak another word, Glenn opened the door. Elsie stood in the doorway with Isaac, who cradled a brown bag in his arms.

Realizing they weren't room service Glenn spoke. "Can I help you?"

"Yes you can, Glenn." Elsie walked around him and into the room followed by Isaac who shuffled his feet along the floor. She stood in the middle of the room and her eyes closed in on Cecilia.

"Who are you?" Glenn asked.

"I'm Elsie." She plopped on the bed. "I'm Cecilia's friend and that's my brother, Isaac." Isaac pulled out a case of beer from the bag and handed it to his sister. Cecilia saw that Isaac looked recovered from his previously wilted features. While he still looked aged, he also looked like he'd recently fed.

"You know Cecilia?" Glenn closed the door. "She hasn't mentioned you to me." He stood, towering over the bed with his hands on his hips.

"I know." Elsie tossed him a can of beer and he caught it unexpectedly. "But I figured since you're in Minneapolis, we can get to know you." Isaac stood next to the wall and gently let his body slide to the ground. His eyes periodically met Cecilia's gaze.

Glenn glanced at Isaac who slurped from his beer. "Cecilia hasn't mentioned you either."

Isaac shrugged at his comment and continued to gulp down the frothy liquid until he emptied the can.

"So how long are you going to stay in town?" Elsie swung her crossed leg back and forth.

"A few days." Glenn looked at Cecilia. "But if there's something going on, I'll probably stay a little longer."

"Sweet. We can show you around town."

"No, Elsie." Cecilia spoke up. "He's not going there."

"Nonsense. I think your boyfriend will like the place."

Glenn eyed Cecilia's strange behavior. "What place are you talking about?"

Isaac opened another can and began to devour the contents. Liquid trails ran from the corners of his mouth and down his white t-shirt.

"Old Farmer's Road." Elsie stood to her feet. "I'm still surprised you haven't told him about that place, Cecilia. We practically live there."

Cecilia cringed at the idea. "You wouldn't like it."

Glenn cocked his head and asked, "Why?"

"Oh, don't lie to him Cecilia." Elsie playfully slapped Cecilia on her arm. "You'll love it there. It's like our own little Santa Monica Pier but without the ocean."

"It's a swamp," Cecilia said with gritted teeth. He was a California boy. He knew nothing of swamps, trees, mosquitoes, and humidity. However, he liked adventure and new places. That frightened her the most.

"What's there?" Glenn asked.

"Death," Cecilia replied.

Glenn looked at her with bulging eyes.

"Stop scaring him." Elsie smiled. "That's not nice."

"I'm not. I'm telling him the truth." She nodded to her own affirmation. "A lot of people have died down there."

"Killed." Elsie corrected her. "But hey, it just the small details, right?"

"That's a little morbid for my tastes," Glenn spoke. "Why would you go down there if people have been killed there?"

"No, it's just..." She couldn't tell him and she cut herself off, afraid of what she might have to reveal. She sulked even further into her darkened worry.

Out of the blue Elsie cheered up and she grabbed Glenn's beer from the nightstand. "You're not drinking?" She held it in the air. From the corner of her eye Cecilia saw her sizing up Glenn while she took a sip.

"Isaac thinks he'll like the place." Elsie wiped her mouth with the back of her hand. "I mean, he practically invited him to visit you."

Cecilia snapped her head in Isaac's direction. She strongly believed that Elsie was behind the phone call, not Isaac. To her surprise, Isaac didn't react to the accusation. Instead he remained sitting with his legs crossed as he drummed his fingers on his knees.

To Cecilia's surprise, Isaac nodded. "He'll have a good time."

"So, it's settled then. Let's go, unless you're too scared to go."

"I'm not scared. It's just a little weird," Glenn replied.

"Glenn," Cecilia pleaded to him, "You don't have to go if you don't want to."

"Cecilia, if not today, then tomorrow." Elsie comment overshadowed Cecilia's answer.

"I'd like to see why you go there." Glenn's brow scrunched. "I mean, you hate scary places Cecilia, so this place shouldn't be all that bad."

Cecilia felt her throat collapsing and the air in the unstable motel room become thick. She didn't know who to trust, and now she doubted if Isaac was the less scary of the two. He knew the horrors that awaited Glenn at Old Farmer's Road. Why would he allow it? Desperate, she wanted to make a run for it with Glenn and take him to Miss Bernadette's house for safekeeping.

"Let's go." Elsie clapped her hand together in victory.

Cecilia's lips grew heavy, like two bags of sand, and her tongue felt as if it had shriveled to the back of her throat, which began to dry and crack. She rubbed her neck, feeling under siege as Elsie placed her arm around Glenn's shoulders. Her thin frame was tiny in comparison to Glenn's built body. She stood next to him and they both looked at Cecilia—Glenn with an expression of uncertainty and Elsie with a look of accomplishment. Her crooked smile always turned her stomach.

"Time's a'waitin." Elsie opened the door and led Glenn out of the motel room.

Alone with Isaac for a brief moment, Cecilia closed her fist and punched him in the face. "What in the hell is wrong with you?" Her hand left a fiery red mark on his cheek.

"He's not as important as you are," Isaac said, as he jumped to his feet.

"Why didn't you tell me that you called him? Why would you call him here?"

Isaac rewrapped his arms around the brown bag. "He's holding you back from you—from me."

Cecilia felt her entire body shiver.

"They all are, Cecilia. I see that as clear as day now."

"Who are 'they'?"

"You'll see soon enough."

CHAPTER TWENTY ONE
Blood on Your Hands

Isaac sped toward Old Farmer's Road, remaining quiet along the way. Elsie, in the front seat, kept her body turned toward the back, immersed in conversation with Glenn who sat with Cecilia. The spoke about the differences between Minnesota and California, the best soda on the face of the planet, and how long Glenn and Cecilia had been dating.

Anytime Cecilia felt that Elsie's questions became too personal, she attempted to change the subject. However, Elsie countered with more questions that Glenn didn't mind answering. A plethora of scenarios flew through Cecilia's mind when it came to what Isaac had planned. As long as she had dated Glenn, Cecilia swore that she would protect him from any sort of danger. However, she couldn't face them both at the same time. For now the charm bag Miss Bernadette had given her rested in her pocket and she placed her hand over it, waiting for the right moment to give it to Glenn for his protection.

Glenn squeezed her hand and she squeezed back. He looked at her and smiled and Cecilia buried her head into the side of his arm. She looked toward the rear view mirror, seeing Isaac quickly glance at her before turning his eyes back to the road. He had avoided eye contact with her since he and Elsie had arrived at the motel.

"I can't wait for you to see the place," Elsie said, her smile widening, extending from cheek to cheek.

"We aren't staying long," Cecilia replied.

Elsie smiled. "I don't expect to."

Isaac turned off his headlights and pulled up to the rusted chain that still blocked cars from driving onto the bridge. He killed the car and they stepped out.

Glenn circled around, viewing the environment around him. He squinted at the bridge. "Are we gonna cross that?" He asked Cecilia.

"I'd rather not," she answered.

"It may look old, but it's safe." Elsie latched onto Glenn's arm and she pulled him along until they approached the bridge. Cecilia moved to catch up with them but Isaac grabbed her, yanking her back.

"Don't touch me," Cecilia said, as she pushed him away.

"I'm doing this for you Cecilia," he said, lowering his voice.

"I doubt that."

"I made her promise me that she wouldn't hurt your boyfriend," he replied.

"I thought she was stronger than you? Is it different now since you fed?"

Isaac pushed his hands into the pocket of his jeans. "I was dying. I had to."

"So who did you kill this time?"

He continued to avoid eye contact.

"Isaac, who?"

"It doesn't matter," he finally replied. "What matters is that you don't have to worry."

"You say that after you drove us here." Cecilia scrunched her teeth. "I'll kill you before you lay a hand on Glenn."

Isaac gave her an unsettled look.

The wind picked up and it blew her hair to the side. She swiped her hair back and watched as Elsie and Glenn began to cross the bridge. She had no choice but to follow them.

"Why didn't you tell me that you spoke to Glenn?"

"Because of the way you're acting now."

"How do you expect me to act Isaac?"

"Relieved," he quickly objected.

"Relieved that Glenn might die down here or relieved that you'll get what you want?" Her shoulder began to throb and Cecilia began to scratch at it. A couple of steps ahead she saw Glenn talking to Elsie.

"So, when did you meet Cecilia?" Glenn turned and looked at Cecilia who walked closely behind him.

"About a week ago, we live next door." Elsie replied. Cecilia shivered from the breeze that became steadily colder. It should've carried warmer summer air.

Glenn slowed his steps until Cecilia walked up to him. He grasped her hand, rubbing the top of it with his thumb. "This place isn't bad, so far. It's different."

A snap of a twig echoed through the air and they all stopped and turned around. Dirt in mini gusts crossed the path, carrying rocks and leaves. The path behind them grew dark and desolate. The trees curved over the path, their branches intertwining and locking to form a makeshift ceiling.

Elsie stood silently, watching the branches sway in the wind.

"You guys expecting someone?" Glenn asked.

Elsie turned back, her expression now filled with peace. "No." She continued to walk. "It's just us down here."

"Okay, I think Glenn has seen enough," Cecilia said, as she pulled him back, but Elsie slapped her hand away.

"Relax, C." She pulled Glenn toward her. "It's not like any of us are going to die down here if we play by Isaac's rules."

They continued on their trek until they reached the opening that Cecilia dreaded. They saw the old wooden shack, still in its contorted position with shattered glass windows and broken steps.

"This is it." Elsie spread her arms like an eagle in flight. "Home sweet home."

Glenn eyed the environment. "Wow. It's old."

But that wasn't the point and Cecilia wanted to let Glenn know the dangers. Standing alongside him, she reached into her pocket to pull out her bag when he walked forward.

"Someone lives here?" Glenn asked.

"Well, used to." Elsie approached the house. "Sometimes I like to believe he's still here." She closed her eyes. "Watching us. Protecting his children."

"Who?" Glenn asked.

"The Old Farmer."

Again, Cecilia walked over to him and tried to place the bag into his pocket. He turned, exposing her secret for a moment, which forced Cecilia to quickly stuff the bag back into her pocket.

"They didn't bother to know him before they slaughtered him." Elsie spoke. "He was a decent man, just misjudged." She placed her hand on the withered railing. "I mean, he didn't choose to be born that way, you know?"

"What way?" Glenn asked.

"The people back then tortured him and hung him from that tree." Elsie turned. "It was all so tragic."

"How long ago?" Glenn asked.

"Glenn, please—let's go," Cecilia quickly spoke up. Again she reached for her bag, but this time Isaac noticed. He stomped back to Cecilia.

"What is that?" He pointed at Cecilia's pocket.

"It's nothing."

"Is that a charm bag?"

"I don't know what you're talking about." Cecilia played dumb.

Isaac forced his hand into Cecilia's pocket and he pulled out the bag. After examining it, he dropped it to the ground and a horrid look overcame him.

Elsie also took noticed and approached them. "What is it?"

Isaac's conduct drastically changed. Now riled up he raised his voice as he spoke. "She has a charm bag from that witch."

Standing in front of Glenn, Cecilia held up her hands. "Please, don't do this." She pushed herself back into his chest, forcing Glenn to step back.

"At first I wasn't going to let my sister hurt him," Isaac replied as he crept forward. "But now, I'm not so sure."

Confused, Glenn spoke up. "What's going on?"

"I was going to give you a choice for his sake," Elsie said, as her lower lip trembled in resentment at her brother. "But now, do you see Isaac? You see that she can't be trusted."

"No! Don't!" Cecilia shouted at Elsie, but her plea went unnoticed. Suddenly Isaac wrapped his arms around Glenn's neck and pulled him back, catching Cecilia's attention.

"I was willing to comprise, to change Glenn so that you could be happy," Isaac grunted, as he spoke. "I was willing to overlook your decision to go to him at the motel when I knew that shouldn't have been a priority."

"Please, don't."

"I'm doing this for you."

Before Cecilia could stop Isaac from hurting Glenn, Isaac quickly jerked Glenn's head to the left, snapping his neck.

Cecilia screamed as she watched Glenn's body fall to the ground. She reached out for him but Elsie placed her hand over Cecilia's mouth, muting her scream. She fought as hard as she could, scratching and clawing at Elsie's face. Isaac stared at Glenn's body.

"You got what you wanted Isaac," Elsie said, as she pushed Cecilia in his direction. "Here's your prize."

"Why!" Cecilia yelled, as she began to batter Isaac's chest. She scratched at his face and a few pieces of his hair became entangled beneath her fingernails.

He halted her attack by moving away from her. "Because he would just be in the way."

"I know how this is going to turn out," Elsie said, as she straddled Glenn's body. "It'll always end the same way, Isaac." Elsie rubbed Glenn's face. "With me having to kill what's yours."

Cecilia screamed again in terror. Tears streamed down her face and feeling lost, she let her body relax, watching Glenn's lifeless, opened eyes. "I'm going to kill you both!" Cecilia cried out to them.

Elsie replied calmly to her threat with one of her own. "You and that witch can try but I promise you. I will gut you and take your stones before I let that happen."

"No, Elsie," Isaac said, as he placed himself in front of Cecilia. "You promised you wouldn't threaten her."

"Get away from me," Cecilia said, lunging at Isaac as he pulled her back.

"Doesn't look like she wants your protection Isaac."

"I said, get away from me!" Cecilia yelled, falling to her knees.

The wind picked up, howling in the night sky. Isaac and Elsie looked to the air and even Cecilia, still in shock, heard it too. A screeching voice, carried by the wind, grew louder and in the bushes an eerie white mist swam across the ground toward them. They stepped back as the pale mist returned, slithering toward Glenn's lifeless body. It swam into his nostrils, expanding his chest, until it disappeared.

Cecilia wiped away her tears and her anger and bitterness grew inside her. As this evil being, their hellish father's spirit, went on the attack, to protect Glenn's body, Cecilia began to drag it across the dirt. "Get out of him you bastard." She screamed at the mist.

Isaac stood up and yanked Cecilia by her arm. "Cecilia stop. You're making this worse."

Cecilia thrust her elbow back, connecting with Isaac's nose. He staggered back and blood poured from his nostrils.

Elsie growled and moved in but he held her off. "No."

Cecilia turned back to Glenn and his wide-eyed stare gaping off into space. His facial features began to contort and his skin began to turn grey.

"Go and get her." Still covering his nose, Isaac motioned to his sister. Still unable to cope with the loss of her boyfriend, Cecilia's legs collapsed under her own weight. The hierarchy between Isaac and Elsie changed. He now seemed to be the one in charge, the maker of their rules. This caused Cecilia to question what had happened after he dropped her off at the motel to see Glenn.

Elsie ran into the trees returning later with someone that Cecilia thought she'd never see at Old Farmer's Road. She dragged Jan, gagged and tied, from the darkness of the trees and tossed her near Glenn's body. Cecilia couldn't help but to look at Jan's bruised face covered in dried blood. She looked frail and decrepit, as if she'd aged thirty years. Her entire body shivered and when she attempted to get on her feet, she stumbled back to the floor.

"There's still some inside this bitch for you to feed on," Elsie said to Cecilia. "And I don't care if you eat or not. Personally, I'd rather you just waste away."

This isn't happening. Cecilia's thoughts raced. She wanted to run, she wanted to get away but she didn't want to leave Glenn's body there. She watched his body continue to shrivel, his eyes lowering themselves into his head. His lips pulled back, revealing his teeth. The skin on his arm flaked and crumbled in her grip. The mist, now with a green fluorescent hue, flew from Glenn's mouth and nostrils, and it disappeared.

"I'm not going to kill her," Cecilia said.

"Fine. More for me." Elsie pushed Jan onto her back and began to feed. After she finished, leaving Jan's body a dried husk, the static voice returned and Cecilia covered her ears, refusing to listen.

Just one more.

One more.

Cecilia ran to Elsie but Isaac quickly stepped in front of her.

"Let her try." Elsie spoke in a distorted, yet flippant voice.

"No," Isaac said.

"Isaac, move out of the way." Elsie said with a hint of hostility in her voice. "I promise to make her death as quick and painless as possible."

"And your own will be slow and full of pain if you harm her," he said, standing vigilant.

Elsie licked her lips and retracted her threat. "Whatever." She kneeled near Jan's body and pulled out a brown leather pocket purse. She opened it, revealing a Minnesota driver's license, two credit cards, and a small card with the name "Derek Ellsy" written on it She read slowly and then handed the card to Isaac.

He looked it over carefully. "This is Robert's brother."

"He dies tomorrow—unless you want to save him too?" she said, rolling her eyes.

The name on the card didn't sound familiar to Cecilia, but she quickly made the connection to Robert thanks to the picture she saw hanging on the wall of Jan's office. That realization she continued to keep to herself. Still her body felt weak and nothing at that moment could take her mind off of Glenn's death. She whimpered and she dropped her face into her hands.

"Don't be ridiculous, Elsie," he replied. "You know he has to die too."

"Jesus, she cries over anything." Elsie stood up. "Make her stop whining."

Isaac reached out to Cecilia but she quickly moved her body out of his reach.

"You know she needs to kill Robert's brother," she said, pointing at Cecilia. "She needs to get her hands dirty."

"I know."

"Do you?" Elsie spoke. "Because from the looks of it, you're the one with blood on your hands. Not her."

CHAPTER TWENTY TWO
First Part of the Plan

Cecilia opened her eyes. She felt a puff of hot breath on the back of her neck and she turned slightly to see Isaac lying next to her.

She found herself in a daze—confused about how she ended up here again, in his bedroom without remembering their walk back to his car after he had killed Glenn. She shot up in bed, her back aching and her mind running. The clothes she wore, a long faded Whitesnake band t-shirt, wasn't her own. Her hair was disheveled from a troubled sleep.

She heard Isaac release a deep and audible breath, and still fast asleep, he turned over and faced her. Cecilia pulled back the covers and quietly slid out of bed, careful not to disturb him. She grabbed a pair of gray slacks from on top of his computer desk, slipped them on, and stood silently, trying to think about what to do. As she watched Isaac, the idea of killing him in his sleep crossed her mind. How easily he could kill her boyfriend and sleep in the same bed with her hours later made her mind run into different directions. How could she trust him when he still decided to follow his crude impulses?

She reached forward, grabbing onto a strand of his dark hair near his ear. He mumbled incoherently and turned onto his left side. She quickly pulled, yanking a few strands from his head. She stared at the strands, hoping that she had enough for Miss

Bernadette. After her quiet act, she tiptoed toward the door, opened it gently, and left his bedroom.

She was greeted with silence. Walking out into the living room, she saw the sun's light seeping between the shut blinds covering the windows. She stepped over trash littering the carpet as she made her way to the front door. The house was an eyesore and it looked like it hadn't been tidied up for days.

When she walked by the kitchen, a horrid smell of rotten food drifted to her nostrils. The kitchen itself looked like a back alley she'd seen in run down cities and small towns. Empty plastic bags, food crumbs, and dried spots of liquid covered the kitchen floor. Half a cup of milk sat on the kitchen counter next to an opened cereal box. Nowhere did she see Margaret or Elsie.

Just making her escape without waking them proved to be a challenge. She couldn't decide what she had to do first once she made it out the front door. She had to tell someone—anyone, about Glenn and the murders, but the only person she could confide in had died at Old Farmer's Road. The police wouldn't believe her, and she couldn't imagine what her parents would do if she told them the truth. She didn't return home after leaving Jan's office and she knew that her mother would be off the rails. Miss Bernadette was her only option.

"Where do you think you're going?"

Cecilia paused at the sound of Elsie's voice behind her. She turned and looked over her shoulder. Elsie still wore the same dirty clothes from the night before. With her hair sticking out in different directions, she looked as if she had slept in dirt all night.

"I'm going home," Cecilia finally answered.

Elsie yawned and crept into the living room. She ran her fingers through her hair, picking out clumps of dirt and flicking them onto the floor. "I don't think that's a good idea right now." She leaned against the kitchen counter. "You might make Isaac angry."

"I don't care what you or Isaac think."

"You should, you know." Elsie's shoulders moved while she laughed silently. "After all, you're the reason why he's turned violent all of the sudden." She then moved to the living room and she threw herself on the couch. "Do you really think you know my brother better than I do?"

"Elsie, I don't care."

"You're going with us, tonight, to visit Jan's friend," she spoke. "You're going to kill him and you're going to like it."

"I'm not going anywhere with you," Cecilia replied.

Again Elsie chuckled. "You will unless you want to get on Isaac's bad side. Believe me, it's a lot worse than mine."

"You think I'd just forget about what he did to Glenn last night?" Cecilia balled her hands into tight fists.

"You better, for his sake—and yours." Elsie continued to laugh.

Cecilia felt her body shake with anger. Her teeth rubbed together and her arms tingled. She envisioned herself placing her hands around Elsie's neck and squeezing until she heard it snap, but what would that prove? Only that she was a killer, just like them. Her branding itched and the scorching sensation returned. She rubbed the area, finding it dry and cracked.

"He got rid of that for you." Elsie leaned her head on the couch. "Can't have his precious Cecilia and her marking covered with that witch's ointment. How else can he have his way with you?"

"You're lying." Cecilia looked toward the kitchen and the utensils sitting dry on the dish rack. She thought about taking a knife and cutting, clawing, and scraping it from her skin.

"After what you saw, do you honestly believe that?" She questioned. "Open your eyes C. I was never the real threat."

Angered, Cecilia swung at Elsie's face. Elsie moved back and Cecilia's fist met air. Elsie promptly stood to her feet and pushed Cecilia back. Her strength made Cecilia stumble over her own feet.

"C'mon, C. I know you want to hit me." Elsie pushed her face forward toward Cecilia. "Think about how Isaac snapped Glenn's neck. Think about how useless you felt and how you couldn't protect him."

Cecilia swung and missed again. In a fit of adrenaline, Elsie jumped up and down before lowering her body. "You feel it now, huh? Do you feel the anger? As Impa we have it, resting just beneath our skin, waiting to explode."

Cecilia continued to swing wildly at Elsie but she met each of her attempts with sarcasm and more teasing.

"Now imagine that but a million times worse," Elsie spoke. "That's what Isaac is. He's all anger, hidden behind his cute, cherub-looking face."

Eventually Cecilia's arms tired and she stopped.

"I've always managed to keep his anger from destroying him. That's what father wanted me to do," she whispered. "Now, I can't even keep him from turning his anger on me."

Cecilia felt the rage inside her wither. For once she listened carefully to Elsie.

"Just like the others he's made that I had to kill, you're just a quick solution to his never-ending problem."

The floor creaked behind them and Cecilia looked over her shoulder, seeing an almost fully awake and naked Isaac glaring wide-eyed at their altercation. He jostled Elsie away from her and helped Cecilia to her feet. "What's going on?"

"We're just having a friendly conversation," Elsie replied.

He looked to Cecilia for any confirmation.

"I'm fine." She wouldn't allow anything, not even Isaac's words of comfort, to overshadow the events of last night. Her tranquil memories of Glenn shattered into broken shards and she felt her anger return. "And don't try to convince me or coddle me about last night, Isaac."

"I wasn't going to."

Cecilia walked to the front door. Behind her she heard his rapidly approaching footsteps. "Stay away from me. I'm warning you." She leaned against the door and turned to face him.

"This is an important time in your life, Cecilia. Why are you so angry with me?"

Cecilia didn't know whether to laugh at his reply or to get away from him as soon as she could. "You're doing this for yourself. You never wanted to help me and you never wanted this to end. All you care about is your well-being and being wanted by someone other than your sister. You're the real monster."

"Don't say that." He looked away.

"I want to kill her." Elsie barked in a pitiless tone. "Doing so would bring me so much fucking joy."

"You don't make the decisions around here anymore, Elsie," he barked at her, silencing her. His swift change made Cecilia move back farther toward the door in a feeble attempt to get away. She saw his face warp and then suddenly change back.

"You will not touch her." He swallowed hard, took a deep breath, and spoke. "I'm not going to tell you again."

"What are you?" The question floated from Cecilia's mouth in fear and angst. This wasn't the Isaac she had grown to know or the person she confessed her feelings to. It couldn't be the same individual who gave her Elsie's hair to give to Miss Bernadette, convincing Cecilia of her pressing threat. No, this person was entirely different to the point that Cecilia felt nothing but anger surrounding him. Isaac tried to comfort her while advancing forward, but Cecilia moved away again.

Elsie slapped her hand on Isaac's shoulder, spinning him around. As she growled, he returned her forced gesture by growling back. With only the side of his face visible to her, Cecilia witnessed the bones moving underneath his skin again and his eyes beginning to constrict back into his skull. His change didn't impress Elsie, but when he reached out and grabbed onto her neck, her features immediately warped back before her transmutation was set.

"Go home," he said again to Cecilia as he unlatched and opened the front door with his other hand.

Terrified, Cecilia opened the door and left without once looking behind her. With her head lowered, she made her way quickly across the front yard and toward her home. She couldn't stop thinking about what Elsie said to her about Isaac. It explained how easily he killed Glenn but the fact that she defended him based on what he said regarding his sister made her feel used.

She had stood by his side, listening to his anger and frustration for anything Impa.

How could he do this to me? She questioned her moral judgment and let her sympathy for him blind the hard cold truth. Death was the only way to stop them and to free her from the madness. Not only did she owe it to herself. She owed it to Glenn, whose withered body still lay where he fell for any wild animals to scavenge. She owed it to Jan who warned her of the impending danger. She also owed it to all of the victims who met their deaths at Old Farmer's Road.

With her mind running rampant, Cecilia didn't notice her mother standing in the driveway holding a bag of groceries. Once she saw her daughter she called out but Cecilia didn't hear her. Only when she slammed the driver side door shut did Cecilia quickly look up from the ground.

Mrs. Richardson's eyes dissected Cecilia with such hostility that she decided to not say anything. "I looked everywhere for you."

Cecilia watched her mother climb the stairs and reach for the door. "Your father was out until midnight driving around, looking for you."

"I'm sorry." Cecilia lowered her gaze. "I was at Isaac's place."

"You weren't there last night." Her mother unlocked the front door. "I've had it with you Cecilia. This has gone on far enough."

Cecilia opened her mouth to speak but before she could, a familiar female voice broke her stride.

"I have the last bag, Whitney."

She looked over her shoulder, seeing Miss Bernadette standing near the trunk of the car wearing bright red lipstick, a flower pattern skirt and a red blouse to match. Her presence gave Cecilia a cold chill and her feet felt as if something had taken a hold of her and kept her from moving.

Before stepping inside Mrs. Richardson took a deep breath. "Things are going to change around here." She walked in.

Miss Bernadette set the groceries on the ground and she brushed the bag's particles from her dress. "Did you get what I asked for?"

Cecilia's eyes wavered. She forced herself to nod, knowing that it would signal Elsie and Isaac's death sentence. "I can't give it to you right now because...well you know, they're probably watching me."

"Actually they aren't at the moment." Miss Bernadette's eyes gradually glanced over at the house next door.

Taken by surprise, Cecilia flinched at the old woman. "How do you know?"

"You don't have to be a witch to know," Miss Bernadette replied. "Give the hair to me."

"How long will it take to work?"

"That depends on when you give it to me."

"Well, here." Cecilia pulled out a knotted clump of both Isaac and Elsie's hair from her pocket. She tossed it at the old woman and the clump floated briefly before landing onto the pavement.

Miss Bernadette picked the clump of hair from the ground and she examined it. "You managed to get his hair as well?" She kicked the bag of groceries toward Cecilia and they skidded across the floor. "Why the sudden change Cecilia? Did you witness something that changed your opinion about Isaac?"

"Let's just say I know more than I want to know."

"This will do." Finding the specimen useful, Miss Bernadette turned. "Oh, and tell your mother I'll start on her pound cake tonight."

****

"A gun has to work. Yeah, I need this. I think this should work."

Derek muttered to himself as he pulled large trash bags full of old clothes and other objects from his cluttered closet. He tossed the bags aside, dropped to his knees, and continued to rummage. He ignored Rosie's knock on the front door and when she entered, questioning his erratic behavior, he pushed her away and continued his search. Again he tossed clothing, hardened by a lack of care, over his shoulder. He stopped briefly at a water-damaged folder, opening it to find a picture of him and Jan in their younger years.

"Derek?" Rosie continued to watch his erratic behavior.

"What do you want?" In all the years he knew her, only recently did he find even the sight of her to be so annoying. She never understood his desires—his dedication to finding out what exactly took place at Old Farmer's Road.

"I can hear you from down the hall." She walked over to him and placed her hands on his back.

"Leave me alone." He stopped in his panicked mode. The corner of a small box stuck out from underneath a pile and he pulled it out. He walked back to his bed.

"What are you doing?" Rosie followed him over to his bed.

He sat down and opened the box. "I was looking for this." He pulled out the 9mm Beretta.

"Is that the gun you said you sold?" Rosie said, sitting next to him. "What are you going to do with that?" Her eyes fixated on it.

"I bought this for Jan." Derek examined the gun. "I would never sell it. It reminds me too much of her." He cradled the gun to his chest and closed his eyes.

Rosie shot him a bewildered look. She hoped he wasn't going crazy. "Yeah, so um how about you put that back?" She tapped him on his forearm.

He placed the gun on his nightstand. "Now, where did I put the ammo?" He dropped to his knees and continued his search, under his bed.

"Derek, what's going on?" Rosie asked in a trembling voice—but he didn't answer. He continued to pull out boxes, trash, and other miscellaneous things including another picture of Robert, covered in dust. He looked at it for a brief moment before returning to his search. Rosie grabbed his arm and tried to yank him back to his feet but he nudged her away with such force that she almost fell over.

"Screw this." She grew angry. "If you don't want to tell me what's going on then," she paused, "then screw you." She marched to the door but before opening it she turned around. "Y'know, I've been here for you. I was there to comfort you when you had no one else." Her upper lip curled in disgust. "And you can't even show me an ounce of respect."

Derek suddenly stopped. He turned to Rosie and remained silent.

"What? You have somethin' to say? Say it then!"

He raised himself to his feet. "Do you believe in God, Rosie?"

Taken aback by the question Rosie shook her head angrily. "What does God have to do with this?"

"Do you believe in God?" he asked again.

"Sure." She shrugged. "Why not?"

"You know I did once," he spoke. "But after I lost Robert, I started to think that maybe there wasn't a God." He lowered his head. "Why would a God allow this to happen to me?"

Rosie relaxed and leaned against the door. "I don't think God chooses who dies and who lives. I mean—if that was the case, then we'd all have perfect lives."

"There's something at Old Farmer's Road." Derek sat on the bed. "Something pure evil, straight outta the Bible."

"Like what?" Rosie sat next to him.

"Demons, devils, I don't know exactly what," he replied. "I just know that it's there and it killed Robert."

"Derek, have you been drinking this morning?"

"No." He gave her a serious look. "I know it sounds too weird to believe. Jan doesn't believe me, but I know and I have to find out proof for myself."

"How are you going to find this proof?"

"I'm going to make Robert's friends tell me." Derek stood up and walked back to the closet. He grabbed a black duffle bag and began to fill it with shirts, socks, and pants. He finally picked up the gun and he tossed it into the bag.

"Derek, they're just kids." Rosie stood up.

"They're murderers." He placed the duffle bag over his shoulder and stomped to the front door. "They're evil murdering sons of bitches." He walked out and scurried down the hall. He looked back once, seeing Rosie standing in the doorway. Regardless if she believed him or not, he was tired of trying to convince everyone around him about the truth. No one believed him, and they never would, until he came back with proof. He hoped that by doing so, he could finally come to some kind of closure for both himself and for the families of the victims.

CHAPTER TWENTY THREE
Kill Her

Without the ointment covering her tattoo, Cecilia felt the hunger and the pain return. It struck her on a phenomenal scale and she retreated to her bed, curling up in a fetal position where she stayed for the remainder of the day.

She desperately wanted to leave, to see how far along Miss Bernadette was in solving the problem. Perhaps she would feel the dark energy escape her body. For now she felt nothing, only pain and the hunger. Shortly after nightfall she heard Isaac tapping at her bedroom door.

Cecilia ignored his suggestion to feed, but even though she didn't agree to go, she couldn't let herself stand aside as Isaac and Elsie went on their hunt for Derek. Her credentials weren't exactly golden when it came to stopping them from killing more people. Her thoughts moved to stalling them, to give Miss Bernadette enough time to finish whatever ritual she had to do to make them vulnerable. Then again, she didn't know how to tell when they would become easier to kill. No one mentioned the warning signs or what to look for.

Isaac knocked harder until she had no choice but to pull back the blinds and open the window. He held out his hand to her, trying to coerce her to come with them. Behind him she saw Elsie sitting in the front seat of his car, looking straight ahead.

"I won't do it." Cecilia shook her head, remaining bent on not involving herself in their planned carnage.

"I don't want to force you," Isaac replied. "I'm not the bad guy here, Cecilia."

"No, you are." Cecilia went to close the window but he placed his hand in the way. "I'm not going with you to kill him."

"Soon he'll find out about Jan and he'll put two and two together."

"I hope he does," she replied. "Maybe he'll stop you once and for all."

His mellowed eyes scouted her face. "No one can stop me, Cecilia." She flinched and again he held out his hand in acceptance. "I know you gave Elsie's hair to Miss Bernadette after you left the house and I know you also took some of mine." His lips curved upward to a smile. "I should be angry with you, but I'm not. You don't see the light at the end of the tunnel but I do. In the end, this will all work out. You'll see."

Stumped by his reply, Cecilia slammed the window frame against his hand, but he didn't budge. "There is no light at the end of the tunnel for us, Isaac—just death. And I hope for everyone's sake that Miss Bernadette finishes what she needs to do tonight."

"She won't." He grabbed her hand. "Now, come with us and let's do this. Don't make me force you."

"You can't force me to do anything anymore. I'm not your puppet."

"If you don't come, Elsie will kill your parents," he replied. "And more importantly, I won't stop her." He gently pulled her, and she made her way through the window and outside, wondering how easy it still was for her to believe a word that came from his mouth. Still, anything was possible when it came to Isaac's split personality behavior. The threat seemed all too real and Cecilia had no choice but to accompany him and his sister on the hunt.

Isaac drove through downtown Minneapolis, heading toward the edge of the city. After the short drive, he parked the car in front of a three story brick building near the I-94 freeway, blocks from downtown Loring Park. He turned off his car and Elsie, sitting in the back seat next to Cecilia, glancing out the window.

Elsie left the car. With Derek's I.D. in hand, she approached the building and carefully read the large white numbers nailed onto its brick surface just near the front doors. "This is the place." A poorly lit streetlight shined on the outside of the building, revealing a cracked wooden front door with shattered glass covered with strips of duct tape. Gray metal mailboxes, old and rusted, hung on the nearby wall. Pine needles and grass covered a weathered Welcome mat. Plastic bottles and empty beer cans littered the front steps.

Cecilia stood by the car and glanced up at the building. Isaac stood next to her and slipped his hand into her own. She turned to her right watching the wind push a brown grocery bag across the sidewalk while three homeless men rummaged through a metal garbage can.

They walked through the unlocked front door. Cecilia shuffled her feet along the black and white tiled pavement. Elsie examined the directory behind a Plexiglass window to the right of the wall.

"Did you find it?" Isaac asked her.

"Yeah."

Cecilia watched Elsie pull out a small pocketknife tucked away in her waist. She handed it to Isaac.

"Just in case your precious gets cold feet."

Isaac held the knife to Cecilia. "Take it."

Cecilia stepped back. "I'm not taking that."

Elsie snatched the knife from Isaac and placed it up to Cecilia's neck "You will take it."

Cecilia held her stance and in fear her mouth trembled the word, no.

"We may not die easily C, but that doesn't mean you can't feel pain."

"Elsie!" Isaac grabbed the knife from his sister. "I've got this."

Elsie fixed her eyes on her brother before she turned and walked in a hurried pace toward the stairwell.

Isaac looked back at Cecilia, sensing her nervousness for being there. He placed his arm around her shoulders.

"Don't you dare." She lumbered forward to get away from him.

They climbed the stairs. Cecilia gripped the wooden railing as she scanned the environment ahead of them. The hot and muggy air smelled of urine. She saw a cockroach run across her path, making her stop in fright. When they reached the first floor, thinking they had reached their location, Cecilia walked into the hallway.

"It's on the third floor," Elsie said, as she continued on her way up.

They followed her until they reached the third floor. Elsie paused before entering the hallway. As she turned her head to the left, then to the right, her hair bounced on her shoulders. "Isaac, you should go down that way." She pointed to their right. "Cecilia, we're going to the left. Look for apartment 323."

They separated. Cecilia remained several feet behind Elsie, anxious that she would turn around and attack her. When they passed the first door, Elsie carefully examined the metallic numbers screwed onto its surface. She silently mouthed the number "313" and continued on her way. They heard the low static sound of a television behind the next door.

"Isaac has always been blind when it comes to pretty girls like you. He always loses control," Elsie whispered as she walked over the brown weathered carpet. "You're not the first girl he's been head over heels for."

"Is that supposed to make me feel better?" Cecilia replied to her.

"No, it should scare you."

"Sounds like you're scared Elsie." As her symptoms grew worse, her head began to pound, feeling as if someone had taken a jackhammer to her skull. "He's finally found a way to take back control from you." She paused and leaned against the wall for a moment.

Elsie glanced back at her. "Hungry, are we?"

The spicy smell of onions mingled together with a pungent odor of garlic ravaged Cecilia's nose, making her feel an urge to throw up right there on the floor. Ignoring Elsie's back talk, she moved forward.

Elsie scanned the numbers on the next door. "I'm not scared of my brother. I'm scared of what he can do." She stopped briefly in front of a door. "Regardless, we always survive." She examined it. "This is it." She whistled to get Isaac's attention.

Cecilia saw only two numbers marking the door as their destination—"32." The only thing that confirmed Elsie's suspicion was the tanned image of the number "3" but, the number itself was missing.

"Everyone dies Elsie. Even us."

"Well you better follow through tonight, C." She waved at Isaac down the opposite end of the hallway. "Unless you want to test that theory." She stepped towards Cecilia and lowered her voice to a whisper. "Isaac isn't as innocent as he claims to be, especially when he's immersed in his anger."

"You're telling me this like I'd ever believe you."

Elsie sniggered with an expansive grin. "Oh you will. That I can guarantee."

Isaac met up with them and Elsie thumbed at the door. With her eyes narrowed, she grabbed the doorknob when Cecilia, without hesitation, moved herself in front of the door.

Elsie swirled around. "Move your girlfriend Isaac or I'll break her legs."

"We can't do this." Cecilia lowered her voice. "You can't just kill him."

"Who said anything about me killing him?" Elsie argued back in a whisper. "That's your job."

Cecilia felt Isaac's hand rest on her shoulder and without acknowledging his touch, she pushed his hand away.

"I swear I'll knock on every door!" Cecilia threatened, as Elsie tilted her head back in laughter.

"Tell the whole building!" she snorted. "Add more meals to the menu!" She held out her hand for Isaac's knife. "Tell them

that you're an Impa and that you need to suck on their insides —
that you need their essence to survive. Go ahead! Tell them!"
She began to knock on the door. "Here, I'll join you."

"Hey, we have company." Isaac quieted their disruption and
pointed behind them and down the hall. Both Elsie and Cecilia
turned around, watching a young Latino woman standing in the
doorway, wearing nothing but a scantily clad pink night gown
with ruffles on the wrist and lower skirt with dark hair pulled
back in a long ponytail. She parted her full lips and puckered
them ever so often, giving them an even fuller look.

"Are you looking for Derek?" the woman asked.

"Yes. Is he home?" Isaac replied.

"No. Who are you?" Her question rolled from her lips as she
licked them. Her right hand slid along the doorway and she
placed her left hand on her hip.

"Where is he?" Elsie asked bluntly.

The woman shrugged her shoulders and her pink nightgown
scrunched along her thighs. She rubbed the back of her left foot
along the back of her right lower leg. "I don't know." She
huffed and crossed her arms in front of her chest. "You must be
the three kids that he's been talking about." Her eyes carefully
examined Elsie from head to toe.

"And you are?" Elsie carefully approached her.

"Rosie." Again her hand slid along the wall as she walked
and she lazily leaned against it.

Cecilia watched helplessly as Elsie continued to probe the
woman for information, hoping that Rosie was smart enough to
crawl back into the safety of her apartment.

"So, Rosie. Do you know where he went?"

She shook her head. "Are you Robert's friends?"

Elsie released a quick chuckle and slowly moved toward her.
"You could say that."

Cecilia continued to watch helplessly as Elsie now stood just
inches from Rosie. Elsie rubbed the soft texture of her clothing,
examining the thin fabric and the twirled ruffles. "That's a pretty
nightgown. Do you wear it all the time to attract simple minded
men—to give them a glimpse of what's between your legs?"

"You should leave." Rosie stood up straight and placed her hands on her hips.

"I know a whore when I see one," Elsie smiled. "Damn, I'm good." Her smile dissipated and in a hurried movement, she pushed Rosie back into her apartment, watching her land between a dark coffee table and a black entertainment center in her living room. Elsie stormed into the apartment with Isaac reluctantly following her, yanking Cecilia in with him.

Isaac closed the door, bolting it shut. "I'll check around." He tossed the knife to Elsie and began to inspect her apartment.

"What are you doing?" Rosie asked in an exalted breath.

Elsie twirled the knife in her hand. "My friend over here needs to find Derek." She nodded in Cecilia's direction. "She thinks she can protect him from us." Rosie attempted to stand but Elsie kicked her back to the floor. "Did I give you permission to get up?"

Isaac approached Elsie, flashing a pink wallet in his hand. "I found her wallet." He tossed it to his sister.

"Rosie Alvarez-Garcia." Elsie read the information off her I.D. before throwing it at her. "So Rosie. Be a good little whore and tell my friend where she can find Derek." She leaned forward.

Rosie scooted back and cursed under her breath.

Elsie flashed her knife. "Speak up." She raised her voice. "We can't hear you."

Rosie spat at Elsie.

"You need some incentive." Elsie wiped the warm thick phlegm from her cheek and rubbed it on the screen of Rosie's television. She grabbed the remote to turn up the volume. "Maybe this will jog your memory." She swiped the knife at Rosie's leg, creating a three-inch gash. Rosie screamed but the sound coming from the television drowned out her voice. Blood began to stream from her wound.

"Elsie, stop it!" Cecilia said, as she grabbed onto Elsie, who easily threw Cecilia off of her.

"Where is he, Rosie?" Elsie flashed the knife at her.

"I don't know where he is." Rosie clenched her teeth in pain.

Cecilia pleaded. "Elsie, she's not part of this."

"Would you shut up, C. I can't concentrate."

Isaac approached them, holding a large knife he'd stolen from Rosie's kitchen. He looked down at Rosie but felt Cecilia's hard stare sticking to the back of his neck. "Rosie, just tell us where he is and we'll let you go."

"I don't know where he is." She screamed back at them.

Cecilia positioned herself in front of Isaac. "You once told me that you were tired of killing and that you wanted it all to end. It'll never end if you kill her."

"He never wanted this to end, stupid." Elsie laughed in her mockery.

"No," Cecilia said. She placed her hands on the side of his face. "You don't have to do this."

Elsie sighed loudly. "This is getting ridiculous. Either you or Cecilia kill her or I'll cut this tramp into little pieces."

Isaac gently removed her hands from his face. "Kill her."

"Put her out of her misery," Elsie taunted.

Cecilia hesitated long enough for Elsie to slash Rosie's arm, opening a long gash. Blood spattered across the television and onto Isaac's face. Soon Isaac joined in, creating a large cut just below her neck. Tears began to stream down Rosie's face and her mouth, propped open, let out a muted scream.

He slashed again and again as Rosie held her hands up in defense. She attempted to slither away from him but Elsie pushed her back.

"What are you going to do Cecilia?" Elsie continued her tormented spiel. "She's going to bleed to death."

Cecilia watched helplessly as their attacks ravaged Rosie to the point that her entire body was covered with blood. It pooled onto the floor beneath them, spreading out toward her own feet.

Isaac slashed again, this time creating a large gash on her forearm. "Kill her. Kill her." He looked up at Cecilia and wiped the trickles of blood from his face.

But all Cecilia could do was cower near the wall, her entire body frozen at their inhumane actions. The sight of Rosie's blood began to push and maneuver her to feed. She couldn't bear to think about how long their victim could take their punishment. If she did nothing, they would go on for hours. However, if she fed she could end Rosie's torment.

She ran over to her. Her fangs dropped seamlessly from her gums and she bit into Rosie's thigh. Suddenly the thrill, the pleasure of feeding returned. She sucked harder and harder, absorbing every drop that she could. She felt Rosie's body convulse under her hold but it wasn't enough to stop the frantic activity. Soon, she would take it all away, leaving nothing but her empty shell.

From her periphery she saw Elsie squat over Rosie as she pushed her knife into her chest. Over the blare coming from the television, Cecilia heard the sound of metal scratching against bone. Elsie then yanked out the knife. Blood dripped from its tip and collected in her hands. Her clothing, saturated in blood, drove Cecilia further back to the living room wall.

"Why did you kill her?" Isaac asked his sister in desperation.

Elsie pointed her bloody finger at Cecilia. "She would've never finished her off." She jumped to her feet and stormed toward Cecilia. "She would've left that for you." She slammed her hand on the wall next to her head, making Cecilia jumped in fear. "She's the biggest mistake you've made in your life, Isaac." The hair on Cecilia's arms stood straight and beads of sweat traced down her neck and into her cleavage.

"Cut the stones from her stomach." Elsie aimed the knife at Cecilia's midsection. "Right here, right now."

"She's mine, Elsie." Isaac said, pushing his sister away from Cecilia with such force that Elsie thwacked against the front door of the apartment.

Cecilia heaved, feeling like the last breath of air had escaped her lungs. She placed her hand over her chest and lowered her head in discomfort. After everything, she'd still fallen victim to her deadly desires.

Elsie dropped the knife and without warning, marched out of Rosie's apartment.

Cecilia let her body slide along the wall and onto the floor. Isaac rushed to her side and tried to lift her to her feet. "We have to find Derek."

"Don't touch me." Cecilia attempted to fight back but Isaac increased his strength.

Isaac held on tight to her as he dragged her out into the hallway. They saw Elsie repeatedly kicking the front door of Derek's apartment. The loud noise echoed through the hallway. She kicked harder and harder but the door didn't budge. Isaac quickly joined her and their efforts paid off. A small dent appeared and it grew into a foot size hole then to a large gaping hole. Isaac kicked higher, near the doorknob and finally the door flew open. Its lock shattered and flew into different directions.

Elsie walked into the dark apartment and rubbed her hand along the wall until she found the light switch. She flicked it on, exposing an apartment in disarray. A bed near the wall, cluttered with cigarette cartons, paper, and a large garbage bag. The floor was littered with clothing, pop cans, dust motes, and other trash. An opened pizza box sat on the desk, the pizza half eaten and the cheese growing mold. The air was hot and thick and smelled of musty clothes. Surprised at the horrid conditions of the apartment, Elsie covered her nose. She walked around the room and into the bathroom. She turned on the light finding the bathroom in no better shape than the rest of the apartment. The base of the toilet, emptied of water, was rusted. The shower was stained and a crust of dirt ran along the top. Mildew collected in-between the cracks of tile.

She stepped out of the bathroom. "Where in the hell is he?" she growled.

"Maybe he went to Old Farmer's Road?" Isaac suggested.

"We need to find him tonight." Elsie approached the side of the bed and searched through the sheets, paper, and clothing.

Isaac cursed. "We don't know where to look." He looked at Cecilia who stood in the doorway.

They heard the distance noise of sirens and Isaac rushed over to the window located on the far end of the room. He pulled back the curtains. "Cops." His breathing grew erratic and he waved his finger erratically. His face, once filled with the look of a deranged killer, was now pasty white with fear.

Elsie pushed him aside and stormed out of the apartment. Isaac looked at Cecilia with uncertainty. He grabbed her and they left the apartment just in time to see Elsie standing outside of Rosie's apartment with a lighter and newspaper in hand. She lit the ends of the newspaper and placed it against the ends of Rosie's frilly nightgown. The flame quickly spread and Elsie tossed the burning newspaper on the couch.

With Isaac and Elsie watching the flames grow, Cecilia saw her only chance at escape. She located the stairwell and without looking back she immediately took off down the hallway, making her way to it. She looked back to her murderous companions who didn't notice she'd left before rushing down the remaining stairs.

In the back of her mind she thought that they'd catch up to her. If they did, she knew they'd kill her, maybe like they killed Rosie. She needed to go to Miss Bernadette. She had to make sure no one else died tonight.

She caught her breath then exhaled in relief upon reaching the door to the first floor. She looked out the small window. Seeing that the lobby was empty she carefully opened the door and peaked out. Through the front door she saw a cop car parked directly in front of the steps of the building, its lights flashing silently. She gathered her bearings, wiped the sweat from her face, and exited the building. She walked by Isaac's car, still parked, and picked up her pace, scurrying down the dark street.

The voice that once harked at her early that night to feed returned. It slithered back into her thoughts in a loud and explosive introduction.

Just one more.

One more.

Cecilia halted in her tracks. Its raspy voice bounced around in her brain like an out of control electric bolt, forcing her eyes shut. "Leave me alone!" she said with clenched teeth, feeling her mouth fill with spit. She bent forward and grasped her forehead, but the voice ignored her plea. It continued and continued, playing its demands in her head like a broken record.

Just one more.

One more.

She forced her eyes to open. As the voice didn't stop, she continued to run toward Miss Bernadette's home. Her destination felt eerily comforting.

CHAPTER TWENTY FOUR
Ding, Dong. The Witch is Dead

Cecilia stood outside, cautious and silently staring at Miss Bernadette's home. The voice continued to attack her mind and at one point her vision blurred in response to its attack. It wasn't enough to make her lose sight of her goal. Anger set in but it wasn't the same anger that now fueled Isaac. The root of her anger spawned from how easy it was for Isaac to manipulate and lie to her about everything. Rosie lost her life due to Cecilia's hesitation and she promised herself that no one else would suffer the same fate after tonight. She didn't want her weakness with the witch to overshadow the fact that they needed to stop Elsie and Isaac before they found Derek. It was the tensest moment of her life.

Cecilia walked up to the front door, expecting the magical barrier to be present, but nothing stopped her. No liquid wall, no invisible force-nothing. When she raised her hand to knock on the door, it opened unexpectedly on its own. Just like the first time, she found the interior dark and unwelcoming. The air smelled of a mixture of burning sage and wood. Just beyond the living room she saw the old witch kneeling in front of her altar in a trance like state. Trying to remain quiet so that Miss Bernadette wouldn't be ripped from her coma like state, Cecilia quietly closed the door, yet the small sound of wood connecting with the door frame caught Miss Bernadette's attention.

"You smell like you've fed." The witch lifted her head for a brief moment before returning to her mumbling.

"How long is it going to take?" Cecilia crept forward. "Right now Elsie and Isaac are out there, hunting someone else. You have to speed up the process."

"I can't go any faster without placing the spell at risk." Miss Bernadette struggled to stand on her feet. Finally she turned to face Cecilia. She held two figurines in her hands, both resembling Elsie and Isaac.

"At least put up your barrier. They're probably on their way here now."

"I'm not afraid of them." She placed the figures on the altar and she walked over to a brown circular table on her right. "Sit." She pulled out a chair.

Still cagey about Miss Bernadette, Cecilia decided to sit. Her eyes wandered over to the two figures. She noticed that both of them were adorned with pieces of human hair. It made her curious about the figure the witch made in her image.

"Where is the one you made of me?" she asked her.

Miss Bernadette smacked her thin lips and smiled. "It's safe. I will hand it over to you once the spell works."

Her answer didn't calm Cecilia's nervousness. Something just didn't feel right, however, she didn't express her suspicions. Not just yet.

Miss Bernadette pulled out a small glass bottle with a red cork from the top shelf of her cabinet. "For now I can give you some more ointment to silence the voice." She pulled out the cork and approached Cecilia.

"So how are you going to get these stones out of my stomach?"

"There isn't any magical way to do that." She dipped her index finger, pulling out a large glob of the yellowish paste.

Cecilia stared at the jar. "So what? You're saying that I have to have surgery?"

"Turn around."

Cecilia followed her orders and now with her back to Miss Bernadette, she felt the witch lift up her shirt and apply the ointment. It cooled against her skin but that feeling was soon replaced with a searing sensation that made her lean forward in agonizing pain. Once finished, Miss Bernadette squeezed the cork back into the bottle.

"Would you like some tea?" She walked toward the kitchen.

Cecilia clashed her teeth together until the pain subsided. Her eyes studied the conditions around her for the figurine that the witch had made of her. She looked under the table and finding nothing there, she searched the cabinets. Finally she saw a large wooden trunk tucked away and opened it. What she found shattered her to her core.

She found her figurine with strands of her hair sewn into it. Upon grabbing it, she closed the trunk and made her way back to the chair. Just like the other two, this one also looked polished and finished; a stark difference from the first time Miss Bernadette showed it to her.

"Do you prefer honey or sugar in your tea?" Miss Bernadette asked from the kitchen.

"Sugar." Cecilia replied. The figure, made out of hardened clay, had two black dots for eyes. It wasn't a masterpiece but it resembled nearly every fine detail of her body, down to the birthmark she had just above her right knee. No one, not even Elsie and Isaac, knew about that.

She heard Miss Bernadette approaching and she quickly stuffed the figurine between her legs and the chair.

"I hope you like orange tea." Miss Bernadette handed her a small white cup. "It's the only tea I have."

"Thank you." The figurine felt uncomfortable underneath her legs and as she shuffled her body to the right, she felt a sharp pain in her arm, causing her to huff out loud.

"Is the ointment too strong?" Miss Bernadette asked.

"No. I'm just...I'm hungry." Her lie worked, for now. Cecilia sipped her tea, keeping her eyes on Miss Bernadette as she walked back to the altar. Repositioning herself again only caused the pain to return, but this time she felt it in her legs. Curious, she moved again and the pain moved to her lower back. Every movement coincided with the doll underneath her. The witch's spell had worked!

"Where you going to tell me or just kill me along with Elsie and Isaac?" Cecilia asked her.

Stumped at her question, Miss Bernadette tilted her head slightly to the right.

"You were never going to give me the figurine you made of me, were you?"

Miss Bernadette turned her upper body toward the trunk. "You've been snooping around." She then faced Cecilia.

"You lied to me."

"No, I haven't. I am following through on what I said I would do."

"You told me that I could be changed back!"

"At first I thought I could until I realized that the threat was much bigger than I anticipated." Miss Bernadette sat across from her. "You see that now, don't you? You understand that they have a bigger influence on you than I could have ever imagined."

"I'm still my own person," Cecilia replied.

"You'd be foolish to think that," she said. "Anger is the ammunition and Impa are the gun, Cecilia. Anger makes Impa react in unruly ways, allowing them to roam free in their dark desires. Elsie's control over her brother's fury has worked for over a century but now he is on the verge of turning into what their father wanted them to avoid."

"So you're saying that eventually we all just lose control?" Cecilia slammed her cup on the table, feeling droplets of the warm tea speckle her skin. "I'm not like them. I wasn't born into this. He made me into this."

"But you are just like them."

Cecilia thought about Glenn, Roger, Amber, Julie, Rosie, and the countless others that had been killed. She continued to tell herself that none of their deaths were exactly her fault. Sure, she participated, but it wasn't her decision. She could never kill anyone without feeling remorse and she didn't kill them out of anger.

"I will show you where you are wrong." She jeered at her. "I will reveal to you the truth." She placed her wrinkled hand on Cecilia's forearm.

Suddenly everything drew quiet and the air carried a smell of lilac and river water. A brisk breeze ruffled Cecilia's hair and darkness enveloped her. The image of Miss Bernadette and her home disappeared, replaced with tall pine trees, dirt, and tall grass.

The change in setting caused Cecilia to hop out of her chair. She called out for Miss Bernadette, who didn't answer her back. She stepped forward, finding the ground soft and uneven with each step. After pushing away dangling, dead tree branches from her path, up ahead she saw the very same spot where they had ambushed Glenn. Somehow she had traveled to the swamp surrounding Old Farmer's Road.

"All Impa are the same."

She heard Miss Bernadette's voice behind her and looked over her shoulder. "How are you doing this?" Her memories brought her back to the motel where she had dreamed of Isaac. She remembered how each image had warped her understanding of the area and of Elsie who had killed Glenn in her dream.

"You all have the same vexed desires inside you."

Cecilia obliged and moved forward but with each step she took, her fear of what would be revealed to her ached in her bones. She approached the shack, which looked eerily different. New boards replaced the old rotted ones. It now stood up straight, and longer boards, missing before, connected to its raised roof to straighten the porch. Time seemed to fast-forward and now night turned into day with the sun's rays beaming down on the revived property like a jealous theater stage light in search of its star.

It focused on an older man, barefoot, wearing torn overalls and a German Shepherd sitting next to him. The dog panted, wagged its tail, and looked up at its master who lifted heavy logs, setting them in a large pile on the side of the shack. The old man wiped his forehead free from sweat and shielded his eyes as he looked up at the sun. He then walked toward the back of his house to a fenced garden where he studied the corn stalks, bursting with large vegetation.

A girl who looked no older than ten years of age ran around from the back, chased by a younger looking boy. Cecilia studied them perfectly, realizing that they were a younger version of Elsie and Isaac. He caught up to Elsie, tackling her to the ground. Pinning her there, his face shifted to reveal the deathly image that Cecilia was all too familiar with. Elsie screamed at him to let her go but Issac continued hold her down. Hearing her plea, the old man rushed over to them and grabbed Isaac by the back of the neck.

"What did I tell you?" He threw Isaac off of his sister.

Isaac landed on his stomach and snarled at the old man.

"You can't let it control you son." He helped Elsie to her feet. "Promise me that you won't let the anger control you anymore." He then kneeled in front of Isaac and with both hands on his son's shoulders he began to gently shake some sense into him. "Promise me."

Again Isaac gnarled at the old man and in return he raised his hand and slapped Isaac across the face. "Say it!"

Isaac's strength at his young age and size surprised Cecilia. He responded to each slap with more anger until he grabbed his father's wrist in mid motion.

His father returned with a stern snarl. "Your mother's lack of control caused her death. Do you want the same thing to happen to you?"

Through her whole ordeal, since the first day she met Elsie and Isaac until now, Cecilia considered Elsie the main source for the evil that the two inflicted upon others, but that was far from the truth. It was Isaac all along.

"You have already brought unwanted attention to us by killing that woman," the old man continued to preach. "And now you want to kill your sister?"

Isaac breathed heavily. "I wanted her."

"Turning the woman into what we are won't bring your mother back." He stood to his feet and held out his arm for Elsie. "No human can curb your anger. Your sister is the only one who can protect you. You must always remember that."

Elsie walked into her father's arms and she nodded.

Cecilia heard the distorted sounds of jumbled voices and leaves crunching. A crowd of armed men appeared from the trees and bushes, carrying pitchforks and ropes. Their style of dress fit the time period—some wore overalls, others were dressed in scraggly work clothes and wool hats. The old man saw them and with bulging eyes he quickly urged his children to run into the trees to hide.

The crowd headed straight for the old man and a voice echoed from their group. "Let us have the boy, Jeb."

The old farmer placed his hands in his pockets and approached the crowd. "Now, you know that I'm not just going to hand over my son."

"He killed that woman Jeb. He ripped out her insides. That ain't normal."

"Ya's family ain't normal!" Another voice ripped from the crowd, as it began to grow more unruly. The old farmer continued his appeal, which went unheard among them. One of them threw a rock, hitting him in the forehead.

The old farmer touched his wound and examined his hand. His eyes dilated at the sight of blood.

"Hit him again!"

Someone threw another rock and it collided with his chest, making his legs give way, and he fell to the ground. They circled him, and one large, overweight man took aim at the German Shepherd with his rifle, pulling the trigger. The shot exploded flesh and fur from the dog's side as it fell to the ground. The overweight man then aimed for the dog's head and his second shot echoed through the trees.

Bleeding and defenseless, the farmer held up his hands in defense. Two of them dragged him toward a large tree as another one from the crowd tossed a rope over the top branch. Near the back of the crowd Cecilia saw a tall dark skinned woman dressed in stained clothing. In her hands she held three figurines that Cecilia had seen in Miss Bernadette's home.

They placed the noose around the old farmer's neck and again one of them asked about the Isaac's whereabouts.

"This is the real story, Cecilia."

Cecilia turned and viewed Miss Bernadette standing behind her. "I thought their father killed the woman?"

"This is the story that Isaac and Elsie have refused to tell you," she replied.

The old farmer's scream brought Cecilia's attention back to the vision. They raised the body into the air and his legs kicked out from underneath him. He grasped for the rope as his tongue protruded from his mouth.

Unable to take anymore, Cecilia closed her eyes. Then there was silence. As fast as it had begun, it ended with the old farmer's corpse dangling from the tree. The crowd, once filled with uncontrollable rage, now stood satisfied with their justice.

The witch stepped forward. "Search the area for his children, especially the boy." The crowd moved through the surrounding forest.

Miss Bernadette spoke again. "Isaac is the killer of all killers. He is the evil that walks among you. Without Elsie, he would be too far dangerous to control."

Cecilia continued to watch as the witch in her image approached the body. She pulled out a small knife and jabbed it into the old farmer's stomach. Then, with her left hand, she punched her way through and pulled out three round stones covered in thick, dark blood.

"My ancestor didn't burn the bones because she knew that without their father, they would roam without any or anything to keep them balanced," Miss Bernadette said. "Elsie knew that as well."

Suddenly an older Elsie and Isaac appeared in Cecilia's view. Elsie, dressed in a bright white dress, sat near a huge mound directly beneath the tree where the crowd had hung her father. She dug through it with her bare hands, pulling out her father's bones one by one.

"She has hidden these bones where no one, not even her brother, can find them," Miss Bernadette spoke up again.

Befuddled, Cecilia placed her hand over her mouth. "I don't know what to do."

"The only thing you can do, Cecilia, is die along with them."

****

The images ended just as swiftly as they'd started. Cecilia found herself back in Miss Bernadette's home, still sitting in her chair across from the old woman. However she felt that her body had grown weaker and she struggled to keep her head up. Her vision tricked her into seeing two images of the witch in front of her and she blinked her eyes, trying to refocus.

"Don't bother. The tea was laced." Miss Bernadette held out her hand. "Now, give me back the figurine."

Cecilia struggled to keep her body up, but she failed. Now limp she tumbled to the ground, revealing the figurine on the chair. Miss Bernadette grabbed it.

"Please." She reached her hand and Miss Bernadette ignored her. She didn't want to die, not tonight. Her urge to live overcame anything that the old woman showed her. She continued to tell herself that what she saw and learned about Isaac and Elsie didn't mean that she would turn out to be as bloodthirsty as they had been.

Using the chair for support, she stood to her feet. Her legs wobbled as she shuffled toward Miss Bernadette.

"Soon, you will be freed from all this." She lifted Cecilia's sculpture in the air and she began to chant.

Without a second thought Cecilia threw her body at Miss Bernadette, wrapping her arms around her midsection. There was nothing propelling her but a need to survive, driving her to do the unspeakable. Unconsciously her fangs appeared and with Miss Bernadette's neck only a few inches from them, she bit down and began to feed.

She heard the witch scream and stumble back while Cecilia still held on. Cecilia felt her body slam against the wall and the pain she felt was soon replaced with an ever more deep inclination to continue her attack. She felt Miss Bernadette's warm essence filling her body and fulfilling the demand that the voice inside her head wanted. Cecilia sucked violently. Miss Bernadette stumbled forward, bumping into the altar, and falling to the floor. The cauldron and its contents tumbled over along with the three figurines. She began to crawl in her attempt to get away, but Cecilia overpowered her and kept her still until she had her full.

When there wasn't any more to suck away, Cecilia pulled back, staring at the carnage she created. Realizing that she had killed for the second time that night, she stood up, covered her mouth, and whimpered.

This can't be my true nature, she thought to herself. I'm not a killer. She grabbed all three figurines and looked around the damaged room. She didn't know if Miss Bernadette had finished the spell or if the two dolls in Elsie and Isaac's image would work against them. She believed that they had to, since her own did a tremendous job of working against her.

"Ding, dong, the witch is dead."

Cecilia heard Elsie's voice and looked at door, seeing her and Isaac standing just outside and on the porch. Their unexpected visit stunned her and she jumped back slightly. Elsie's locks were pulled back in bun and she wore tight-fitted blue jeans and a pink shirt. A cigarette dangled from the corner of her mouth.

"I didn't think you had it in you," Elsie said, as she twirled a knife in her hand.

Cecilia hid the dolls from them by moving her hands to her back. When Isaac walked in, his face showing that he too was surprised by what he saw, Cecilia made sure she kept her distance from him by standing against the farthest wall from them. "I know what you did Isaac." Her lips trembled.

Isaac stood by the altar, quieted and unresponsive.

"It was never Elsie. It was you."

Isaac finally spoke. "Now you know why I need you." He held out his hand. "Now you know why I can't abandon my sister."

"You're a monster." Cecilia rubbed her hands over the dolls, trying to find the two that belonged to Isaac and Elsie.

"I never said I wasn't," he replied.

"Where are the figurines?" Elsie asked.

"I'm not telling you."

Elsie lunged at her. Quickly Cecilia squeezed Elsie's clay manikin and watched as Elsie stopped her advance. She leaned over in pain and the knife fell from her grip.

"No more threats. No more violence. We're going to do this my way." Cecilia watched as Isaac hesitated. She released the pressure and Elsie stood up.

"You bitch," she snarled at her.

They heard the sound of a distinct click coming from behind them. Derek stood in the doorway, aiming a loaded 9mm Beretta in their direction. Cecilia breathed a sigh of relief as Derek responded to the scene with an order.

"Don't move or I'll shoot. All of you—hands up. Now."

Elsie defiantly placed her hands on her hips. "Fuck you."

"Now!" He turned the gun at her. Still they didn't raise their arms.

Derek's eyes moved to Miss Bernadette's shriveled body on the floor. "What in the hell did you kids do?"

"You already have an idea." Elsie crossed her hands in front of her chest.

Derek wavered his gun between all three of them. "I won't tell you again."

"Shoot if you have to." Elsie stepped toward him and she held out her arms to the side. "I dare ya'." Her lips moved in a vicious snicker.

Derek's arms grew straight and he lifted the muzzle to Elsie's head. "I will shoot you," he replied. "Now step back."

Unafraid, Elsie continued her approach, forcing Derek to lower the muzzle to her chest. With his index finger on the trigger he took the shot. Elsie's chest caved inward and she fell back. Both Cecilia and Isaac jumped at the noise of the gun echoing through the air. Seeing her opportunity to escape, Cecilia took off toward the door.

Isaac launched at Derek with a scream and Derek moved aside, striking Isaac on the back of his head with the butt of his gun, forcing him to the floor.

Cecilia ran from the house, still grasping onto the clay figures. She didn't know where she was headed to, but she needed to get as far away from Isaac and Elsie as possible.

Derek picked up his pace and ran after her. In seconds he caught up to her and shoved the muzzle of his gun in her back, making her stop in mid-stride.

"Don't shoot." She begged. "I'm one your side."

"Like hell you are." Derek caught his breath and he forcefully grabbed her by the arm.

"You don't understand. We have to run. We have to get away from them now!"

"What are those?" He reached for the figurines in her hand but she pulled away which made him point the gun at her face.

"This is the only way to stop them." She nodded emphatically. "Just don't kill me. I'll tell you everything but first, we have to get out of here."

"Oh, you're going to tell me everything all right." He gripped her violently by her arm. "Starting with what the hell is going on." He dragged her out of the front yard.

****

Isaac sat up and then lifted himself off of the ground. His tongue glazed over his lips, covered in blood, and he spat, trying to clear his throat. He looked back at Elsie who still lay motionless, the front of her shirt covered in blood. He limped over to her. This wasn't good. He thought that his sister had finally met her death and for a moment, he rejoiced.

He felt as if he could scream at the top of his lungs and jump to the heavens in celebration. Now he had the chance to finally be released from her. No more orders, no more rules, and no holding back. No longer did he need to feel confined to what he did best. She wouldn't be around to try and tell him what to do. Finally, he saw an end to his sister's ridiculous leadership.

However, it couldn't be that easy. It never was when it came to his sister. She had taken plenty of bullets for him in their long existence. Taking one more to the chest wasn't anything new. Still, she would remain out long enough for him to pursue Cecilia and take back what he strongly believed belonged to him. With Cecilia's scent still lingering in the air, he headed for the front door when he heard a low snivel from his sister.

He sighed and rolled his eyes, watching Elsie come back to life. She slowly lifted her body from the ground and after regaining her footing, she glared down at her chest. He had missed his moment when he could have ripped her open and taken her stones for himself.

"That actually hurt this time." Elsie looked down at her shirt and upon seeing the blood, she cursed.

"It's the figurines," Isaac replied. "That witch actually did it."

"Impossible. She doesn't have our hair unless..." she thought, as her eyes rapidly moved about the room. Finally, they settled on him. "You gave it to her, didn't you?" She slammed her hand into his chest, pushing him back. "What in the hell were you thinking?"

"Killing you was exactly what I was thinking," he said, pushing her back.

Elsie caught her breath and tilted her head back. "You don't mean that."

"I do mean it," he replied. "Getting you out of the way is the best thing that can happen for me."

She looked at him in disbelieve. "It's your anger talking."

"Why do you always blame that? What's so wrong with being angry?" He argued back.

"Those backwater hicks tortured and killed our father because you didn't see anything wrong with being angry."

"He was weak, Elsie." Isaac looked away. "Maybe if he lost control, he'd still be alive today."

"So it's his fault that we're in this predicament? You're the one that gave Cecilia my hair." She folded her arms. "How did she get yours?"

"Never mind I said anything." He walked to the door.

"Father wasn't weak. He was smart." She followed him out of the house and onto the front porch. "He knew how and when to react. You don't." Standing behind him, she let her head rest on his back. "I'm not upset with you. You have to realize that what you're doing is risky. No one else can complete you. It's just you and me, baby brother—until the end." Then she walked around him, facing him. "And that might be tonight if we don't find Cecilia."

"I'm not going to kill her."

"Fine. Then don't. But Isaac, you have to think clearly now. We need to get those figurines."

Staring back into his sister's brown eyes, Isaac sighed and nodded. He still felt that his sister didn't understand. She would never see his side of the issue. He thought long and hard. "Her family."

Elsie tilted her head slightly.

"Let's start with her family."

CHAPTER TWENTY FIVE
Tattoo

With Derek at the wheel, the Lincoln Town Car pulled into the parking lot of the Sunnyside Motel, just an hour outside of Minneapolis. Throughout the car ride, Cecilia held tightly onto the figurines, refusing to have them anywhere near his reach. When they arrived, he placed the car in park, turned off the ignition, and he kept his attention straight ahead.

Besides the fact that he had kidnapped her, the gun sitting on his lap made her regret taking a chance to escape. She could easily take him, like what she did to Miss Bernadette, but that wouldn't help her issue. Desperate, she needed help.

Periodically she looked at him out of the corner of her eye, noticing his uneasiness. His chest heaved, slightly lifting his sweat-soiled shirt. The perspiration he collected after he wiped his forehead with the back of his hand dripped from his fingertips.

Moments went by until he finally moved, flipping down the visor to grab a small picture stuck in its pocket fold. "Do you know who this is?" He flashed the picture of a male wearing a Minnesota Twins baseball cap, smiling at the camera.

"No." Cecilia sniffled, assuming the image was Robert, Elsie and Isaac's friend who disappeared from Old Farmer's Road—

the same person that Jan questioned her about last night before they killed her.

"This is my brother, Robert. I took this picture a month before he disappeared," Derek replied. "We always got into arguments because I love the Yankees and he was more of a Twins fan."

"I'm sorry. I've never met him, if that's what you want to know."

Derek's silence rattled the already tense atmosphere.

"Are you going to kill me?"

"Not if you answer my questions."

Cecilia reached for the door handle, jiggling it to open the door but it didn't budge. Derek yanked her arm, pulled her away from the door. He pointed the gun at her, sticking the muzzle against her temple. "I will shoot you like I shot your friend." His hot breath, reeking of alcohol and cigarettes, steamed the side of her face.

"I've already told Jan what I know."

"She said you were sticking up for Isaac. Why?" The gun's muzzle pressed deeper into Cecilia's skull.

Cecilia cried out. "I'm not sticking up for him now."

He wiped away the beads of sweat littered his brow and traveled down the side of his face. "I want to know everything about that damn place," he demanded. "And I want to know everything about Elsie and Isaac."

Feeling her fear increasing, Cecilia quickly retorted, "Elsie isn't dead."

"I shot her square in the chest. She's dead."

"She's not dead. I wish to God that she was." Her statement sounded more like a hope and not a reality. "We aren't normal. We aren't human."

Derek readjusted his grip on the gun.

A huge lump filled Cecilia's throat, making her swallow loud enough to hear. She didn't know which way to break it to him and however she did, he probably wouldn't believe her anyway. "We feed on the living."

"Like zombies?" He placed his finger on the trigger.

"No... not zombies. We're..."

"What?"

"First it started with the tattoo and..."

"Wait a minute." Derek interrupted her. "Tattoo?"

Cecilia nodded. "It's on my shoulder."

Derek pulled back his gun and waved the muzzle to the left. "Turn around," he ordered.

Cecilia turned, facing the passenger side window. She felt Derek's callused hand grip the back of her neck, yanking her forward as he lifted up the back of her shirt. She waited, feeling her body tremble at what he planned to do next. She tried to focus her gaze through the fogged passenger side window, hoping to see that they weren't alone in the parking lot, but it was empty. A semi sped down the freeway with its headlights illuminating the road for a few seconds.

"Robert had the same marking." Derek's rough fingers glazed over a small liquid substance covering the tattoo on her back. He quickly lowered her shirt and ordered her to face him. "What does it mean?"

"It's supposed to tell us apart from the others," Cecilia answered.

"What others?"

"Impa."

Derek placed his gun in the pocket of his weathered jacket and he unlocked the door. "Be quiet and don't do anything." He grabbed her left wrist and got out of the vehicle, yanking Cecilia across the driver seat.

"You don't understand. We have to get out of here before they come."

"I said be quiet." Derek twisted her arm up her back, lifting her to her toes, and they began to walk to the entrance of the motel, heading toward Room 114.

When they reached the door he unlocked it and slid his hands up and down the wall in search of the light switch. Once he found it, he turned it on and pushed Cecilia into the room.

The brackish air carried an old musty smell. The small room came complete with only a twin bed, an old tube T.V. that sat on top of a three-drawer dresser, and a lamp with a titled nightshade the table next to the bed with its sad, flattened pillow. Dark stains covered the tan walls.

Derek slammed the door behind him and pointed, with the gun, towards the bed, indicating Cecilia should sit. She straggled over to it and sat as he pulled out a pair of handcuffs from his back pocket. He grabbed her arm, cuffing her right wrist to the wooden bed frame.

"What the hell is an Impa?" he said, as he towered over her.

"You don't have to handcuff me. I'm not going to run."

"Tell me what the hell is an Impa." He repeated his question.

The metal had already begun to dig into her skin. She wanted to start her explanation with the night Isaac made her into one, but she decided to start with their father instead. "Elsie and Isaac were born a long time ago—centuries ago. Their father, Jeb, was the old farmer from Old Farmer's Road." She struggled with the handcuffs. "Impa aren't human. They feed on the essence of their victims to survive. The age slowly and you can't kill them easily."

"Unless you have those things, right?" Derek pointed to the three figurines resting on Cecilia's lap.

"Yes. That was what I was doing when you came to the house. Miss Bernadette is a...well, she was a witch who was going to help me kill them." She paused. "But I killed her."

"Go on," he said.

"They did the same thing to me that they did to Robert. They changed us by feeding us these stones. It's what makes us what we are," she said. "If we don't eat, we die."

"So those dolls or whatever they are. If I burn them, they'll die?"

Cecilia didn't answer him immediately and he kicked her in the shin. "Answer me."

"I think so."

"You don't know?"

"I don't know if Miss Bernadette finished the ritual or not."

"Maybe you should've found out before you killed her." He reached for them and Cecilia blocked his advance. Angrily, he snatched Elsie's figurine from her grasp and glared at it. "Say I believe you. Why don't you just destroy these things now?"

"I want whatever it is inside me to go away." She looked down at her swinging feet kicking the side of the bed. "The witch wasn't going to cure me. She was going to kill me. Just like she was going to kill Robert when he went to her for help. But if I have these, then I can at least hold off Elsie and Isaac while I find a cure."

Derek continued to stare back at her with empty eyes. She saw that his mind had trouble processing the information she just told him. Eventually, he stood up from the bed and walked over to the duffle bag lying on the table near the front door. "I knew something was wrong with Robert." He zipped it open and began to dig. He pulled out a bottle of whiskey and set it on the table with a thud. He twisted the cap and took a giant gulp, wiping the excess alcohol from his lips, and then his fingers. "Jan didn't believe me but I swore to her that there was something we couldn't explain going on at that place."

Cecilia looked away. He didn't know that Jan was dead and she decided to keep it that way. "That's why I need your help."

He took another gulp.

"Elsie and Isaac forced Robert into this. They made him into a murderer, like they did me."

"Robert wasn't a murderer."

"But he had to kill to survive."

"He wasn't a murderer!" Derek threw the bottle at the wall above the bed. It shattered and pieces of flying glass peppered Cecilia's back. The brown liquid slid down along the wall.

Cecilia shuddered and scampered across the bed as Derek ran at her. He gripped the back of her neck and pushed her onto her back. She felt the cold steel of the gun pressing between her eyes and waited in terror for the bullet to exit the chamber and bury into her brain.

"So you don't die easily." He breathed deeply with his lips extended back and his teeth clenched. His eyes were wide and his pupils dilated.

"They're coming for me." Cecilia spoke in a low, shaky tone. "And when they get here, they will kill us both but not if we kill them first." She had to make him believe. She was bent on it. "They killed your brother. I had nothing to do with his murder, I swear it."

Derek closed his eyes as if in thought and his grip lifted, leaving Cecilia to wonder if what she'd just said somehow seeped into him. He lowered the gun and stepped back. His face, once angered, now showed signs of anguish. His hand shook and he placed the gun in the pocket of his jeans. He slammed his hand on the bed, rattling its surface.

"Thank you." He sat on the bed and gaped at her with tear filled eyes. "I just wanted one person, besides myself, to say it." He placed his face in his hands.

His behavior confused her but at least he had put the gun down. "They're coming, Derek," she said. "Maybe not tonight, but tomorrow or the night after. Either we do something if we stay here, or we leave. Now."

"I need to tell Jan." He stood up from the bed. "She can help." He walked to the window and pulled back the white curtains to get a view of outside.

"Did you just hear me? She can't help you."

"She wants this solved as much as I do." He looked back at her.

"She can't help us, Derek."

He continued to stare back at her.

"She can't help us because she's dead."

CHAPTER TWENTY SIX
Freed

Cecilia opened her eyes. A dark oval stain on the white stucco ceiling of the motel room came into view. She stretched her arms and feeling the cold hard steel from the handcuffs rubbing against her skin, constricting her movements, suddenly brought her back to reality. To her left she saw Derek standing near the window, peering out from between the long thick curtains.

He pulled the curtains back farther and sunlight blasted through the small room, stinging her still sleepy eyes. "You were talking in your sleep last night," he said.

Cecilia turned and looked straight ahead. She wished that the past few days had been a dream. With the threat of Elsie and Isaac looming over her, and Derek holding her hostage in a filthy room against her will, she didn't understand how easily she could've fallen asleep at a time like this. She raised her upper body and leaned back on her shoulders. With her legs she moved the bed sheets aside.

"You kept saying, 'Just one more. Just one more.' Robert used to say that." He looked back at her. "While you slept, I thought a lot about what happened last night and what you told me. I still didn't believe it until I saw your face change right before my eyes."

Cecilia examined her face with her hands, finding her skin saggy and wrinkled. She pulled at her hair noticing that white had invaded its color. She didn't know what was worse—the fact that he watched her sleep or the fact that she had aged overnight.

Derek walked across the room toward the coffee maker located in the bathroom. She heard the faucet turn on as he began to fill the pot with water. The smell of fresh coffee filtered the air as he turned on the maker to brew.

"What's happening to you? Is that part of being an Impa?" He appeared from the bathroom, staring at her.

Cecilia looked around the bed, searching for the figurines. Unable to find them, her eyes darted back to Derek. "What did you do with them?"

"I hid them." He reached into his pocket, pulling out a yellow Post-It note. "I found this stuck to the door this morning. It's for you." He handed it to her.

She took the note and read it out loud. "Join us and your parents for festive activities at the shack." She looked up from the note. "They have my parents. You have to let me go."

"How do they know you were here?"

"They always know where I am," she replied. "You have to let me go."

"Let's get something straight." He sat on the edge of the bed. "One. You're a murderer. You killed God knows how many other people. I assume you killed or participated in Jan's death as well. Two. You're not human, so why should I trust you? Three. How do I know that once I let you go, you won't try to kill me?"

"You have the figurines." She began to struggle with the handcuffs. "You have the upper hand."

"So now you're saying that they do work?"

"Maybe. I don't know." She continued to yank at her handcuffs. "What else do you want me to say?"

Derek placed his forefinger over his mouth to quiet her. "I have a better idea. I'm going to kill them right now." He stood up from the bed and he walked over to a black book bag in the middle of the floor. He unzipped it open and pulled out a small flask. He took a swig, feeling the vodka burn the back of this throat as he swallowed hard.

"If you do that, I won't find out where they took my parents. You don't understand. They will kill them if I don't go."

He took another sip from his flask and leaned over her. "I understand more than you know." He pulled out a small key from his pocket and began to unlock the cuff from her wrist. "I'll take you, but only because of them. I don't want to see anyone else get hurt."

Now freed, Cecilia hesitated to move from the bed, fearing what he'd plan to do next. "What are you going to do after that?" She asked in a shaky voice.

He stared hard at Cecilia. "Kill you all, of course."

CHAPTER TWENTY SEVEN
Killer of All Killers

The car lights shined brightly on the rusted metal chain blocking the parking lot from the bridge. Derek turned off the car and opened the door. "Remember what I told you. Don't try anything."

Cecilia nodded and stepped out of the car. The plan he revealed to her on their way wasn't solid. He was hell bent on storming into the area armed with his right hand gripping his 9mm and his left hand holding tightly onto the figurines. To her, Derek had unconsciously set them up for failure. However, she didn't tell him that. The only thing she wanted was to make sure her parents left the area, unharmed.

This was the moment she's been waiting for, her chance to wipe the Earth clean of this evil, but she wasn't nearly as ready as she wanted to be.

He opened the trunk of his car and grabbed the figurines. Almost immediately Cecilia heard her wrist crack and she gripped it in pain. "Be careful," she snapped at him. The pain was an eerie reminder of how close Miss Bernadette had come to killing her. Now her life rested in the hands of a drunk, obsessive man she didn't trust.

After placing the dolls in a brown bag, which he stuffed under his right arm, Derek pulled out his gun and waved it at her to start walking. They crossed the bridge and continued down the path. The humid air made Cecilia's shirt stick to her sweaty back. They hadn't traveled far until Derek also began to sweat. His head constantly moved from left to right and if Cecilia slowed her footsteps, he'd prod her forward her by sticking his gun's muzzle into her right arm.

They approached the rock cropping. Big, black spray painted letters, which she'd never seen before, covered the white pasty surface.

This way if you want to see your parents alive again.

The warning made her pick up her pace, almost leaving Derek by the rocks. He caught up with her before the path curved to the right. When the area became too dark for normal eyesight, he whipped out a flashlight and handed it to her. He then took out his flask, unscrewed the top, and took a sip.

"Do you always drink?" Cecilia asked, as she turned on the light and shined it straight ahead.

"Drinking keeps me calm." He offered the flask to her.

"I don't drink," she replied. "Well, not that anyway."

"Yeah, I forgot." He screwed the lid back on and stuffed the flask back into his pocket.

Silence followed their exchange as they continued into the dim swamp. Cecilia could only imagine what nonsense was running through his shattered mind or how he had mentally prepared himself for this encounter.

The wind blew and the thick bushes around them swayed under their influence. The hard branches of the pine trees shuffled and opened up, revealing the clear night sky, which allowed the moonlight to brighten the path like a searchlight. It extended its glow to the shack located straight ahead of them. It looked exactly like what Miss Bernadette had showed her in her vision. It was still quaint and new, as if time had done nothing to wither its boarded surface.

Upon seeing it, Derek stopped. "This is where they live?"

"Yes."

"And Jan was killed here?"

Cecilia found herself struggling to answer.

He pulled out his gun and rammed it into her back. "You first."

Cecilia made her way to the porch. A paper sign, nailed to the front door read: "Come Inside." Weary, she climbed the wooden steps and looked back at Derek who still remained a few feet from the entryway.

"Keep going," he ordered.

The interior looked abnormally clean and fresh. Yellow flowered wallpaper had replaced the dingy, dusty walls she'd seen the first time. A large polished oak table took the place of the old termite-ridden table with three legs. On the top sat a vase filled with long stemmed roses.

"I don't understand," Cecilia said, as she walked forward in a confused state. "It's like they somehow brought this home back to life."

Derek wiped his hand on the surface of the table, finding no dust.

They heard sobbing coming from the next room. She squinted, seeing her mother on the floor with her arms tied behind her back and a thick gag in her mouth. Cecilia quickly ran to her assistance.

"Mom, are you okay?" Cecilia pulled the gag from her mother's mouth and watched as a string of spit dribbled down to her chin. "Where's Dad?"

Trails of dirt partially covered her mother's bright red cheeks. "He killed him." She wept.

Cecilia moved to untie her mother's arms when she heard slow footsteps ahead. Looking up she saw Isaac standing just beneath the doorway, glaring at her. The thought that he killed her father moved her to race toward him. He easily shoved her back.

"Yes, get angry. Show your mother your true face." He grabbed Mrs. Richardson and pulled her toward him, wrapping his arm around her neck.

"Why did you kill my father?" she yelled, as she moved forward, but Isaac simply adjusted his hold on her mother.

"Why not? He wasn't a good father, Cecilia," he replied. "I did you a favor. You're better off without them." His eyes moved to Derek. "What is he doing here?"

"You son of a bitch," Derek gasped.

Cecilia felt her breathing turn shallow.

"I asked you. What is he doing here?" Isaac yelled. He stared carefully at the brown paper bag underneath Derek's arm. "He has the figurines? Give them to me."

Derek pointed his gun at Isaac and in return, she moved her body in front of it. "Don't. You'll shoot my mother." She returned back to Isaac. "Let her go. I promise, I'll do anything you want me to do."

"It's too late for that." He walked backwards, dragging Cecilia's mother toward the kitchen.

They followed Isaac closely—out the back door and down to the cellar. They waited until he descended before moving again. As he backed down the stairs, Mrs. Richardson's feet hit each step with a loud thump. Derek opened the bag, but Cecilia stopped him.

"Not yet. Not until we know that Elsie is also down there."

"We need to see if all these dolls work," he replied back.

"After I get my mother back. Now please," she said in a sorrowful voice, "don't do anything."

A flickering light brightened the cellar's darkness and Derek looked in, seeing movement in the glow.

"Fine." Derek ordered. "You first."

Without hesitating, Cecilia climbed down the stairs. Her eyes immediately adjusted to the dark interior. She saw Isaac drop her mother into the middle of a circle outlined with white chalk. A lantern hung from the ceiling and long metal chains clung to the walls. Candles illuminated each corner of the cellar. In the corner she saw a pruned body on the ground with its back facing her. She hastily approached it and upon turning it over, she noticed that it was her dead father. Cecilia looked at Isaac with fresh tears in her eyes.

Derek raised his weapon at Isaac.

"I'm sure Cecilia told you that shooting us won't work," Elsie said, as she walked out of the shadows that filled the back of the room.

Derek turned his weapon toward her. "It's worth another try."

She folded her hands across her chest, a cheeky grin covering her face. "We weren't going to eat you tonight but since you're here," her cheek bones began to move underneath her skin, "we might as well."

Mrs. Richardson wailed at the sight of Elsie's transformation. A shot rang out and Elsie fell to the dirt floor. Curled smoke floated from the muzzle of Derek's gun.

"Like I said. It was worth another try." He repositioned his sweaty grip on the handle and turned his attention toward Isaac, who didn't move.

Cecilia grabbed her mother by the arm and dragged him away from the circle. "Do it now." She screamed at Derek.

He opened the bag, grabbing the three figurines. Isaac launched his body at Derek as a horrifying scream escaped from his mouth.

Cecilia began to untie her mother, careful to keep her eyes on the brawl between them. Derek punched Isaac across the face and pushed him against the wall. He raised his gun to shoot, but Isaac knocked his hand out of the way, scattering both the gun and the figurines across the ground.

Cecilia located the figurine made in her likeness she ran for it, but Elsie, now on her feet, tackled her before she reached it. Overpowering Cecilia, her face continued to warp, but this time her arms began to change as well. Long strands of dark fur exploded from the skin on her forearms and her face. The section around her mouth pushed itself out, cracking and stretching her jawbone. Her teeth fell from her gums as sharp fangs replaced them. Her nose widened and turned black as her eyes grew steadily in size, the pupils now bright red. A string of spit hung down and settled on Cecilia's forehead.

"I'm so going to enjoy this," she said, her voice coming out dark and garbled. Her fingernails, now sharp and pointed, pushed into Cecilia's stomach.

Derek rushed over to his gun just before Isaac. He pulled the trigger and the bullet entered Isaac's upper arm, his body colliding with Elsie, pushing her off of Cecilia.

Pain engulfed her midsection, and weakened, Cecilia scurried across the dirt floor with her eyesight on her figurine. She heard Derek pull the trigger again and when looking back, she saw a portion of fur blow into the air. Elsie had fully changed into the hellhound that Miss Bernadette had told her about. On all fours, the beast growled and slouched forward, like a hunter narrowing in on its prey.

When her figurine was within her reach, Cecilia reached out for it, but Isaac suddenly appeared, placing his foot over her wrist. Stopping her, he grabbed it and stared at it for a moment before speaking. "I wish things would've been different Cecilia. I really do."

"It can be if you just stop this." She looked up at him. Not only did he have her figurine in his possession, but had his sister's as well. "You can do it, Isaac. You can stop her and be free from her." She held out her hand to him. "I'll help you. We'll find a cure together."

Derek emptied the clip into the hellhound's body. Dark blood poured from each wound and the dog's legs crumpled. It fell over and began to change back. Derek went to reload his weapon and Isaac snatched it out of his grip, tossing it into the corner of the room.

Cecilia pulled herself up from the floor. Now at a standstill, Derek and Cecilia had no choice but to wait and watch for Isaac's next movements.

He looked to his sister, fully changed back, as she managed to stand to her feet. Noticing that he had her figurine, she held out her hand. "You got it!" Her face lightened up. "Give it to me."

"Then what?" Isaac caressed the doll. "Will you continue to control me?"

Elsie dug her finger into a bullet hole in her chest, pulling out the shrapnel. "Of course not. Just give it to me so we can kill them and get this over with."

Isaac looked back at Cecilia. "I don't think so, Elsie." Holding her figurine between her hands, Isaac began to tear it apart. The surface began to crack and Elsie screamed before it shattered into two large pieces.

A cloud of dust billowed from Elsie's mouth and nostrils, shooting into the air. She wobbled before dropping to her knees in paralyzed pain. Isaac caught her in his arms before she fell to the ground. He held her, not paying any attention to Derek, who made his way to Isaac's figurine located on the floor next to him.

"I'm not your puppet anymore," Isaac said as he pushed back the strands of Elsie's hair from her face. "I'm finally free from you." He punched into her stomach and edging his way deeper, he latched onto the stones and yanked them from her flesh. He studied their bloody texture before he pushed Elsie's dead body away from him and stood to his feet.

Cecilia had a sliver of a moment to change her mind about Isaac's future. He had finally pulled away from Elsie's influence but if what Miss Bernadette said was true, this meant that he now had no one to control him and guide him. It made him more dangerous and unpredictable like in his early years before his father's death.

Holding onto Isaac's figurine, Derek looked at Cecilia and immediately she knew what he was going to do. She screamed out for him but she was too late to stop his action. He raised his hand and slammed the Isaac's figurine into the floor. The noise of hardened clay shattering caught Isaac's attention.

However he didn't scream nor did he look in pain. Unlike his sister, dust didn't escape from every orifice in his body. Instead his full lips culled back into a vast, frenetic smile, which made Cecilia and Derek stare, confused.

"Why isn't it working?" Derek asked, frantically looked at Cecilia. "You said it would work."

She couldn't find any explanation except for the fact that maybe Miss Bernadette had only finished the ritual for her and Elsie's puppets. However, Isaac hadn't concerned himself with his own doll throughout the entire confrontation. He must have known, and Cecilia wondered how he had gotten that information.

Isaac walked to Derek with a hint of confidence in each step. He placed his foot over the remains of his effigy and pressed down. Without so much as a word he forced Derek closer to him and bit down into his neck.

Cecilia limped toward her mother in an attempt to shield her from the horrors. Her mother embraced her and they sat, huddled together, watching Isaac finish off Derek quickly. Afterwards Isaac stumbled back, enriched with Derek's essence as it traveled through his body. His eyelids fluttered and his legs shook. He searched Derek's shrunken body, finding his flask. He then let go, letting the body fall to the floor.

He opened the flask and instead of taking a sip, he sniffed its contents. His nose crinkled and he tossed it over his shoulder. And then he focused his sight on Cecilia and her mother.

"It should have worked." Cecilia said, allowing her rage to flutter inside her. "Why didn't it work?"

Isaac juggled Cecilia's figurine in his right hand. "It would've worked if that was my hair." He squeezed and Cecilia's body buckled in pain.

Somehow, she managed to remain on her feet. "It was yours. I took it from you." She pulled away from her mother.

"That's what I like about you Cecilia." He now stood inches from her. "Naive, trustworthy—you stand up for what you believe is right and you help your friends and family."

"But that was your hair!" She replayed that morning in her mind, trying to understand how she could've made such a horrendous mistake. When her thoughts turned to the argument he had with his sister, her lips wavered in response.

"See, I knew you'd try to take my hair eventually." His hand grazed her cheek and she pulled back, disgusted. "They all do at one point or other. Wigs are one of the greatest inventions of all time."

"What do you really want, Isaac?"

"What I want is to find someone who won't try and control me. Someone who can understand me without any hesitation or rules," he replied. "I thought that someone was you." His eyes moved to Mrs. Richardson. "But I see now that I was wrong, just like Elsie said I was." He looked back at his sister's corpse. "She was always right." He ground his teeth. "I hated her for it."

Cecilia tried to stop him again but he squeezed her figurine harder and this time she couldn't avoid collapsing to the floor. She watched as her mother tried to run for the stairs but Isaac yanked her back by her hair, tilting her head to the ceiling. He bit into her and began to feed.

She yowled at him to stop and spare her mother, but with each scream, he squeezed her figurine harder. Her lungs constricted and her body convulsed until she felt paralyzed. Unable to move, she watched feebly while her mother succumbed to Isaac right before her eyes.

Instead of letting the body fall, he carefully laid Mrs. Richardson's corpse onto the floor. He sat down next to Cecilia's bruised and worn body and rested her body on top of his legs. "Thank you, Cecilia." He traced her lips with his fingers. "Thank you for finally opening my eyes. Thank you for helping me get rid of Elsie once and for all." He placed his hand over her stomach and a high shriek escaped her mouth. "And thank you for setting me free."

"Isaac, don't." Tears moved from her eyes and down the side of her face.

"Shh. Don't cry," he replied. He gently pushed his hand into her stomach, ripping back her flesh. "I won't forget you for as long as I live," he grunted as he grasped onto the stones in her stomach, "which will be a very, very long time."

EPILOGUE
Epilogue

"This is what I wanted to show you."

Freddie pointed to a large dirt mound. He looked up at the blue sky, shielding his eyes from the bright sun.

"This is retarded," his girlfriend, Jada said, as she walked toward him. "You brought me all the way out here for this?"

Freddie knelt on the ground, and with his hands he began to pull back the dirt. "Just wait for it."

Jada stood behind him with her arms folded across her chest. She tapped her foot impatiently and then spoke again. "The last time you said that, we ended up in the middle of nowhere during a tornado watch."

"Relax, Jada. We won't get lost out here." He continued to dig. "We're only half an hour from the city."

Jada looked around. A year ago the city of Minneapolis had decided to cultivate the land around Old Farmer's Road. They started by demolishing the old bridge, replacing it with a sturdier one made from concrete and steel, leaving enough room for the Light Rail which would zoom through the area once they had cut down the large pine trees and replace them with condominiums and townhomes. They had already started just north of the bridge, building two new business complexes.

"This is the most stupid thing you've done in a long time," Jada said. "If you knew you had to dig, why didn't you bring a shovel?"

"Because I was told not to bring one."

"Who told you?" She repeated.

"Jada, I found this place a week ago. It was just here, uncovered." Freddie continued to wipe away the dirt. "Once the city finds it, they're going to destroy it."

"So what?"

Slowly the image of a brown wooden door appeared. Freddie sat back, admiring his hard work.

Jada rubbed her fingers on the rotten wood. "Is this a cellar?"

"It used to be connected to an old house down here," he replied. "It was the first thing the city tore down." He grabbed onto the rusted metal latches and pulled. "A farmer and his family lived down here over a century ago." He grunted and pulled until the metal chains snapped, breaking away from the door.

"Fuck." He wiped his brow.

"Oh, I heard about that," Jada started to laugh. "They used to call this place Old Farmer's Road, right? Didn't people die down here?"

"Yeah, about fifteen years ago." He stood up and began to pound on the wooden door with his feet. He continued until finally his foot broke through. A rush of hot, musty air escaped which made them both cover their nose. Freddie peered into the darkness. Cobwebs hung from the entrance and mossy wooden steps lead down into the darkness.

"You're not going down there, are you?" Jada asked, pointing to the steps.

"Shhh," he said to her. "Listen and watch."

They stared into the darkness for what felt like minutes before Jada cleared her throat.

"I don't hear anything, Freddie."

"Just listen and watch, Jada."

She lingered until catching just a quick glimpse of something moving in the dark. "What was that?" She said, as she moved back, frightened.

"Don't be afraid," he replied. "It won't hurt us."

"This place is freaking me out," Jada said, as she stepped back. "Let's go."

Freddie eyed her. "C'mon, Jada. We just opened it."

"Close it and let's go," she barked.

"Fine." Freddie grabbed onto the door and before he could close it, they heard a sound of shuffling footsteps echoing from the darkness.

"Now, I know you heard that, Freddie."

"Yeah, I did."

A voice interrupted them from the darkness. "Just one more." Freddie stepped back.

"Just one more." The voice spoke again.

"Hello?" Freddie called out.

"Just one more."

"How did you get down there?" Freddie spoke at the darkness but they received no reply.

"If someone is down there, we need to get help," Jada said, slapping at his shoulder.

"No," the voice retorted.

"Who are you?" Freddie called out again. "How did you get down there? Are you by yourself?"

The voice suddenly changed its tone. "Please, please. Can you help me? It's dark down here."

"Sure, sure." Freddie called out to the voice. "We'll go and get help." He then whispered to Jada. "Sounds like it's a guy."

"He sounds really young," Sally whispered back. "Freddie, stay here. I'll go for help." Jada quickly took off back to the road.

Freddie returned his attention to the voice. "Help is coming soon. Don't worry. We'll get you out of there."

"No, don't leave me," the voice called out.

"My girlfriend went." Freddie said, in a reassuring voice. "I'm staying right here."

"Jada isn't with you?"

Freddie stopped. "How do you know her name?"

The voice didn't reply back.

"Hey, I'm talking to you. How do you know her name?"

"I know everything about you, Freddie."

He stepped back. "Who are you?"

The voice paused and then spoke. "Isaac. My name is Isaac."

ABOUT THE AUTHOR

A veteran of the Armed Forces, Isaiyan Morrison was born and raised in Minneapolis.

Her passions include writing, reading, and researching historical events.

She also spends her time gardening, playing video games, and hanging out with her three cats and beloved Pitt bull.

She's the author of The Deamhan Chronicles and the novel, Old Farmer's Road.

Made in the USA
Middletown, DE
11 December 2022

18068418R00139